An UNCERTAIN ROAD

Center Point
Large Print

An UNCERTAIN ROAD

ADVENTUROUS HEARTS • 1

ABBEY DOWNEY

CENTER POINT LARGE PRINT
THORNDIKE, MAINE

This Center Point Large Print edition
is published in the year 2025 by arrangement with
Wild Heart Books.

Copyright © 2024 by Abbey Downey.

All rights reserved.

The characters and events in this fictional work are the product of the author's imagination. Any resemblance to actual people, living or dead, is coincidental.

Unless otherwise indicated, all Scripture quotations are taken from the Holy Bible, King James Version.

The text of this Large Print edition is unabridged.
In other aspects, this book may vary
from the original edition.
Printed in the United States of America
on permanent paper sourced using
environmentally responsible foresting methods.
Set in 16-point Times New Roman type.

ISBN: 979-8-89164-627-8

The Library of Congress has cataloged this record
under Library of Congress Control Number: 2025936648

To Emilee, my wildflower, with hopes that you'll grow to be strong, fight for your dreams, and rely on the Lord.

An UNCERTAIN ROAD

Chapter 1

June 1905
Philadelphia, Pennsylvania

Couldn't you make it a few more blocks?"

As useless as it might be to talk to an automobile, doing so made Flora Montfort feel better about being stranded on the side of the street. She screwed the cap back onto the radiator and stepped away from the car as smoke billowed around her, covering her driving coat and hat with a fine layer of grime.

Sending a reassuring smile to her mother-in-law, Isabelle, who waited in the car, Flora blew a loose strand of hair out of her face, determined not to smear more grease on herself if she could help it. There certainly wouldn't be enough time to scrub it off before joining the celebration dinner for her brother and his fiancée that evening. She and Isabelle had already missed the beginning due to several wrong turns she took on the way into town, but if they hurried, they could be there for the rest. Resisting the urge to kick her smoking, hissing automobile, she chewed on her lower lip as she tried to decide what to do.

"Flora, *ma chère*, can it be repaired?"

From her seat in the open touring car, Isabelle

fanned a plume of smoke away from her face. Stately and elegant, Isabelle Montfort possessed features and a French accent so like Flora's late husband Henri's that she could envision how he would have been mocking her ineptitude by now. His mother, on the other hand, looked genuinely concerned, another confirmation that helping Isabelle start a new life in America was worth the immense effort of moving back to Flora's home country. "Of course. No need to worry."

While the statement was technically true, Flora couldn't make the repairs alone on the side of the road. She examined her beloved Decauville again. The car had been a gift from Henri the year before his death, and she hoped it would be part of her new independent future. If they continued the drive, she risked permanent fatal damage to the engine. But the car was still running, even if it sounded rough. She was sure it was only a few more blocks to Owen's house. After driving from New York City almost entirely on rutted dirt roads, couldn't the car make it a bit farther?

As she glanced at Isabelle's furrowed brow, resolve settled over Flora. She would get them to Owen's house. She would find a way out of the mess Henri left them in. And she would see Isabelle live out the rest of her days in comfort, as the dear woman deserved to.

Flora returned to her seat. "I don't have the tools to make repairs here, but I think it's cooled off enough to finish the drive. For now, let's get to Owen's house so we can celebrate with him and Aggie. I'll worry about fixing the car later."

Setting the vehicle into motion, Flora spent the next few minutes praying that the Decauville would keep running. Four blocks to go. Three blocks. Two.

After the last turn, she released a sigh of relief. The lovely home Owen had described in his letters came into view. The Italianate-style house featured a magnificent square tower and the rustic stonework Owen had told her was common in the area. A wide, curved porch welcomed visitors to sit in the shade of the large trees that lined the street. The neighborhood was picturesque, perfect for a young couple preparing to start a family before long. A burst of pride warmed Flora's heart. Her brother was proving already that he would care for his family better than Henri ever had.

Flora found a spot along the street to park the car and helped Isabelle step out onto the ground. By the time they turned to face the house, Owen and Aggie were standing outside the open front door with an older couple flanking them. If only there had been time to freshen up before facing the people who would be Owen's new family. As it was, Flora smoothed her hair into place the best she could.

Her reluctance dissipated the moment her

younger brother dashed forward and enveloped her in a hug. "Flora, you made it! I was worried."

Crushed against his chest, Flora smiled at the concern in his voice. He was one of the few people who had ever worried about her. "The car overheated and forced us to stop. But I'm so thankful to be here now. I've missed you."

They pulled apart, and Owen greeted Isabelle as if she was his own family. Then he led them to the porch, where Aggie and the older couple waited. Owen's grin threatened to split his face as he slid his fiancée's arm through the crook of his. "Flora, you remember my beautiful Aggie. And these are her parents, Albert and Mary Harrison."

Mr. and Mrs. Harrison welcomed them with as much enthusiasm as Owen had. Aggie managed to slide her arm around Flora's waist without untangling herself from Owen's touch, the kind of feat easily managed by those in love. She was as beautiful as Flora remembered from their first meeting almost a year ago, sporting a spotless lace gown with her hair in a stylish swirled pompadour. But she was far from snobbish, despite the family's obvious social standing.

Aggie pulled Flora close, her perfect features glowing. "I'm so glad you're here, Flora. Having grown up with only brothers, you have no idea how thrilled I am to have a sister now."

Flora couldn't help but respond with a smile.

"I only had brothers, too, so we'll learn about sisterhood together."

Aggie giggled as Owen led her toward the door. "Let's not leave the rest of our guests waiting, shall we?"

Inside, voices from farther down the dim hall confirmed the presence of Aggie's extended family and friends. Another moment of reticence hit Flora. "Owen, could Isabelle and I clean up before we join the party? I'm a mess after poking around in the car on the road."

Instead of Owen's, a different deep voice rang through the hall. "I suppose that's why ladies shouldn't poke around in cars."

Needing to see who would be so rude before even meeting her, Flora stepped around Owen. She found herself looking up at a tall man, lean muscle filling out his tweed jacket and matching vest nicely. His hazel eyes held her gaze with no hint of shame over his unsociable behavior. This man might be quite good-looking, but he was also showing a distinct lack of modern thinking. Flora couldn't stand the insinuation that cars were only for men. She'd been fighting that common opinion ever since Henri first convinced her to get behind the steering wheel. He might have had selfish reasons for teaching her to drive, but she'd proven herself more than capable, despite being a female.

Before she could sort out which retort might let

this fellow know her exact feelings on the matter, Aggie swatted the man on the arm and rolled her eyes. "Honestly, Jensen. Just because you hate cars doesn't mean no one else should drive them. It's admirable for a woman to be self-sufficient enough to get where she needs to go."

The man didn't miss a beat, as if they'd already had this conversation more than once. "It's not getting where she needs to go that's the problem. It's getting there safely. You know as well as I do that those machines are lethal."

Waving him off with one hand, Aggie turned back to Flora. "Please, don't mind Jensen. He's like another brother, complete with overprotective instincts. Let's pretend the meeting didn't start this way and make introductions instead. Flora, this is Mr. Jensen Gable, my father's right-hand man. He grew up with my brothers and me, so he's as good as family. Jensen, may I present Owen's sister, Mrs. Flora Montfort, recently from France, and her mother-in-law, Mrs. Isabelle Montfort?"

The others all acted as if Jensen had been eccentric rather than insulting, so making an attempt to be civil was probably the best way to keep from ruining Owen's dinner. Flora summoned the best smile she could manage. "How do you do, Mr. Gable?"

Aggie beamed as if she'd solved a national crisis and clapped her hands together. "You must call him Jensen, Flora. We'll all be family once Owen and I are married."

Jensen nodded when Flora looked toward him for confirmation. "It's nice to meet you, Jensen."

Expectant silence filled the hall, but she refused to return the favor of allowing him to use her given name. She was done with letting men's behavior go unchecked while she remained agreeable and pleasant. Until Owen's wedding was past and he was settled, Flora would try to steer clear of this man and his incorrect opinion about cars and the women who enjoyed them.

Putting aside the awkwardness of Mrs. Montfort's silent refusal to allow the use of her given name, Jensen offered a slight bow to greet the two ladies. But inside, he was dying to find out why the younger Mrs. Montfort had been working on a car on her way there. Owen had mentioned his sister was driving her own vehicle, worrying that an accident could be the cause of her delay. It turned out he was right to worry, as Jensen had assumed. Everyday driving was far too great a risk for anyone, much less two ladies alone in an unfamiliar state. Why was he the only one who saw that Owen was a fool to have let his sister do it?

As Owen gathered the newcomers to show them rooms where they could freshen up, Jensen couldn't help examining Owen's beloved sister. Along with Owen's effusive praise for her intelligence, her resourcefulness, and her kindness, Jensen had heard of her adventure-seeking ways and how her late husband had taken her along on all sorts of dangerous ventures.

From that part of the description, he'd expected the type of cloying, fortune-seeking female he was used to seeing at auto races. There had always been a few women who craved the thrill of being with a man who risked his life for fame and glory. But they'd been easy to spot, always clinging to a top racer's arm or following one around while gushing compliments in an effort to get his attention.

Now that she was in front of him, Mrs. Montfort appeared to be the exact opposite. He got a closer look as she passed him in the narrow hall, her head barely coming up to his shoulder and the skirt of her sensible plaid suit brushing his leg.

While she was quite pretty, her air of independent confidence and easy grace added to her compelling looks. But it was the flash of temper in her eyes when she glanced up at him that intrigued Jensen. The women who followed around race car drivers didn't usually have strong opinions about much except wanting the men to notice them. He had a feeling Mrs. Montfort was bothered by his original statement and would have expressed her thoughts if it wasn't for her brother and the Harrisons standing right there.

Why was he disappointed that she didn't?

After the newcomers disappeared upstairs, Jensen followed the Harrisons back into the parlor, where family and friends had gathered to celebrate the upcoming nuptials. Jensen found a spot to stand next to Mrs. Harrison's chair, where he always preferred to be during social events. Despite her failing mental condition, she often made more sense than anyone else in society.

Having shown his guests to their rooms, Owen soon returned, pausing by Jensen and regarding him with an expression that made Jensen's throat go dry. He'd seen that look before. Owen was thinking about the family business and planning something that meant change. "You know, Jensen, I hate to bring up work during a party, but Mr. Harrison is set to make an announcement, and I wanted you to hear it before it's public knowledge."

Yes, this was going to be the conversation he'd been dreading. Jensen was aware enough of his shortcomings to recognize that he'd made a mess of every position Mr. Harrison had tried to put him in at his successful sporting goods store. Jensen wasn't cut out for managing employees, for paperwork, for dealing with indecisive customers. He was cut out for one career, but that was out of the question.

Leveling a look straight into Owen's eyes, Jensen waited for him to come out and say what he had to say. He'd been expecting this moment since Aggie announced her engagement and Mrs. Harrison's health further declined.

Owen shuffled from one foot to the other, then drew a breath, as if gathering his wits. "Mr. Harrison and I are meeting Monday to work out the details of me taking over for him after Aggie and I return from our honeymoon. He's ready to retire from running the company. But I'll have to make a strong impression on the board. I can't continue employing someone who isn't helping us move forward, no matter how much I like him as a person."

Jensen tried not to let Owen see how hard he had to swallow before he could respond. "I don't hold any hard feelings. I knew I'd run out of chances at some point."

Owen's face scrunched in confusion. "Then why haven't you found another job already?"

Was there a way to answer that wouldn't dig up long-buried, painful secrets? That wouldn't force him to admit he was only good at working on cars, but he could never touch one again?

A commotion at the door was the most fortunate distraction he could have imagined. The Montfort ladies swept into the room with Mr. Harrison, who began introducing them to the other guests.

Owen reached out to squeeze Jensen's shoulder. "I didn't want you to hear that news without me letting you know personally. But there's more

Mr. Harrison has to say and it might be the opportunity you've been waiting for."

Owen joined his sister while Jensen let himself sag back against the ornate paper-covered wall.

From her seat, Mrs. Harrison reached up to slide her fingers into his. "My dear boy, I wish you didn't have to struggle so."

Doing his best to smile at the kind woman who'd stepped in when his mother died, Jensen nodded. "So do I."

She cocked her head to one side, eyes far away in an expression he knew meant her mind wasn't in the present moment. "Perhaps Gregory can help. He's very good at running Albert's store. He could teach you."

Pain shot through Jensen so hard and fast that he couldn't breathe for several heartbeats. As it always did on the rare occasions Gregory's name came up, Jensen's mind started playing memories of that day. As if it were happening in front of him, he saw the young errand boy, Sam Kelly, running toward him with the bad news. Twisted, torn metal at the site of the accident. Archie Franklin, Gregory's rival in the race, smirking as he walked away unscathed.

Jensen squeezed his eyes shut, trying to regain his composure. Mrs. Harrison didn't know she'd brought up old hurts. If Gregory had been there, none of this would even be a problem. He would be running the store and Jensen could follow whatever dream he wanted. Instead, Gregory was dead, and Jensen was directionless. He'd spent the last five years trying to make up for Gregory's absence—for his part in that tragedy—by helping to make Harrison Goods a success. But he was failing. Now Owen would take the reins of Harrison Goods and Jensen would be without a job, a failure in the eyes of the people he cared for most.

And all because of one stupid, youthful mistake.

"Oh, hello. Have we met?" Mrs. Harrison raised her voice, and Jensen finally forced his eyes open to find Mrs. Montfort standing nearby. She'd changed into a form-fitting lace gown, the light pink creating a dramatic contrast with her dark hair and eyes. But those chocolate pools were narrowed now, darting back and forth between him and Mrs. Harrison. Had she caught any part of the conversation? Did she know who Gregory was?

Thankfully, she didn't ask. A gentle smile graced her face when she turned to Mrs. Harrison. "Why yes, but only for a moment. I'm Owen's sister, Flora."

Mrs. Harrison brightened. "From France!"

"Yes, that's right." Mrs. Montfort radiated compassion and grace, and Jensen's heart warmed toward her. Anyone who took the time to be kind to Mary Harrison was worth keeping around.

Then Mrs. Montfort glanced up and met his gaze. Her smile flattened. Was she still angry about his comment earlier? He should probably apologize, but he'd meant it. No one ought to go poking around in an engine if they didn't know what they were doing. Lives were on the line any time an automobile was involved. Why did he need to sugar-coat that reality?

He opened his mouth, searching for a truthful way to smooth it over with her, but the graceful tapping of silver on crystal caught their attention. Mr. Harrison stood at one end of the parlor with Owen next to him, beaming like a proud father. A pang hit Jensen without warning. He'd hoped Mr. Harrison would look at him like that when he took over Harrison Goods.

Silence fell over the room, and the family patriarch began his announcement. "As many of you know, Owen here has proven to be quite an asset to Harrison Goods. So much so that he's agreed to take on the responsibilities I've shouldered for years so that I can retire by the end of the summer."

An approving murmur rose from the guests. Jensen caught a proud smile on Mrs. Montfort's face as she watched her brother. Near the front of the room, Aggie was beaming. Everyone was proud of Owen, it seemed.

Mr. Harrison waited for the noise to die back down before continuing. "As he takes over the planning for the future of the company, we've made a decision that I'm very excited about. While we're doing well selling sporting equipment, Owen and I both see the wisdom in continuing to reach for the next wave of public interest. It was brought to my attention some months ago that rival companies have thrown their hats into the auto racing ring. We feel that's a smart decision, and so we've been preparing to start a Harrison Goods racing team. The shop we'll use to build our cars is nearly complete, so hiring will begin immediately."

Delighted clapping filled the air, but Jensen felt as if the floor had dropped out from under him. Why couldn't he find the wall to support him again? He stumbled from the room, not even caring who saw him about to fall apart. The hallway was quiet and dim, the perfect place to stuff the surge of panic back down into his chest.

Racing. Mr. Harrison, after living through the pain of losing his oldest son to a racing accident, was unfathomably starting an auto racing team.

Jensen straightened as the truth settled in. It was Owen. There hadn't been a word of this until Owen started taking over some of Mr. Harrison's tasks and talk of him running the company started. The man must have no idea of the horrors that accompanied racing. Mr. Harrison should know better, but he was so focused on retiring to care for his wife that he might be swayed to go along with anything.

Owen had done this.

And it was up to Jensen to fix it.

Chapter 2

As Mr. Harrison's announcement sank in, Flora took in the excited faces all around her—except for one. Jensen's skin had gone ashen. He fumbled for the wall behind him as if needing support, then abruptly dashed from the room. Aggie claimed he hated cars, and he'd made it clear earlier that he felt they were unsafe. But even with that knowledge, his reaction seemed rather dramatic.

Owen and Aggie waded toward her through congratulating guests, reaching her side with grins spread across both their faces. Owen leaned close. "I had a feeling you would be delighted by this announcement, and your expression confirms my suspicion."

"I love the idea, Owen. I'm proud that you were part of making it happen." Flora hesitated, planning her next words with care. Mr. Harrison's last comment about hiring for his racing team had stuck in Flora's mind, feeling very much like the opportunity she'd been praying and trusting God for. But she'd have to tread lightly or risk her inspired plan being denied before she had a chance to pursue it. "Do you have any racing team members in place?"

"Not yet, although we have some mechanics

in mind to ask. The construction crew recently completed the last few updates needed to make the shop functional, so we haven't started that process."

A shrewd look crossed Aggie's face. "Flora, didn't your husband race cars in France? I'm certain Owen mentioned you have an interest in the sport."

Memories struck Flora with unexpected force. Even two years after their last race, she could feel the rumble of the engine sending vibrations through her body, the jolt of hitting ruts in the road at high speed, and the sound of Henri's voice in her ear, urging her to push the car faster because an opponent was gaining on them. His motivation for encouraging her to race might have been selfish, but those moments when she felt he believed she could win had kept her going through the rest of their rocky marriage.

Flora swallowed around a twinge of worry that the truth would change Aggie's anticipation of their future relationship. Society women didn't often understand those who didn't conform to their ideas of appropriate feminine pursuits. "More than an interest. I was the driver in races while Henri rode along as the mechanic."

Rather than showing condemnation, Aggie brightened, more excited now than a moment ago. The tension that had been building drained from Flora's shoulders. "Owen, it's perfect. You have a driver you can trust right here. That's a wonderful start to hiring for your team."

But Owen didn't appear to share his fiancée's excitement. He put a calming hand on her arm. "I'm not sure that's the best plan, dear. Flora lost a great deal due to racing. I don't know that she's planning to return to it."

Her brother's eyes met hers, and Flora's heart sank at what she saw in them—an appeal for agreement and support. He didn't want her to drive. Could she find a way to convince him it was what she wanted, what she needed most at this moment? Henri may not have left enough of his family fortune for her and Isabelle to live off of, but he had blessed Flora with the skills to build a career in racing. If only the world wasn't so opposed to women doing what they loved if it was deemed unfeminine.

Then again, Owen seemed to be more worried about her emotional response to racing than the propriety of it. His wordless appeal reminded Flora of their childhood when the two of them had to face their cruel older brother, Clement, alone. Owen had often borne that look as he encouraged Flora to go along with whatever method he was trying to use to soothe Clement so they wouldn't be punished again. Flora forced herself not to assume the worst. She and her brother had hardly been together in person for any amount of time in the years since she'd married Henri. If they could discuss it, she might be able to convince Owen that racing—and the money that winning could bring in—would be welcome in her life.

Until she could speak to him alone, she focused on another matter. "I'm a bit worried about Jensen. He left in quite a state while Mr. Harrison was speaking. Should someone check on him?"

Aggie sighed. "I expected as much. I'll go see to him. You two stay here."

She floated out of the room, managing a polite excuse whenever a guest tried to engage her in conversation before continuing toward the door.

Once she was out of earshot, Owen ran a hand through his hair. "I suppose you have something to say about the racing team and Aggie's suggestion."

A group of young ladies—cousins of Aggie's, if Flora remembered correctly—squeezed past her on their way to the door, throwing effusive thanks and goodbyes at Owen as they went. He had the worst timing. It would be impossible to have such an important conversation here. "Could we discuss it later? Perhaps when there are fewer people around?"

Distracted by an older couple calling his name as they prepared to leave, Owen nodded. "Excellent idea. Thank you, Flora." Before he even finished speaking, he'd turned toward the couple and started walking them to the door. "Oh, Mr. and Mrs. Kendall, are you leaving?"

His voice switched from that of brother to host as they went, and Flora couldn't help a proud smile. He would make a wonderful heir for Mr. Harrison—that couldn't be argued.

The room soon emptied. A few guests stopped to say goodbye to Flora, but mostly, she was left to her thoughts. Thoughts of racing, of Henri, of the foolish financial decisions he'd made that left her and Isabelle in rather desperate need of an income. She remembered his easy smile when they first met. He'd been so different from Clement, with his threats to marry her off to the next old man he owed a gambling debt to if she disobeyed him the least bit. Meeting wild, exciting Henri on a trip to Europe had seemed like the perfect escape. But he'd turned out to be overbearing and foolish in a different way.

Owen, however, was proof that kind, responsible, honorable men existed. Knowing him, Flora couldn't doubt the truth of it. But that didn't make it easy to believe there were many more like him.

Before long, the only remaining occupants of the parlor were the close family. The Harrisons and Isabelle settled on a sofa near the fireplace. Aggie, Owen, and Flora all found chairs facing them. And Jensen—who had returned looking less ill but still grumpy—stood by the fireplace, twirling a crystal glass of water in his hands.

Mrs. Harrison glanced at Aggie, her eyes

clearer than they'd been earlier in the party. "My dear, remind me when Fred will arrive?"

Aggie directed a soft smile at her mother. "On Thursday. He'll be here in time for dinner with his wife, Beth. You remember her, don't you?"

Mrs. Harrison looked affronted, in her right mind again now. "Of course, I remember my daughter-in-law."

Next to her, Mr. Harrison slid his arm around her shoulders in a comforting gesture. "There's one more item to add to our schedule. I was hoping to wait for Fred and Beth, but I'm afraid with the wedding events, most of the week will be too busy. I'd like to arrange for all of us to tour the racing shop. Would tomorrow after church be acceptable to everyone?"

Nods and murmurs of agreement went around the small circle. Except for Jensen, whose scowl deepened. "I apologize, but that won't be possible for me. Perhaps another time."

Flora expected Mr. Harrison to accept the refusal and move on, but instead, he removed his arm from around his wife and leaned forward, resting his elbows on his knees. "We would love your support for this family venture, Jensen. Can't you spare a few minutes to join us?"

Red began to tinge Jensen's cheeks as every gaze in the room locked on him. How awkward that he was being put on the spot in such a way. But then, Flora was hardly one to understand the dynamics of a healthy, loving family. Perhaps this push and pull between family members *was* normal.

Aggie jumped in, her sweet, even tone perfect for calming the tension that was rising in the group. "Please Jensen, it will be a quick tour. This is a big step for Harrison Goods, and you're an important part of the company and our family. We want you to be there with us. And you could give input on increasing safety measures in the facility."

Would he give in? Flora waited with the others while conflicting emotions chased each other across Jensen's face. What was it that caused him to dislike cars so much that he would disengage from those closest to him over a mere visit to a racing shop? Would she get to know him well enough to find out?

The desire to discover more about Jensen was unexpected. His dour outlook reminded her a bit of Clement, which should have been an immediate cause to get as far from him as possible.

But Jensen Gable intrigued her. His loyalty to the Harrison family was especially intriguing. She could appreciate the way he doted on Mrs. Harrison. And it was hard not to be drawn to a man with convictions as strong as his, even if she didn't agree with them.

After a long pause, Jensen's expression settled

into resolve, and the tension broke in the room. "I'll join you at the shop. But only so I can see for myself that safety will be a priority."

The next morning, Jensen made every effort to listen to the minister at the church the Harrison family had attended for generations. But he'd never found the elderly minister's sermons interesting in any way. Ever since Gregory had been taken from them, church attendance had been a struggle—one Jensen more and more often chose not to fight. He preferred to keep what faith he had left to himself. Mrs. Harrison had implored him to join them for a few weeks while the family was together to celebrate Aggie's wedding, though, and he could never say no to her.

Glancing down the pew past Aggie and Owen, he caught a glimpse of Mrs. Montfort on the far end. She didn't look nearly as uninterested as he felt, instead hanging on the minister's droning words. Why did her attentiveness spark such fascination in him? He had the urge to find her after the service and ask what was so riveting, what she was learning from the sermon that he was missing. Would her opinions about faith be as strong as her determination to drive herself everywhere?

Jensen shook off thoughts of her and let his gaze stray to the sun slanting through a stained-glass window next to him. He had much more pressing problems than an errant attraction to the sister of his soon-to-be supervisor.

One of those problems was about to face him head-on that afternoon.

The service finally ended, and the family all gathered at the Harrison home for a quick lunch, laid out by the cook, Mrs. Kern. Jensen rushed through his meal so he could take a moment to peek into the kitchen and thank the aging woman for her work. She'd always snuck him bites of the tastiest treats as a child, and he'd loved her for it ever since.

At two o'clock that afternoon, Jensen gathered with the others in front of a tidy brick building two blocks from Harrison Goods. Mr. Harrison beamed with pride when he saw Jensen examining the well-designed exterior, with the words *Harrison Goods Racing* painted in huge white letters around two arched bay doors facing the street. He nudged Jensen with eyebrows raised. "Are you impressed that I pulled this off without anyone in the company knowing?"

Jensen frowned. This venture was hardly a laughing matter. "I don't know that impressed is quite the word, sir."

Undeterred, Mr. Harrison made his way to the entrance on the side of the building and turned to address the group. "I'm thankful each of you could join us today. I hope you'll see the care and effort that went into making this building a template for the future of auto racing. We consulted many drivers, mechanics, and team owners in the process of planning it, and I believe that will serve us well. Let's not waste any more time. Please come in."

Jensen didn't expect the pang of regret when he realized he hadn't been one of the mechanics Mr. Harrison had involved in planning the shop. Not that he would have agreed to participate in this scheme. But he would have appreciated being asked.

Conflicted, Jensen followed the others into the shop, their footsteps echoing through the space as Mr. Harrison switched on the lights. It was a far cry from the chicken coop at the back of the Harrisons' property he and Gregory had commandeered to build their cars in, with dirt floors, grimy windows that let in little light, and a distinct lack of space. This was what an elite racing garage should look like. Electric lights hanging from the ceiling brightened every inch of the smooth concrete floors. There was enough space in the center of the room to work on at least four cars at once. Every imaginable mechanic's tool hung in orderly rows above workstations lining the walls. It was a dream.

But cold reality splashed over Jensen when he caught a glimpse of a Peerless touring car in the back, awaiting a crew of reckless adventure-seekers to pilot it to their deaths. He squeezed his eyes tight against the all-too-familiar vision of flames engulfing an inverted car as men rushed toward it in the futile hope of saving a life. This shop was no dream, after all, but a nightmare where human lives were at stake.

He had a job to do here, and that was to stop this foolishness from happening.

Looking past the state-of-the-art equipment, he peeked into corners and under worktables while the others exclaimed in delight over the shop.

Finally, Mr. Harrison strolled over to join him. "Jensen, what do you think? Is it up to your standards?"

The entire group seemed to hold their breaths at once. He knew what they wanted to hear. But he couldn't say the right words just to make them happy, not when lives could be at risk. "What fire prevention methods do you have in place? What about ventilation during chemical use? I haven't seen a single first-aid kit. I can't imagine you'd be willing to open this shop without planning for employee safety first."

It might not be enough to stop Mr. Harrison from opening the shop altogether, but at least asking questions might delay him long enough that Jensen could convince the man this was reckless.

While everyone had their eyes fixed on him, Jensen felt Mrs. Montfort's gaze most prominently. Out of the corner of his eye, he could see her bewilderment. Of course, she wouldn't understand his intentions. Most people thought of cars as either unnecessary inconveniences or exciting innovations. Unless they'd seen firsthand the damage these vehicles could inflict at high speeds, they had no idea the danger posed every time a person climbed into one. He could tell Mrs. Montfort was part of the latter group. It would most likely take a tragedy for her to realize how misplaced her passion for cars was.

The sound of the side door opening again echoed through the room before Mr. Harrison could address his concerns. Jensen had to blink several times to decide if he was seeing what he thought he was. Framed in the doorway, Sam Kelly had grown in the years since Jensen had last seen him. But that flaming shock of red hair was unmistakable, bringing back visions of the young boy who ran errands for drivers and crews at the impromptu races they held on country roads and open pastures. He'd been the one to deliver the terrible news about Gregory. Now he stood almost as tall as Jensen and was built more like a farmhand than the gangly errand boy Jensen remembered.

Mr. Harrison welcomed Sam with delight, offering a brief introduction to those in the group who didn't know him. Sam greeted everyone with professional poise, even shaking Jensen's hand, although his roguish smile was the same as always. Jensen waited through the small talk, desperate to know why Sam was there. Had Mr. Harrison gotten the young man tangled up in this racing mess?

Mr. Harrison eventually got to the point, explaining Sam's presence. "I've put out some inquiries about men who would be good options for our new team, and Sam's name came up more than once. I'm sure even Jensen couldn't argue that his years of experience in racing make him an excellent candidate to be a mechanic for us. Sam, have you come with an answer for me?"

Nodding, Sam appeared far more mature and capable than Jensen ever would have imagined the ragamuffin boy could have become. "I'm sorry, but I had already agreed to be a mechanic for another race team right before you contacted me. If I'd known, you can be sure I'd have chosen you, Mr. Harrison. Gregory was the kindest driver I ever met, and it would be an honor to work for a team carrying on his work."

Mr. Harrison's expression hardly changed, but Jensen could see him holding his emotions in check. Whether it was the mention of Gregory or the disappointment of not getting Sam to work for him, Jensen couldn't be sure. For his part, there was no relief that Sam had declined the job, only worry over the fact that he was already entrenched in this wretched sport.

Owen had made himself a spot next to Mr. Harrison and Sam, following the conversation with interest. "I'm almost afraid to ask, Sam. Are you working for Ronald Dorman? We learned of his racing plans last year."

The name settled everything into place in Jensen's mind. Ronald Dorman was the owner of Harrison Goods' strongest competition and Mr. Harrison's lifelong rival. The knowledge that Mr. Dorman had started a racing team put this situation into perspective. Jensen had to confirm his suspicions. He waved one hand to encompass the entire shop. "Is that the real reason for this stunt? Did you two pour company money into a dangerous game just because Ronald Dorman is doing it?"

A heavy silence filled the shop. Though he'd thought he was doing well at keeping himself under control, it was clear from the expressions around him that his disgust had shown through. He ran a hand over his face, working to get himself together. This was why he stayed far away from cars at all costs. He couldn't even manage his emotions around them, much less make rational, safe decisions.

Owen shifted from one foot to the other. "It's not a stunt. We came up with the idea as a way to keep up with Mr. Dorman, yes. But we're also confident this will launch Harrison Goods into the modern era. Like it or not, cars are the future of transportation. We'd rather get involved early than be late."

Sam cleared his throat, reminding everyone that he was there. "I don't suppose I'm meant to hear all this, being Mr. Dorman's employee and all. I respect you folks enough that I wanted to stop by and deliver my news in person, but I'll be going now."

Regret cooled Jensen's frustration. He'd made everyone uncomfortable again. "Before you go, I believe I can speak for all of us when I say that we'd like to celebrate your . . . opportunity. Tell us about it. When will you start racing?"

Sam perked up at the chance to talk about his new job. "In a few weeks. Mr. Dorman has had teams run at some small local races, but our first big event will be the Glidden Tour starting in July."

Mr. Harrison cocked his head in a gesture Jensen knew all too well. It meant a plan was forming in his mind. "I've heard about that one. It's an endurance race, correct? Run over several days with check-ins each evening along a pre-determined route, if I remember right."

Enthusiasm radiated through Sam's every move as he nodded. "Yes, sir. Ten days, to be exact, heading north from New York City through several states, then returning to the American Automobile Association headquarters."

Mrs. Montfort joined the conversation, her

excitement matching Sam's. "I'd love to hear more. I enjoy long races. I drove in the Paris-Madrid race in 1903 with my late husband as the mechanic. We had an excellent start position and might have won our weight class if not for a broken axle near the end. But ten days—that would be a challenge for any team."

Jensen's mind went hazy, and he had to take a moment to orient his thoughts. She didn't simply enjoy the thrill of being at a race. This woman drove the race car herself. With her husband. What kind of man encouraged such reckless folly? His mind flew back over their previous interactions and her obvious love of racing, seeing it all in a new light. How had he missed the signs of another person who loved the speed and freedom racing brought as much as he did?

And how was he going to continue fighting for the safety of those he loved if her passion for racing kept them all moving forward with this nonsense?

Chapter 3

Next to Jensen, Flora heard the whoosh of air leaving his body when the truth about her involvement in racing slipped out. She was so intrigued by the idea of this Glidden Tour that she had forgotten how people tended to respond to a female race car driver.

But after several years of facing down biased men on the track, Flora knew what to do. She squared her shoulders and refused to look in Jensen's direction, instead focusing all her attention on Sam. It was plain as day from his expression of admiration that he didn't share the common opinion that women should refrain from any sort of excitement in their lives.

His words backed up her observation. "Mrs. Montfort, I'm impressed. Do you plan to continue racing here? Are you working for Mr. Harrison?"

Flora tried to maintain a light smile, but the fact that she longed to answer *yes* was hard to ignore. A silent plea rose from her heart. *Lord, please let me race again. Give me a way to support myself and Isabelle.*

Glancing over with interest, Mr. Harrison saved her from needing to come up with a graceful response. "Owen, I'm surprised you didn't think of this. We'll have to discuss the possibility of

Mrs. Montfort driving for us. For now, though, we haven't hired anyone. I hate to rush you out, but I promised our family a short tour of the shop, so we better get to it."

Mr. Harrison walked Sam to the door with a friendly hand on his shoulder, then started his official tour.

A mix of emotions accompanied Flora through the space. It was thrilling to see the advanced machinery Mr. Harrison and Owen had invested in for their shop. She longed to spend more time with some of the equipment, trying it out to see how much easier the new technology would make mechanical adjustments.

But at the same time, her heart ached. Despite the excitement Mr. Harrison and Aggie showed when they learned about Flora's racing experience, there were so many reasons for her to fear the possibility of driving for their team was only a silly dream. More than one racing organization had started barring women from entering. Men on teams sometimes refused to work with a woman or quit altogether if the matter of a female driver came up. She wanted the venture to be a success for Owen, which meant he needed the best crew—one that could create opportunities and partnerships instead of forcing doors to close.

Maybe it was better if she struck out on her own to drive so no one she cared about would feel the sting of any repercussions from her choices.

Flora ran her fingers over the smooth, shining wood of a worktable. Next to her, Isabelle smiled. "This is a lovely space to work. Will you consider it if you're given the choice?"

Dear Isabelle, always thinking of Flora's preferences. Her mother-in-law didn't deserve the mess Henri had left them in. The older woman had spent years caring for her ailing husband and handling Henri's immature impulses. Isabelle always claimed she should have been sterner with Henri as a child, but his angelic face had made it impossible. After the years she'd been married to him, Flora could understand that. He'd had a way of entrenching a person in his view of the world, which he considered his playground with no consequences for his actions. It was enjoyable to go along with such a vibrant man for a time, but it made the crash back to reality all the more difficult.

He was wrong. There were indeed consequences. But sometimes they fell to the people left behind.

Trying not to let too much sadness tinge her smile, Flora shrugged. "There's much to consider before answering that question." As usual, she would have to be practical. If racing wasn't going to provide enough secure income to support the two of them, she would have to give it up.

Flora's gaze roamed the magnificently appointed shop. As much as she wanted to protect Owen's business from her choices, a team with the financial support and clout of Albert Harrison behind it might be the only one that could convince the racing world to allow a woman into their ranks. The Harrison Goods racing team might be her best option, after all.

That truth niggled in the back of her mind for the rest of the shop tour.

It shadowed her thoughts for the next several days.

The hours she spent helping Aggie finish preparations for her wedding were all eclipsed by the realization that Flora's choices were as limited here as they had been in France. Few teams would choose to hire a woman. If Mr. Harrison wanted her to drive for him, she would be a fool to refuse the opportunity.

But what would Owen say?

With only a few busy days remaining until his wedding and honeymoon, she'd barely seen her brother through most of the week. Owen hadn't made any effort to return to the subject when they were together. Flora would have to make the time and confront him with her plan before Saturday, or she might lose the chance altogether.

On Thursday evening, Flora, Owen, and Isabelle went to the Harrisons' home for a garden party celebrating the arrival of Fred Harrison and his wife. It wasn't a long ride, but the differences in the neighborhoods were clear. Flora was admiring a lovely park Owen called Rittenhouse Square when the carriage slowed in front of one of the largest homes, a towering mansion built out of pale marble with large arched windows lining the front.

The driver stopped the carriage under one of the pavilions that flanked either side of the home, letting them out in the covered entrance. Flora hadn't realized quite how well Aggie's family had done with their sporting goods store, but it was clear that Owen was marrying into the kind of fortune Flora had enjoyed. Before Henri squandered it all, anyway. This home could stand alongside any of the most fashionable houses in the Paris district where the Montforts used to live.

The door opened to reveal a stately but kind-looking butler. "Good evening, Mr. Lewis, ladies. Please follow me."

The three of them followed the butler through the house and out to the backyard, where the party had been set up to take advantage of the warm evening. The back of the house was much more relaxed than the front, with bay windows, a curved balcony, and a beautiful octagonal greenhouse that led to sprawling gardens.

Owen strode straight to his bride's side, Aggie's cheeks flushing when he dropped a kiss on her lips. For a few moments, Flora found the nearby beribboned fabric awning sheltering a group of musicians to be the most fascinating thing in the world.

Finally, the couple put a little space between themselves, and Flora could stop feigning interest in the decorations. She smiled as Mrs. Harrison came forward with her hands outstretched. "Flora, it's a delight to see you again."

The Harrison matriarch was fully in the present this time, not slipping in and out of the past as she had been at Owen's house last week. She let Mrs. Harrison take both of her hands and draw her toward the clump of family members. "The pleasure is mine, Mrs. Harrison. Your home is quite lovely."

Mrs. Harrison beamed at the praise. "I'm so pleased everyone can be here to greet our dear Fred and his wife, Beth. They'll be out to join us in a few moments."

The whole family seemed excited about the prospect of seeing the youngest brother and his wife.

Mr. Harrison put his arm around his wife. "Of course, we can't begin until Jensen arrives home from the store either."

"Well, wait no more."

Heat crept up Flora's neck when Jensen's deep voice rumbled close behind her. Her heart fluttered in a disturbing way, one that reminded her of the intense infatuation that led her to impulsively marry Henri. She turned to find

Jensen standing inches behind her, dashing in a navy-blue sack coat and straw hat. His eyes met hers for the briefest moment before he stepped around her, a warm spark evident as he took in her pale-green lingerie dress. His arm brushed her shoulder, the contact so quick she would have missed it if not for the lingering tingle that made her breath catch in her throat.

The men greeted Jensen while Aggie and Mrs. Harrison chatted with Isabelle, so Flora took the chance to slip off to the side, allowing a few extended family members who had arrived to take her place. She watched the Harrisons welcome a variety of aunts, uncles, and cousins with smiles of genuine delight.

She'd never seen a family where every member was as loving and joyful as the Harrisons. After her messy childhood, marrying Henri had seemed like a dream, with his doting mother and his initial kindness to Flora. But it hadn't taken long at all to discover he was only kind when he got what he expected from people. Henri was used to getting his way, Flora was discovering what it was like to get hers for the first time, and neither ever wanted to give in. It had been a terrible combination. Any disagreement turned into an explosive argument.

The Harrisons cared for those around them with a generosity Flora admired. That was the type of person she knew God wanted her to be. Finding a balance between giving to others and not being used by people like Clement was the problem.

As a few more family and friends streamed into the garden, footsteps on the brick path alerted Flora to Jensen's approach.

He stopped in front of her, shifting his weight from one foot to the other as he spoke. "I'm glad I found you alone for a moment."

He paused and cleared his throat, looking as though he was struggling to find the words he wanted. Curiosity nearly got the best of Flora as she waited. What on earth could he have to say to her that was so important?

Several family members reached them and stopped to greet Jensen, who then introduced Flora to them. Finally, they were alone again and he found his voice. "I couldn't help noticing your interest in the Glidden Tour when we were all at the shop the other day."

That was not at all the opening she'd expected. "Yes, it's a delightful concept. I'm sure you heard me say that my late husband and I raced together, so the sport is near to my heart."

Jensen's gaze roamed the garden, never once coming near to meeting hers. She took a moment to examine him, from blond hair that was almost but not quite perfectly in place to large scarred hands that spoke of years of hard labor. That detail caught her by surprise. She'd assumed his work at Harrison Goods meant he was accustomed to sitting behind a desk or greeting customers all day. What had led him from physical labor to a career in the store?

For a moment, his eyes landed on her, and the intensity of them brought her mind right back into the conversation. "It seemed as if you might be thinking of driving in the tour yourself."

Was he worried about her? Or did he disapprove of a woman driving? "I must admit, the idea appeals to me. I would love to build a career in racing. But I'm striving to make wiser decisions moving forward, and I don't want to rush into racing again at the first opportunity if it isn't the best choice."

There was no mistaking the relief on Jensen's face at her response, and it irked her. She was certain now that he was more disapproving than concerned. "What difference does it make to you whether or not I drive, anyway?"

Her question was poorly timed. Before he had a moment to respond, a commotion by the house distracted them. Flora didn't know the young couple who were being surrounded by guests, but she could assume by the joyous exclamations filling the garden that they were the beloved Fred and Beth. Jensen immediately went to join them, leaving Flora to mull over the motive for his questions without the possibility of getting any answers.

• • •

Jensen let out a slow breath. At least he didn't have to come up with an answer that wouldn't make Mrs. Montfort more defensive. Thank goodness for Fred's excellent timing. As he headed back toward the house to greet the young couple, Flora marched toward the path that snaked through Mrs. Harrison's flower garden. Had he upset her that much, or did she not have any interest in meeting the new arrivals?

Focusing on Fred and Beth, Jensen finally made his way through the crowd to greet them.

Fred grinned, as friendly and cheerful as ever, and reached out to give Jensen a warm hug. "There he is, my big brother."

Jensen mumbled a greeting, but the words shattered the joy he'd felt moments ago. He wasn't Fred's brother. A statement like that would make people think Jensen was trying to fill that role in Fred's life when he had no right to. It should have been Gregory getting a hug from Fred and greeting his bride.

But Fred's enthusiasm was impossible to argue with. Jensen summoned the best smile he could, returned the hug, then moved on to welcome Beth with polite small talk. Anything to turn the conversation from straying toward Gregory. "How was your trip? You made good time despite the delay, it seems."

Beth exhibited a calm warmth that was the

perfect foil for Fred's exuberance. "The train had to make a brief repair. I love to travel, so I didn't mind one bit. It allowed us time to see the most charming little town in rural West Virginia. The mountain view more than made up for the lost time."

His heart swelling, Jensen couldn't help smiling at how perfect this woman was for Fred. They were very near what he'd consider too sweet, though, when their eyes met and they both melted into silly grins. Jensen hated to give up time visiting with the young man he'd hardly seen these last few years, but maybe it wouldn't be so terrible if Fred and Beth decided to take their delayed honeymoon this summer as they'd talked about. There would be benefits to them taking a trip now, even if it cut their time at home short. Namely, that their saccharine expressions wouldn't make him ill.

As more extended family stepped up to greet the newcomers, Jensen found himself scanning the flower garden for Mrs. Montfort. He didn't see her, meaning she'd either returned to the party, or she'd found Mrs. Harrison's special bench tucked in the one spot with plants tall enough to provide privacy. The only question was why Jensen felt the urge to go find out if she was there.

Mrs. Harrison clapped to get the guests' attention and announced the refreshments were ready, causing people to flock toward a row of tables laden with a variety of light foods fit for a warm evening outdoors—cakes, cookies, tiny sandwiches, fruit, lemonade, and tea. Jensen had his eye on the ices, though he hoped Mrs. Harrison had provided flavors besides her favorite of cucumber.

Musicians seated in simple wooden chairs near the house provided gentle background music as the guests milled around talking and eating. Perhaps he could slip out before the dancing started. He was the furthest thing from an eligible bachelor, with no fortune or family name to draw husband-seeking ladies and their mamas to pursue him. Spending hours dancing with women who were only biding their time until a wealthier man noticed them was never his idea of fun.

Instead, he ate while watching many of the younger guests take up positions to play lawn tennis and croquet, then he went in search of Mr. Harrison. Talking business would be preferable to watching others enjoy frivolous amusements from the sidelines.

What he ended up finding was Mr. Harrison, Fred, and Owen. The three men stood in the middle of a small circular terrace built into the garden path, surrounded by hedges and deep in animated conversation. Before he could decide whether to walk away or join them, Fred caught sight of him and waved Jensen over.

As he approached, Mr. Harrison spoke in the firm voice he used in the Harrison Goods board room. "It's an opportunity I can't pass up, Owen. I'm not asking your permission to speak to your sister. I'm simply asking your opinion of whether or not she would be interested in the idea."

Fred moved toward his father to let Jensen into the circle. "Jensen, we're discussing an idea Aggie and I devised before she came out to the party."

Glancing around the group, Jensen read a variety of emotions on the men's faces. Whatever this plan was, it was already causing friction. As the youngest in the family, Fred had been rather spoiled, giving him the ability to talk his family into nearly any scheme as an adult. What was it now, and how did it involve Mrs. Montfort?

Unlike the other two, Fred beamed with excitement. "I've come up with the perfect wedding trip to surprise Beth with. Neither of us enjoys playing tourist. Following a guide around crowded attractions is hardly our idea of fun."

No doubt, whatever Fred had devised would be the exact opposite of a calm, reserved honeymoon walking through historical sites and touring gardens. "So what is it?" Jensen asked.

A familiar mischievous look crossed Fred's face, forming a knot in Jensen's stomach. There was more going on here than a simple trip. Fred held up a finger to Jensen. "Let me find out one thing first." He turned to Owen again. "Do you think your sister will be willing to at least consider it?"

Owen fidgeted with the buttons on his loose jacket. "Most likely, she would. But that doesn't mean this is the best time to bring it up to her. I'd hoped she could spend some time settling back into life in America. She's been through so much."

A cleared throat stopped the cryptic discussion. The men turned to find Flora standing behind them with her arms crossed and eyes blazing. "And what's being planned for me here?"

Mr. Harrison and Owen had the decency to look humbled. Fred, however, jumped forward and drew her into the group. "Ah, you must be Mrs. Montfort. Aggie told me all about you. No plans are being made for you. We were explaining to your brother our intention to ask if you might be interested in helping with my idea for a surprise wedding trip for Beth. I'll need both you and Jensen to pull it off."

At the inclusion of his name, the knot in Jensen's stomach turned into a rock, weighing on him and making his response gruffer than he intended. "Just tell us your idea, Fred."

The light in Fred's eyes dimmed, bringing guilt to churn up Jensen's stomach around the rock. He'd never been able to blame anyone in the Harrison family for doting on Fred. The younger man's infectious optimism made even Jensen want to keep him happy. Especially after Fred's actual brother had been taken from him at only fifteen, leaving Jensen to fill the gap, no matter how unworthy he was to do so.

Jensen softened his tone, trying to let a more pleasant expression warm his words. "We need to know what you want before either of us can decide if we're interested."

Fred clasped his hands together, almost bouncing as he spoke. "As I was saying, Beth and I aren't traditional tourists. We both crave a bit of adventure before we settle down into family life. So I thought we could arrange to field a team in the Glidden Tour. Aggie told me Ronald Dorman is putting a team together, and with our new shop nearly ready to open, I see no reason why Harrison Goods shouldn't also run it. Beth and I could ride along, as many people do in reliability tours."

Jensen had to force back another harsh retort. Even for Fred, this was asking too much. And Mr. Harrison seemed to be considering this nonsense, even supporting it. Would he really encourage another son to risk his life in a car race?

But Fred wasn't done. "Now, I know you're not keen on racing, Jensen. But that's where your help would be invaluable. Because of your history with racing and your concern for safety, you're the perfect person to ride along as our mechanic.

And the moment Aggie told me Owen's sister raced cars, I knew we had the best team right here ready to go. Jensen, Mrs. Montfort, what do you think about being our driver and mechanic in the Glidden Tour?"

Chapter 4

I would consider it."

"Absolutely not."

Despite them speaking at the same moment, Flora heard Jensen's refusal loud and clear. Considering Fred's exuberant, hopeful expression—that of a man ready to give his bride the trip of her dreams—how could Jensen say no without even thinking it over for a moment?

But it didn't take long to see that the group was divided in their opinions of Fred's idea. Jensen and Owen both scowled, while Mr. Harrison looked torn. Fred's face fell, and he looked as if he was preparing to argue his point. It was up to Flora to resolve the standoff before it turned into an angry fight, much like every discussion with Clement ever had. "Fred, it's a charming idea. There are women who love and appreciate an adventure now and then, and if Beth is one, then the Glidden Tour will be an excellent choice for your trip. But are you certain you need me and Jensen specifically? Perhaps you could go with Mr. Dorman's team?"

Judging by the shock that emanated from the group, she'd said the wrong thing. Mr. Harrison's face went from a furrowed brow to a set jaw and tight lips quicker than the Decauville starting a race. "You wouldn't know, of course, but Ronald

Dorman is not the type of man I want anyone I care about to associate with. He'll do anything—and stomp on anyone—to get ahead. My son and daughter-in-law will not be riding along with his team."

Fred took the opportunity to begin his arguments. "I've thought through this thoroughly. There's no one I trust more than Jensen to make sure our car runs well and that we're safe for the entire tour. It's expected to be a grueling drive, and many teams will face mechanical problems, so the best mechanic is vital. And Mrs. Montfort, when Aggie mentioned your driving experience, I made a telephone call to an acquaintance who is familiar with racing in Europe. He confirmed that you and your husband had quite a bit of success, didn't you?"

Flora's heart swelled that he'd heard a good report of her racing career. "We did win much of the time. And please, call me Flora."

With a knowing grin, Fred nodded. "Indeed. And while the mechanic is important to keep things running, it's the driver who leads the team. Beth and I know nothing about cars. We need an experienced driver we can trust, and you are certainly that. Plus, I've heard that your Decauville is durable and built to stand up against the fastest cars out there. If we're going to go on this trip, I'd like to see us make a race of it, and a good car will be an advantage."

The little corner of Flora's heart that had jumped with excitement when she first heard about the tour came to life again. But the way Owen was chewing at the inside of his cheek drained the joy from the moment. The last thing she wanted was to alienate the only family she had left. Could she make him understand how important this was to her? "Owen, I don't want to agree without your support."

"And I don't want to control you, Flora. But I'm concerned about you chasing wild adventures again. I'd rather see you settle down a bit."

Her heart was already becoming set on doing the tour, and Owen simply must understand. She stepped forward to face her brother. "It's hardly wild. The tour barely qualifies as a race. Remember, Sam Kelly told us it will be ten days, with check-in points where everyone has to stop. So speed won't matter as much as consistency. Keeping the car running and avoiding obstacles on the road is what will determine the winner. I know I can do my job well, and if Jensen is the mechanic Fred claims he is, his part shouldn't be a problem either."

All eyes turned back to Jensen, who raised both hands as if to ward them off. "Oh, no. I'm not doing this. I refuse to participate in racing anymore, and despite what Mrs. Montfort claims, anything with a timed ending and a winner is a race."

At that moment, Aggie approached the group, wrapping her arm around Owen's. "Dearest, it's time to send off some of our guests. Join me at the house?"

Nodding to his intended, Owen locked eyes with Flora. "Don't commit to anything until we have a chance to talk. Please."

Aggie whisked him away before Flora could argue. She stamped down a tendril of frustration, wanting to be angry that he wouldn't let her make her own choices. But she knew deep in her heart that his intention wasn't to control her. If they were going to have a healthy relationship in the future, they should figure this out together. Flora turned to the group of men still standing around her. "I'll talk with Owen and let you know what we decide, Fred. But I'm certain I can convince him. He won't want to keep me from doing what I love."

As if it was already decided, Fred and Mr. Harrison started chatting about details related to the business side of the tour, things such as the finances and how they should advertise the racing team. But Jensen muttered, "You're a fool to take this lightly. Lives will be lost in this fiasco."

Turning to face him, Flora finally had a target for her frustration. "It's a tour, not a cut-throat race. It will be leisurely and friendly. How do you consider that dangerous?"

Jensen fixed his intense gaze on her, and Flora

caught her breath at the pain etched across his face. He felt so strongly about this that there must be more to it than simple concern for safety. "Anytime fools get into cars intending to beat each other to a finish, it's dangerous. Anytime the point is to get somewhere the fastest, it's dangerous. If you've raced as much as Owen says you have, you're sure to have seen that."

Flora refused to let unbidden memories of Henri's death distract her. Accidents happened, but that was no reason to stop living her life. "Yes, I do know the risks, better than you could understand. That proves my confidence in this tour is not foolish. I know what's at stake, and I still believe this is worth doing. My opinions matter as much as yours. Why is that so difficult for you to accept?"

Her words were met with silence, but voices beyond the two of them brought Flora's awareness back to the party still going on. She'd let herself get too invested in convincing Jensen and forgotten this was an event where she should be supporting her brother. "I apologize. This isn't the place for such a discussion. I'll talk with my brother, and then I'll make my decision about the tour. But perhaps you ought to discuss it with someone, too, and consider why you're so set against a tour that exists to promote safe driving conditions."

Flora turned and held her head high, intending

to pass Jensen and return to the front of the gardens where Owen and Aggie had gone. But she found herself glancing up into his tight, scowling face as she squeezed by him on the narrow path. He started to reach out—to stop her retreat? Instead, he muttered again, for her ears only. "I'm sorry for calling you a fool. You're the furthest thing from that."

A shiver worked its way up and down her spine as he dropped back a step and allowed her to continue on her path. What a confounding man. First, he treated her like an idiot, then he looked at her with such intensity and complimented her intelligence.

There was indeed something at risk if she was going to spend any amount of time with Jensen Gable. The tour might not be dangerous, but keeping her heart from becoming enchanted with a man who didn't want anything to do with her was a hazard she might not be ready to face.

Jensen watched Flora join her brother and his fiancée with conflicting emotions. Astounding that the woman would even consider continuing to race if she truly knew the damage it could cause, the lives it took. It was beyond his understanding how anything could still draw her to the sport if she'd seen the cost associated with it as she said she had.

At the same time, her strength and willingness

to take on the adventure were the exact characteristics Jensen found lacking in so many women. Confidence like Flora's was more attractive than it had any right to be. Not to mention her intelligence and kindness. Spending any amount of time with her was going to be as dangerous as the race itself. The last thing he needed in his life was a woman who loved automobiles.

He turned to find Fred and Mr. Harrison both staring at him. Fred grinned knowingly, but Jensen shook his head. "Whatever you're thinking, stop. Let's get back to this racing business. Why would you want to subject your wife to such an event, Fred? I know you could find a wedding trip that isn't a dreary tour but also doesn't put both your lives at risk."

For the first time in a long time, Jensen saw Fred's confidence falter. "I'm preparing for a life in the ministry, Jensen. We'll never be living lavishly. I haven't told Mother yet, but our visit here will be much shorter than we planned. I've been hired by a church that needs a minister in a month. This is my chance to give Beth an entire adventure in a few short days without spending beyond our means."

Fred's earnest face told Jensen all he needed to know about how important this was to the younger man. "But a race, Fred? Isn't there anything else you could do?"

Mr. Harrison finally spoke up, twisting his

fingers together in obvious agitation. "It's partly my fault, Jensen. You were right at the racing shop. This is mostly because of Ronald Dorman. If he gets the upper hand in racing and the sport takes off as I believe it will, a good showing in races would cement his company as the sporting goods store of choice for teams. Harrison Goods will always be second after that. We'll risk losing customers and contracts, everything that keeps us going." He fixed Jensen with the gaze of a father, not the owner of a sports empire. "It would mean so much for our business—and our family—if you would help us."

A throbbing pain started in the back of Jensen's head, and he tried to relax the muscles he'd been clenching. He should explain why this was so hard for him, why he felt he was being forced into choosing between the family he loved and the sport he hated.

But they'd gone through the same loss he had and seemed to have healed far more easily. Would they understand that he was frozen in place by his own stupid actions? If he told them the entire truth, would they ever forgive him for his part in Gregory's death?

Just like every other time he'd asked himself those questions for the last five years, the answer Jensen came to was no. He looked at his companions. "I doubt I'm going to be able to talk any of you out of this. But why are you set on involving me? I'm sure you could find another qualified and far more passionate mechanic."

When his voice came out as a rough croak, Jensen wanted nothing more than to find a quiet space to be alone so he didn't have to face this. But Fred wasn't going to let it go. He stepped close and put one hand on Jensen's shoulder. "Any good mechanic won't do. We need the best. You may not admit it, but that's you. When Gregory died, you promised me you'd be like the brother who was taken from me. Well, a brother would do this with me. *My* brother would do this."

Jensen had to work to relax his hands, which had clenched into fists at the mention of Gregory's name. Fred had some nerve, leveraging Jensen's love for Gregory and guilt over his death to get his way, even if he didn't know about the deep level of remorse Jensen lived with.

The worst part was that it was working.

Looking into the sincere, imploring eyes of the two men he loved most, Jensen's resistance broke down. "How can I live with it if something happens to any of you, Fred?"

A grin broke out on his dear friend's face, so much like Gregory's that Jensen's heart lurched. "That's why you'll be along with us. With you there, nothing will happen. If Mrs. Montfort agrees, we'll be all set. You'll see, Jensen. It'll be the trip of a lifetime."

Without waiting for further arguments, Fred stuck both hands in his pockets and ambled toward the house, where the rest of the family stood with their guests. He looked so pleased with himself that Jensen nearly rushed after him to refuse to do the race. But Mr. Harrison took the opportunity to clench the deal. "I know you're opposed to this, Jensen. But I hope you see how much is riding on the team doing well in this tour. Events like this have the potential to make or break companies."

Jensen was at his limit of being convinced. "Yes, in the automobile industry. This doesn't have to have anything to do with a sporting goods company. We sell baseballs and football helmets and tennis rackets. What bearing does auto racing need to have on us?"

Running a hand through his hair, Mr. Harrison looked weary. "I didn't want to burden Fred with the details, but it's more than the desire not to come in second to Ronald Dorman. The truth is, he's been stealing away our customers for months. Whole teams have switched to using his products because he somehow gives them lower prices than I can afford to give. Last week, we lost a bid to provide all the baseball gear for the Philadelphia Athletics next season. We need new sources of revenue, and there's plenty of equipment I can stock related to racing. Driving gloves and goggles, dusters for the ladies, custom items like horns. I can see an entire industry opening up around it. And Harrison Goods needs to be involved."

Against his better judgment, a thrill raced through Jensen. An industry supporting auto racing? To his younger self, that idea would have sounded like a dream.

Now? It was more like a nightmare he was being dragged into against his will.

Mr. Harrison, knowing Jensen as well as any father, must have sensed the war within him. "I know you swore you'd never race again after . . . after the accident. We've all watched you snub anything to do with cars altogether. But they're going to be a large part of the future, like it or not. I won't force you if you're still opposed. I'll even try to talk Fred out of it. But it seems to me, something like the Glidden Tour—with its focus on increasing safety for drivers—might be something you could support."

Any fight left in Jensen fizzled into nothing. If he was going to have to accept that cars would become more and more popular for everyday driving—which seemed to be the case—then he also had to support efforts to promote safety. It was the least he could do to make up for what happened to Gregory. There was only one thing left to say.

"Fine. I'll be your mechanic."

Chapter 5

"I can't understand why you want to race again, Flora." Standing by the fireplace in his parlor, Owen wanted an explanation, one Flora had already tried to give twice.

Fighting to hold back her frustration, Flora rubbed her hand over the back of her neck. Lashing out would only halt the conversation and turn it into an argument. She had years of experience hiding her true feelings from the men in her life, but she hated having to do the same with Owen now. "It's an opportunity for me to do what I love, Owen. Can't you be happy for me and support what I want to do?"

She'd assumed he would. Since the moment Fred brought up the possibility of her driving, she'd gone over and over the facts so she would be ready to talk it over with her brother the moment they returned to his house. Joining the team for the Glidden Tour was a good choice for her. Owen usually championed her cause, no matter what it was. He was the one person in her life who saw and understood her. Clement had always been the one to shut the door on her dreams. Henri was kinder at times but no less controlling or more interested in her dreams than Clement had been.

Was Owen going to join their ranks?

Isabelle looked on from a chair by the large front window with her sewing in her lap, meeting Flora's gaze with calm understanding. Flora had confided in Isabelle about her oldest brother's cruel ways soon after marrying Henri. And Isabelle often admitted how selfish her son was, even if her tendency to spoil him was part of the problem. Her advice to Flora had always held peaceful, practical insight into the ways of men. Would she stand with Flora on this subject?

Clearing her throat, Isabelle glanced between Owen and Flora. "I hate to see siblings at odds like this. Flora, you should tell your brother why you must run this race. The true reason why."

Flora's first response was to shake her head. She didn't want to admit why she needed to build a career in the first place. Owen would offer to give her the money she and Isabelle needed. He wouldn't understand her desire to earn a living for herself, to be completely independent for the first time in her life, to make every choice on her own.

But Isabelle's slight nod reminded Flora that the woman was usually quite wise. Maybe it wouldn't hurt to reveal her position to Owen. He'd always been the kindest man in her life. Would he accept her desire for a racing career, even if he didn't understand it?

Sitting in one of the chairs near the fireplace, Flora gestured for Owen to join her. He dropped carelessly into the other chair, causing it to creak under his weight and bringing a smile to Flora's lips. This was still her beloved brother, the one who made her feel loved and secure when they were children. He had even seen and understood her need to get away from Clement, even if her method was more impulsive than his. She could trust him.

"I don't need to remind you what it was like for us growing up with Clement in charge of our family affairs. But I'm not sure you can ever know the fear I experienced as a female with no say in my life for all those years."

Owen's eyes softened, and he reached out to take her hand. "I always thought you had a worse time of it than I did. At least I had some options, even if they weren't good ones. But what does that have to do with driving a race car?"

Flora shook her head. "Patience, Owen. I'm getting there. I'm sure you know by now that my marriage to Henri was, more than anything, a way to keep Clement from marrying me off to the next old man he needed a favor from."

She paused to glance at Isabelle, hoping her words wouldn't hurt the dear older woman. As much as she'd seen his flaws, Isabelle was still Henri's mother and mourned him more now—two years after his death—than Flora did.

To her relief, Isabelle smiled and started gathering her sewing supplies. "It is getting late and I'm quite tired from the lovely party. I'll leave you to finish your talk. *Bonne nuit.*"

They returned her wish for a good night and watched as she shuffled from the room. Flora's heart ached over how much older Isabelle looked now than when they'd first met only a few years ago. She'd lost a husband and her only child in that time, and the grief had marked her permanently.

Once she left and silence fell over the room, Flora focused her full attention on her brother. "Henri was passionate and exciting. I didn't believe he wanted to use me like Clement used everyone around him. But over time, I saw how he would get so consumed by his desires that he didn't take the time to consider what I might want. He wanted to race, but he was better as the mechanic than the driver. So he decided—without asking—that I would drive the cars, and he insisted on teaching me."

Flora paused to swallow as her throat constricted. She'd never told anyone the entire story, and it was more difficult than she'd imagined. "At first, the races were thrilling, and I did love it. But after a while, I wanted to stay home and start a family. Before his last race, we quarreled over that very thing. It's the reason I stayed home, to show him he could race without me.

That I could have a baby, and he would still win races as he wanted."

Words to describe those days eluded Flora. It was surprisingly difficult to express the things her heart had desired that were no longer a possibility. "That hope is gone now, of course. Despite our difficulties, the one good thing our marriage gave me was a love of racing and the knowledge that I have a real talent for it. If I'd been driving instead of letting him go alone that day, I doubt that accident would have happened. Henri might still be alive."

Again, she had to stop. Owen scooted his chair closer to her and wrapped his arm around her shoulders. "Flora, I'm sorry. I had no idea you felt that way. You must know, deep down, that it isn't your fault he died."

Sniffing against the tears that threatened to fill her eyes, Flora shrugged. "I do know that, even if I question it sometimes. But there's more I need to tell you. Henri's selfish choices continue to impact me and Isabelle. He bankrupted us before his death. The Montfort family fortune was long gone by that time. So racing is more than a desire for me, it's a necessity. It's the only way I can make a living and give Isabelle the comfortable life she deserves for her last years. The only way I can keep my independence."

Standing, Owen paced the room several times, running one hand through his hair as he did. "I would never want to stop you from doing what gives your life purpose. And I understand your desire to forge your own path. But Flora, this isn't any race. This is two weeks of dangerous roads, unknown obstacles, and strangers you may not be able to trust. Can't you pick an easier type of racing, at least? Soon enough, we'll be running teams on the dirt tracks that have been springing up across the country."

"You know as well as I do that no race is safe. And I won't be alone facing all that. I'll have people who are family to you by my side." Searching for the words to show him what was in her heart, Flora stood and moved to look out the window at the dark, empty street. "Too many men think women don't belong in sports. I could put in an application and try to enter another race myself, but even before Henri's death, female drivers were being denied entry to races in Europe. I'm certain that's the case here, as well. If not, it will be soon. Mr. Harrison's respectable name might be the only thing that gets me a spot in the tour in the first place. I need to run this race now and start making a name for myself that can't be denied."

Pacing again, Owen spent a few minutes in what looked like deep thought. Flora let him sort through all she'd said. Finally, he turned to her, clearly having come to a conclusion as the hint of a smile played around his otherwise-serious expression. "All right. I won't try to dissuade you from racing. But I will require frequent communication. And your absolute promise that you won't take unnecessary risks."

Delight flooded Flora. She hadn't needed his permission, but she'd longed for his approval. Leaving the window, she wrapped her arms around Owen. "I'll do my best. And think how grand it will be when you can brag that your sister won the inaugural Glidden Tour. You'll be the envy of Philadelphia."

Owen laughed, returning her hug. "I'll be glad if I can say my sister is happy and living the life she wants. That's what you deserve."

On Friday afternoon, Jensen shifted in his desk chair, looking around the office and wondering how much longer it would be his. Owen had yet to assign him a new position in Harrison Goods—not that Jensen was anxious to make the change. Maybe he should go ahead and volunteer to unload the wagons that brought crates of merchandise. That was the only job in the company he hadn't tried yet. Surely, he couldn't be a failure at that.

A knock at the door broke into his thoughts. Jensen opened it to find Owen standing on the other side, shuffling from one foot to the other. Was this it? Was it time to face his fate?

Returning to his seat, Jensen gestured for Owen

to join him. "What can I do for you today?"

Owen's fingers twitched out a beat on the arm of the chair he had dropped into. Jensen might have to come up with some small talk to break the tension, the silence stretched out so long. But finally, Owen spoke. "Flora and I spoke last night about Fred's idea for the Glidden Tour. Have you decided if you're going to ride along as the mechanic?"

Jensen's shoulders tightened. This was the last thing he wanted to talk or think about. "I've been convinced to participate."

Owen's eyes narrowed as if he was trying to read Jensen's mind and figure out the statement that, admittedly, had come out a bit cryptic.

Well, if they were going to discuss it, Jensen might as well be honest. "It's the last thing I want to do. Racing isn't for me. But Fred is set on going with or without me. And I can only imagine the trouble they would get into without someone who at least recognizes possible threats."

"Ah." Owen leaned back in the chair, looking much more relaxed than when he entered the room. "You're going along to watch out for their safety. Excellent. I have a request for you along those same lines."

"What would that be?"

"Flora is set on driving. She's excellent at it, don't get me wrong. But much like Fred, she tends to put her goals over concern for safety.

You would think after her husband died in a racing crash, she would be more cautious, but it seems to have pushed her toward even less prudence."

A pang hit Jensen in the stomach. Her husband had died while racing? Had it been like Gregory? He had an unexpected desire to talk with her and let her know she wasn't alone in that grief, but it was hardly his place to do so. "Then what's your request for me?"

"Since you're already watching out for Fred, try to keep Flora in line too."

A snicker escaped Jensen before he could stop it. Owen's eyes widened, and Jensen remembered this man would soon be his boss and part of his family. "I'm sorry, but it seems that might be more than one man can handle. I haven't spent much time with your sister, but I can tell she's quite set on taking care of herself and won't hesitate to demand her right to do so."

Owen rubbed his face with one hand. "I know. That's exactly the problem. She is capable. But that doesn't mean she's invincible. I've already lost my parents and my brother. If something happens to Flora, I'm left with no family. I need her to make it through this safely."

The way his voice broke when talking about his sister's safety softened Jensen's resolve yet again. "Why don't you ask her not to do it?"

Owen sighed. "I did. We had a long discussion.

But in the end, she's a grown woman, a widow who would rather build a career than sit and watch everyone else live their lives. Driving in this tour means the world to her, and I want her to be happy. But I also want her to come back unscathed."

If anyone could understand that sentiment, it was Jensen. He felt the same way about Fred. Understanding seemed to be growing between himself and Owen. "Since I have to be there anyway, I'll try to keep your sister from doing anything dangerous. She'll be the one driving, of course, but I'll do what I can to protect her."

Owen's shoulders relaxed. Pushing up from the chair, he stuck out his hand to shake Jensen's. "Thank you. I hoped you would understand my concern, and I can see that you do. I'll rest better knowing someone is caring for Flora. I'll see you tomorrow at the wedding."

Owen exited the office, leaving Jensen alone with his thoughts again. That was not where he wanted to be for any amount of time. Piling up the ledgers that would have to wait until Monday morning, he left, taking the back door to avoid anyone flagging him down with questions on the shop floor.

Once outside, he stood for a long moment, looking out across the neatly trimmed grass. How had he gotten so caught up in everyone else's plans that he was now responsible for three other people in a ten-day race to see who could break their neck the fastest?

Footsteps on the sidewalk heading toward the building caught his attention after only a few breaths of cleansing fresh air. He wanted solitude but could hardly ignore his boss. "Hello, Mr. Harrison."

The older man stopped next to him. "What brings you to loiter by the back door, Jensen?"

He couldn't explain all the nuances of that subject, so he settled for a simple reply. "I needed some fresh air. It seems like it might help sometimes." Jensen let his gaze stray across the grounds again.

"Yes, I know that feeling well." Mr. Harrison's voice was quieter and more serious than Jensen expected.

"You sound as though you could use a few deep breaths too. Is Mrs. Harrison having a good day? Even with all the preparations for the wedding, she seems to be thriving more than usual."

Stuffing his hands in his pockets, Mr. Harrison rocked back on his heels. "She loves a party, to be sure. It seems all the planning has helped focus her mind rather than tire her out as I expected. I only hope she doesn't regress once Owen and Aggie leave for their trip and it becomes a reality that her daughter will have her own home. You'll have to keep up your frequent lunches with her as you were in the habit of doing before this wedding took over our schedule. At least she'll take comfort in that routine."

"I wouldn't miss the chance to spend time with her for anything." He stopped himself before adding that he'd hate to miss a visit when any conversation might be the last one where she remembered him. Mr. Harrison didn't need a reminder of that possibility. "Perhaps Fred and Beth's presence will help her with the transition to Aggie living in her own home."

Mr. Harrison shrugged. "It might. I'm thankful they'll have the next few weeks here before you all leave for the tour." A long pause stretched out as Mr. Harrison looked to be planning his next words. "How do you feel about the tour after some thought, Jensen? I know you're hesitant, but can you see that my team needs you?"

Unfortunately, that was all too clear. "Yes, I understand your reasons for wanting me to go. I wish you would all drop this nonsense, but I know that won't happen. So I'll go and do my best to keep everyone safe."

Mr. Harrison clapped his hand on Jensen's shoulder, an understanding look on the older man's face. "I had a feeling that would be your response. But my prayer is that you'll find a way to release some of that dependence on the idea of safety and enjoy the trip. Take joy in the driving, the thrill of doing well, even the pride of winning if that opportunity arises. My boy, there's so much more to life than getting through it safely."

The words felt like a gift, but one that Jensen wasn't sure how to operate yet. He tucked them into the back of his mind. Mr. Harrison might be right, but Jensen had already promised to look after the safety of his teammates, and he couldn't go back on that now. If they survived the coming weeks, there would be time to consider adding more enjoyment to his life later.

Chapter 6

The morning of Owen's wedding was perfect. The sun rose in a crystal-clear sky with birds chirping and squirrels racing each other across the lawn in front of Owen's house. Flora spent too long watching the little creatures scurry around while memories of her own wedding day flitted through her mind. It had rained, stormed even at times. She'd been drenched by the time she arrived at the church, and her shoes hadn't dried out the entire day. Henri had looked dashing as he waited at the altar for her, though, and at the time, she thought that was all that mattered.

How wrong she'd been.

The maid's knock at the door to bring a breakfast tray shook her from her melancholy comparisons. Owen wasn't wrong about choosing Aggie. She was kind and strong and part of a wonderful, loving family who embraced Owen as their own. His marriage would be as different from Flora's as his wedding day was proving to be. She could rest in the knowledge that her brother had found a love that would last his lifetime.

So why did she feel such melancholy?

Flora rushed through her preparations, sliding on her favorite gown, a dove-gray silk with gold embroidery and chiffon sleeves that would be perfect for the hot day. Then she and Isabelle joined Owen in his carriage to go to the church. Seeing her beloved younger brother dressed in a fashionable suit, eyes shining with joy and anticipation, Flora was overcome for a moment. "Owen, I'm so happy for you and Aggie. I pray you'll have the best life together."

He embraced her, lingering over the hug. "And I pray for you to find the same happiness, you know."

Her heart clenched and tears rose unbidden. She shook them away. "Mine will have to come without a marriage attached. But I'll find it. There's no need to worry about me."

When they arrived at the church they'd attended with the Harrisons on Sunday, Isabelle went inside, but Owen hesitated. Flora stopped with him. He rubbed his hands on his trouser legs as they stood together. His thoughts must have moved on to the impending ceremony. She remembered when the reality that she was getting married hit at her wedding. It could be an anxious moment.

But then Owen turned to her with a huge grin lighting his face. "Let's go in. I can't wait to see Aggie."

He led the way up the stairs, then disappeared into a cluster of men who would stand up with him, including Fred Harrison. Flora joined Isabelle and Beth across the foyer as they waited for the seating to begin.

Beth looked delicate and lovely in a simple, flattering pale-pink silk gown. She leaned close to Flora. "Don't you just love weddings? All the fashion and romance? I could attend one every day."

Flora's instinct was to disagree. In her experience, weddings were a way to secure one's place in the world, not a dreamy celebration. Yes, she'd thought herself in love with Henri at first. But it had soon become clear she didn't know him nearly well enough for such depth of feeling. It had been a convenient infatuation, at best.

This was her brother's special day, and she'd already realized how different it was from her wedding. "I suppose there is much to enjoy." But the fearful, trapped feelings that accompanied her own marriage hovered in her mind, refusing to let her enjoy this day.

Beth laughed, a light, airy sound that fit her delicate looks. The doors to the sanctuary opened, and the ladies moved forward to find their seats. The pews were decorated with opulent garlands of exquisite white flowers. Matching bouquets in large vases surrounded the altar where the couple would stand.

The sanctuary filled within a few minutes. The musicians started up a familiar march, and all eyes turned to see the bride's and groom's attendants making their way down the aisle. Flora's gaze followed their progress until Jensen walked past, mere feet from her. He was dressed to perfection in the same long black jacket, black trousers, and white bowtie that the other men wore. But unlike the rest, his expression was solemn, as if he regarded his position as best man with the utmost seriousness.

Once they were all in place, Owen and the minister took their spots. Then the music changed, and once again, the guests turned toward the back. Aggie and Mr. Harrison made their procession with deliberate steps, the bride glowing in a white silk gown covered in layers of lace with a delicate veil trailing behind her.

The ceremony began with the minister speaking for some time about love, drawing from the usual Scripture passages that Flora had heard a hundred times. No doubt, the words were meant to sound romantic and uplifting. Normally, she cherished the reading of God's word. But all she felt right then was the constriction of the choices she'd made. Her marriage hadn't been one of love as she'd thought it would be, and the fault for that foolish, rash decision could only be placed on her.

In the background of her thoughts, the ceremony went on with Owen and Aggie exchanging their vows. But Flora had to wonder if this was what the rest of her life would be like, watching others fall in love without experiencing it for herself. Had she squandered her only chance by marrying the first man that wasn't her brother's choice?

A sniffle from Beth brought Flora back to the present. The ceremony was nearly over, with vows made and rings exchanged. Flora glanced at Jensen, whose attention was riveted on the couple next to him. Was that the sheen of tears in his eyes? Was he that much of a romantic, deep down somewhere?

Flora shook off that thought. It didn't matter if he was. She had no reason to be so intrigued by the idea that he could be longing for love as much as she was. Jensen hated the sport that was her passion in life. He despised the kind of risks that made her feel the most alive. If love was in her future, it wasn't with Jensen Gable. She'd already married a man who was far too different from her. If she were ever to wed again, it would have to be someone who valued all the things she did. She wouldn't doom herself to a life of strife again.

The minister finished the service and finally directed Owen to kiss his bride. The congregation sighed as the couple sealed their commitment and then walked back up the aisle with the wide, joyous grins of newlyweds. The wedding party followed them to form a receiving line, and the guests began filing out. Flora, Isabelle, and Beth waited, letting everyone else go before them.

After the last guests had left the church, the family members convened at the Harrison home for a reception and to send Owen and Aggie off on their honeymoon. Flora found herself sitting with Isabelle on one side and Jensen on the other as servants brought dish after dish to the long table in the Harrisons' dining room. Happy conversation flowed around them, but Flora preferred to listen, not in much of a mood for small talk.

When Isabelle turned to ask Fred a question, Flora snuck a peek at Jensen to find him staring at the glass in his hand. He must have felt her scrutiny, though, because he spoke without looking at her. "Mr. Harrison has arranged to have your Decauville taken to his shop first thing Monday morning. I hope you don't mind. He didn't want to risk more damage by driving it until we can fix the overheating issue. If you'd like to oversee the work, you're welcome to join us at the shop around ten o'clock."

Oversee the work on her own car? Flora would usually respond with irritation to a comment like that, one that assumed she had no ability or interest in repairing her vehicle herself. But Mr. Harrison had already asked her to let the new crew use the repair and the process of setting up the Decauville for the tour as practice for their future race cars. And she couldn't be too angry when his arrogant comment got her mind off of weddings and love gone wrong. "I wouldn't miss it. I can't wait until the car is back in good working order."

Jensen raised his eyes to meet her gaze, his fingers continuing to turn his crystal glass around and around on the table. "Are you still sure you want to do this? The entire engine needs to be rebuilt to get the car running again, then we'll have to prepare it for the trip. Not to mention, the intensity of the race itself. It's a big commitment."

"Are you trying to dissuade me again?"

The air around them shifted when his eyes lighted with humor. Flora's breath caught, the unfamiliar amusement making him even more captivating than usual.

"I've been told it won't do any good. Should I continue to try?"

Letting a coy smile turn up her lips, Flora shrugged. "I don't see any use in it. You've heard correctly. Once I decide on something, I don't back down."

The lingering smile Jensen sent her flipped Flora's stomach in ways she hadn't experienced in years. She was flirting. With a man she could not afford to fall for, but whom she would be stuck with for most of her time over the next six weeks. If she didn't get herself under control, a rash decision might seal her fate again.

• • •

In the Harrison Goods garage, Jensen ran one hand through his already messy hair, mentally cursing the high early-July temperatures that made the building an oven. It didn't help that for the three weeks since the wedding, he and Mrs. Montfort had argued every day over the Decauville, debating what changes to make so the car would perform its best during the tour. Every chance she got, Mrs. Montfort pushed for anything that would add speed without considering the impact on safety and endurance. She knew plenty about what it took to get a race car to go fast. But her vehicle's capability didn't always translate to the best setup for the conditions, a fact she either didn't seem to understand or wasn't willing to accept.

Standing beside her behind the car, he once again repeated the phrase he'd already uttered a thousand times. "But the car has to get through ten days of rough driving, Mrs. Montfort. Keeping it together through all that is more important than being in front."

She faced him without hesitation, hands balled into fists and pressed against her hips. Dressed in what he guessed was an old blouse and skirt covered by a heavy leather apron she'd borrowed from the line of them hanging by the door, she looked quite capable of handling herself in the shop. As intriguing as the idea of a woman who could hold her own with a racing crew might be, despite her competent appearance, she probably didn't even know which way to hold a wrench.

Mr. Harrison had secured her promise that the shop crew could make all the mechanical changes to the car, giving Jensen a reprieve from Mrs. Montfort attempting to meddle with the setup behind their backs and causing problems in the process. But still, a smear of grease from the engine compartment had somehow appeared on her cheek, tempting his hand to reach up and wipe it away. He was getting to be skilled at forcing those wayward desires deep down, pretending—even to himself—that they didn't exist.

Bringing his mind back to the discussion, he tried to find a way to deny her proposed change to the car that wouldn't make her dig in even more. If he'd learned anything about her in the many afternoons they'd spent together working on the car, it was that this look meant she intended to get her way. He listened for a moment as she explained her reasoning. "A light car is a fast car. That steel plate underneath is so heavy. We'll be much faster without it."

Her idea sounded good in theory, but the reality was often different. Jensen prepared to stand his ground. This was a battle she wasn't going to win. "But the entire purpose of it is to protect the more delicate parts under the car from rough road conditions, which we will be facing every day on the tour." He kept his voice as even as he could manage. "It's an integral safety feature, and many of the other cars won't have that protection. It's a benefit to us and it's staying."

She stared him down long enough that Jensen started to get distracted by the color of her eyes. Were they more like the chocolates Mrs. Harrison was fond of or the rich, dark leather of his favorite chair in the Harrisons' library? His wayward thoughts paid off this time, causing him to inadvertently wait long enough that she grew frustrated.

She threw up her hands and turned back to the car. "We'll discuss this later. For now, we should give it another test drive to make sure everything functions well in this kind of heat."

Jensen dropped the lid back over the engine compartment while looking around the shop. It was empty and silent except for the sounds of the city at dusk that drifted in through the open bay door. His heart sank as he realized all the crew members had left while they'd been facing off. He'd done well avoiding it to this point, but this might be the moment when he had to climb into the car, something he hadn't done in five years. "Maybe you didn't notice, but today is Independence Day. The rest of the crew have left for their well-deserved time off. We have the rest of the week to finish up the changes and test it all you want. Leave the drive for tomorrow."

Ignoring him, Mrs. Montfort hopped into the driver's seat, a joyful glint sparking in her eyes. "I had forgotten about Independence Day. I missed the fireworks and parties while I was in France. There's something about the exuberance of our American rebel spirit that's unmatched anywhere else."

And there was something undeniably appealing about a vibrant, beautiful woman sitting in the driver's seat of a car. When they weren't fighting, he had to admit that spending time with Flora Montfort was more fun than he ever expected. When he'd let Fred convince him to do this, he wouldn't have believed he would enjoy having Flora in the shop, nor that he would anticipate seeing the fire of passion for racing light up her face.

Still sitting in the car, Flora patted the passenger's seat. "Get in. We'll do a quick test drive, and that will give us more time to fine-tune things tomorrow. It's getting late, but I'll hurry so you won't miss the celebration."

Jensen tried to move toward the car, but his feet refused to obey. Of course, he'd known when he agreed to this that he would have to get into the car. But he'd thought he might feel more prepared when the time came, that working on the car every day would give him a sense of familiarity that would make it more natural to open the door and step inside.

Instead, his knees were likely to buckle if he tried to lift a foot.

Mrs. Montfort's eyebrows raised as she waited. "Are you coming?"

His pride wouldn't let him say no. Then he would have to admit to her that he was terrified of riding in a car again. So Jensen forced himself to open the passenger side door. Then he managed to get one foot onto the running board.

You can do this. Just get in the car.

Mrs. Montfort watched him too closely, eyes narrowed as if she could read what was going on in his mind. Leaning across the seat, she rested one warm hand on his fingers, which gripped the dashboard. "Jensen, I've never seen you get in the car. You always have one of the other men ride along with me when we test drive it. Combined with your . . . interest . . . in safety, I'm beginning to wonder if you have a fear of cars."

He wouldn't call it fear . . . more a paralyzing distaste. Either way, the result was the same. He looked like a weak fool. "It's just been a long time, Mrs. Montfort."

When he glanced up at her, he didn't see the judgment or mockery he expected. She looked concerned and caring. Her mouth opened, and she drew a breath as if she wanted to ask more about it. He swallowed hard. There was no way he could explain the situation to her. The unspoken rule in the Harrison family was that they didn't talk about what happened to Gregory.

To his relief, she leaned back and offered a soft smile instead of more questions. "It's past time you start calling me Flora. If you'd like."

Holding her gaze, he decided her brown eyes weren't the same as chocolate or soft leather. They were a special, warm shade all their own, one he very much enjoyed examining.

She couldn't know what his hesitation stemmed from, the connection of this moment to the one that had changed his life forever. But even without knowing, she managed to convey the right amount of compassion. He drew strength from that and managed to force his body into the seat next to her, hoping his rough voice was loud enough she could hear his response. "I'd like that very much. Flora."

It was nice to say her name, but almost overly familiar at the same time. Less than a foot separated them, and that swath of air was charged with a peculiar energy as they held each other's gaze, both as serious as could be. He hadn't expected such intensity when she finally felt comfortable enough to allow him the use of her given name.

Flora turned away first and started the car. Before he was quite ready, they were moving. Outside the shop, the streets had filled with revelers celebrating the holiday. Boys chased girls with small popping fireworks, making the girls squeal in mock protest when they were caught. Older people sat on their porches, smiling at the sights. Young parents gathered their small children close as they went in search of a good viewing spot for the fireworks show.

But amidst it all, Jensen couldn't shake the strangeness of being back in a car.

As Flora accelerated, his chest felt as though a boulder sat on it, making full breaths impossible, which was torture in the heavy July heat. The seats in the Decauville were not wide, leaving very little room between the two of them. Every time she turned the wheel even a little, her arm brushed his.

Over the distance of a dozen city blocks, the car ran perfectly, as Jensen expected after the work they'd done that day. He found himself settling into the rhythm of the movement, the speed not bringing back terrible memories as he'd assumed it would, but instead feeling like freedom. That was one of the few good things he remembered from five years ago.

Darkness had fallen by the time Flora stopped on a side street to turn around so they could go back to the shop. At the same moment, the first blast from the fireworks show rang out.

Raising his voice so she would hear him over the engine and the explosions, he pointed toward the sky. "Why don't we stay a few minutes and watch?" They had an excellent view right where they were.

Her eyes warmed again, reflecting the sparkles above. She nodded and turned off the engine, the silence between them only marked by pops and bangs. As the moment grew more intimate while they sat in the dark alone, Jensen did his best to scoot toward the door, giving her as much space as he could squeeze out of the seat.

But that didn't mean he could distance his mind from awareness of her. They sat together in silence for a long time while Jensen watched Flora gasp and cheer with a charmed smile, along with all the other spectators.

"This is madness and pure joy mixed together. I'd forgotten how it felt," she said.

"Yes, there's nothing more American than expressing yourself with loud, uncontrolled passion."

Her smile faded into pensiveness. "That's quite accurate. You say it as though it's a bad thing, but compared to what I've been accustomed to, it's a lovely way to live."

Something in her words reminded him of Gregory, who had also believed in living out what he loved without apology. Familiar tightness gripped Jensen's stomach, and his breathing hitched. "It's not all lovely. That independent streak leads to trouble more times than it needs to."

Glancing at him, Flora tipped her head to one side, as if she was trying to decode his statement. He cleared his throat, wishing he could take those words back. They paved the way for her to ask questions, to push at his secrets. He was letting her in far more than he ever imagined he would. He needed to put space—emotional and physical—between them before she dug too deep and uncovered the one truth he needed to keep to himself.

A particularly loud boom reverberated through the streets. Flora's gaze lingered on him for another second, then she turned away to watch the fireworks light up the sky in shimmering tendrils again. Jensen, however, could only think about how close he was to revealing a part of himself that must stay hidden. If the truth about Gregory's accident got out, the Harrisons would never forgive him. He would lose the only family he had left in the world, the only people he'd felt were on his side since his parents died. He was on the verge of losing his job, and he had no passions or plans to pursue. He couldn't lose the only good thing he had left.

No matter how much he enjoyed her company or how attractive he found her—both in looks and heart—he had to keep Flora out of his life.

Chapter 7

Four days after the Fourth of July, anticipation rose in Flora's heart as she drove toward the towering New York City skyline. Philadelphia wasn't exactly a small town, but compared to Paris or New York, it felt like one. Flora preferred the vibrant feel of a big city. For all the struggles she'd gone through there, Paris had been a wonderful place to live. New York felt similar, while also having its own unique atmosphere.

But more than that, this was the beginning of something new for her. This opportunity would give her the purpose she'd been missing for most of her life.

In the back seat of the car, Fred and Beth exclaimed with delight over the sights they saw driving through the crowded city streets. Beth, especially, seemed as taken with it as Flora was. "Look at the size of those buildings! I love the variety of architecture. And the fashion is sublime. I saw a woman wearing the most charming feather-covered hat back there. Oh, Fred, maybe someday we can settle here."

The couple went on for some time about the different things they loved. But not everyone in the car was excited. Flora glanced at Jensen, who sat in silence next to her. "What about you? Are you as in love with the city as the rest of us?"

While they'd spent plenty of time together in the days since the fireworks display, Flora couldn't remember a single conversation that wasn't about the Decauville. Jensen hadn't even fought her the least bit on the final setup for the car, as she'd assumed he would.

The hours it had taken to drive from Philadelphia to New York City had consisted of Fred and Beth talking to Flora over the clatter of the car's engine while Jensen kept to himself. Was he worried about the tour, or had she said something wrong? She'd gone over and over the moments they'd shared watching the fireworks and could only remember feeling more connected to him than at any other time in the weeks since they met. Whatever had caused him to withdraw, it surely hadn't been her.

Now, Jensen shifted in the seat, his voice barely loud enough for her to hear. "Philadelphia is almost too busy for me. This is . . . so much."

Flora looked around at the multitude of horse-drawn vehicles that clogged the streets, mixed with fewer automobiles, but still more than she usually saw in one place. New Yorkers streamed down every sidewalk and into the streets, all walking with purpose. The buildings were magnificent to look at, but also blocked any view of the horizon. It wasn't hard to imagine some people might not enjoy the electric energy and could feel claustrophobic. "It's only for a few days. We'll be on the road Tuesday, and then it will be rural driving for most of the tour."

Fred leaned forward to join the conversation. "Beth and I have some sights we'd like to visit before the tour starts. The Statue of Liberty, one of the theatres, a day at Coney Island."

"And shopping, if we can fit it in," Beth added.

Even while looking ahead at the road, Flora could tell Jensen's shoulders tensed at their enthusiastic plans. Perhaps she could smooth the way between their exuberance and his obvious need for something quieter. "Don't schedule too much. We'll want to get some rest and leave time to make sure everything is ready for the race. It's going to be a grueling ten days on the road."

Jensen nodded. "I vote for rest and preparation."

Fred bumped Jensen's shoulder with his elbow. "Oh, don't say that. We'll have time for both. Please, don't make me disappoint my bride, who wants to experience a little of New York City while we're here."

Flora was sure Jensen would shrug him off and lean into his preference for their time in the city. To her surprise, he relented without any further convincing. "Fine. We'll see a few things over the weekend. But Monday is all business. We have to be ready for the tour."

Not caring whether he noticed her scrutiny, Flora watched Jensen's face for as long as she could have her eyes off the road. His lips pressed into a tight line, but when he turned her way, he didn't look angry. What had possessed him to agree to several days of sightseeing so easily?

As if reading her confusion, he leaned closer so he could speak for her ears alone, his shoulder pressing against hers. "Don't look at me like that. I've never been able to deny Fred anything. He's the little brother I never got to have."

There was that sweet charm she'd like to see more of. "Were you that close growing up?"

He responded slowly, as if he needed time to form each word in his mind. "Fred and I weren't, not until I was older and could see how important it is to cherish those you love."

Before she could think through whether it was a good idea or not, Flora let the truth she'd just realized slip through her lips. "That's why you agreed to this, isn't it? Fred asked."

Was that pink tinging his cheeks? A horn blared and several horses nearby neighed in panic. Flora spun the wheel to steer the car back into the appropriate lane, mortified that staring at Jensen had nearly caused her to crash them into a wagon. Maybe Jensen remaining aloof would be better for their chances of staying safe during the race, after all.

Flora let the conversation go and kept her focus on the road until they arrived at the famous

Waldorf-Astoria Hotel, where Mr. Harrison had arranged for them to stay before the race started. The building was imposing, the red stone-and-brick exterior all one could see when standing near it. Turrets and ironwork decorated the upper floors, drawing attention to its staggering height.

Beth gawked as they disembarked from the car and started for the front door. "Will we stay in places this nice the entire tour? I could get used to this luxury."

Flora suppressed a grin at Fred's look of dread. Was he about to find out his wife had much finer taste and expectations than he'd thought? A glance at Jensen showed the same amusement written on his face. His eyes met hers, and for a moment, they were united in their humor. If only all of their time on the tour could be this companionable. But Flora had a feeling the friction they'd experienced while preparing the Decauville would resurface as soon as they started the race.

The group separated inside the opulent lobby, retiring to their rooms for the night with a plan to meet in the lobby in the morning to start their first day of sightseeing. Flora's single room was small but beautifully outfitted with a wrought-iron bedframe, several comfortable chairs, a chest of drawers, writing desk, and access to her own private bathroom.

After a lovely night in one of the softest beds

she'd ever slept in, Flora rose and looked over the selection of clothing she'd brought for the tour. She chose a light-weight white shirtwaist paired with a simply embellished black skirt. It would be practical and comfortable for a day of taking in whatever adventures awaited them at Coney Island. A plain straw hat with a black band completed the ensemble.

Downstairs in the lobby, Jensen occupied a settee near a towering fireplace, unlit on a morning that already promised stifling heat. His casual jacket fit like a glove, showing off those broad shoulders and muscular arms that Flora had caught glimpses of when he worked in shirtsleeves in the shop. Flora swallowed, remembering the warm pressure of his shoulder pressing against hers yesterday in the car.

Jensen glanced up and saw her standing there awkwardly. His eyes traveled down her outfit with slow scrutiny. Her cheeks heated at the appraisal even as she wished she could know what thoughts were running through his mind when he looked at her.

As if realizing what he was doing, Jensen straightened and raised his gaze to meet hers. "I haven't seen Fred and Beth yet. You're welcome to join me to wait."

Forcing herself to ignore the emotions swirling in her chest after the intense way he'd looked at her, she sank into the plush cushion with a sigh.

"All that bumping around in the car wears on a person more than expected, don't you think?"

Jensen quirked one eyebrow. "It's only going to get worse as the days wear on and the road conditions deteriorate. If you're not up to that challenge, we should withdraw now."

The instant Jensen's words hit the air, he wanted to pull them back. Flora's lovely face crumpled, draped in disappointment he'd caused with his carelessness. He'd been so flustered when he looked up and saw her standing by him in that outfit. It hugged every inch of her body, putting her curves on display in the most appealing way without being at all improper. Frankly, she was breathtaking.

And that knowledge hit him so hard and fast that he'd grown cross. Then he'd taken it out on her. Why was gruff and angry his first reaction to being caught off-guard? "I'm sorry, Flora. That was unkind of me. Do you think we should hunt down some cushions to make the seats easier to sit on for days in a row? There's not much we can do about the bouncing, I'm afraid."

Flora sat for long enough that she must be angry with him. He didn't blame her one bit. What else could he say to smooth over his mistake?

But then she turned to face him, not angry but with a little hurt still lingering in her eyes. His mind emptied. He'd done that. He'd hurt her.

There was no smoothing it over. Her voice was a little quieter and not as cheerful when she finally responded. "That could be helpful, especially for Fred and Beth, who probably don't know what they're getting into. But I'd thank you to remember that this isn't my first race. Nor my first multi-day race. I'm aware of the challenges we'll face."

At that moment, Fred and Beth came down the wide staircase, arm in arm.

Flora rose from the settee in a cloud of floral scent and waved to them. "Good morning. Are you ready to enjoy a day at the beach?"

Jensen kept to himself how much that was the last thing he wanted to do. New York was crowded and unpleasant, filled with noise and smells and too much of everything. He was anxious to get on with the race for no other reason than to get out into the open again. But first, he had to get through the two days of sightseeing he'd promised Fred and Beth. Starting with Coney Island, which was sure to be one of the most crowded spots in the city on such a warm, clear summer day.

But the others all looked delighted. Beth chattered as they boarded an express train that took passengers straight to the park, going on about all the things her friends had told her they shouldn't miss at Coney Island. "Miss Adelaide Warren said we can't miss the Fighting Flames show. It's supposed to be spectacular. For adventure, my sister recommended Shoot the Chutes, although I'm not certain I'm brave enough to ride those flimsy boats down such a steep slope. She said the height at the top is breathtaking."

"What about the beach?" Flora was next to Jensen, and he had to crane his neck to see her. So he almost missed the veiled amusement on her face as Beth went on about so many attractions that there was no way they would be able to see them all in one day.

Beth must have missed the expression entirely, as she responded in complete earnestness. "Oh, that, too, of course. The beach is the entire point, isn't it?"

By the time the half-hour train ride to Dreamland was over, Jensen was ready to quit the day altogether. Passengers—more than the occupancy limit for the train car, he was sure—had crowded in tight, pressing the group together on all sides. It was a relief to disembark and walk a few blocks to the park. But judging from the vast number of people streaming into the main entrance, crowded would be the theme of the day.

The four of them paused to experience the spectacle in front of them before entering the park. Beth, cheeks pink from the sight of the half-naked angel statue towering thirty feet above the main entrance, stared at the figure despite the inappropriateness. "My friend Mrs. Lasley said they installed this new entrance to bring attention to the Creation Show. There was some controversy over the state of her, as I'm sure you can imagine."

They made their way through the entry point, then spent some time wandering the boardwalks, the women delighting over items in shop windows and the many unique sights that spilled out of the attractions. Beth eventually led them to one of her first choices, the Galveston Flood Show, a building constructed with distinct square towers and huge stars carved into the sides.

Inside, the atmosphere was more hushed than the busy walkways. They took seats in the auditorium and were soon wrapped up in the enthralling tale of the flood that occurred five years earlier. The town of Galveston had been recreated in miniature, and through performance tricks, was destroyed by fake floodwaters. The narrator displayed surprising skill in setting the dramatic yet serious tone that such a devastating real event deserved.

As the waters rose to engulf the tiny town, a gasp rose from next to him. Jensen peeked at Flora to find her eyes riveted on the scene and lips parted in distress. He had to fight the urge to put a comforting arm around her. Or to remind her that it was all done with tricks and those miniature people weren't real, anyway.

Once they departed, Beth led them through other attractions along the Dreamland boardwalks. They stopped at another of her most desired shows, Fighting Flames, where they watched firemen work tirelessly to put out a false fire in a row of tall building facades. Then they rode gondolas through replica Venetian canals.

To finish off the morning, they walked through Bostock's Animal Show, a circular-fronted building that reminded Jensen a bit of photographs he'd once seen of the Colosseum in Rome. Inside, they marveled with the rest of the audience over the circus acts. Flora gasped as a trainer surrounded himself with thirty lions. "How brave he must be to do this multiple times every day."

Fred shrugged. "He trains them, so he must know them well and be confident they won't hurt him."

Jensen had a different take. "Or he's foolhardy enough to take careless risks with his life believing nothing bad can happen to him."

Flora met his eyes, looking for all the world as though she was trying to solve an enigma. It was a vulnerable feeling, to know she wanted to decode his deepest emotions. For the first time that day, Jensen was thankful for the brisk pace Beth set for them. He had no desire for Flora to have time to puzzle the secrets out of him.

Finally, Beth directed them to Feltman's for

lunch. It should've been a relief to sit in a quiet restaurant for an hour and eat. But the massive building with dining room after dining room was every bit as crowded and loud as the walkways outside. Still, the day was half over. That was progress.

Beth was quite pleased with all they'd seen so far. As they waited for their food, she gushed, "Oh, isn't this the most marvelous start to a wedding trip, Flora? I can't wait to tell my friends every single detail. I'll have to write it all down this evening so I won't forget a thing."

Fred leaned forward with his eyes glued to his radiant wife. "What do you have in mind for this afternoon, darling?"

"What about a walk on the beach?" It was Flora who spoke up, to Jensen's surprise. She'd been on the quiet side most of the morning, letting Beth lead them all around without argument. But it looked as if this particular request was very important to her.

Without thinking, he found himself directing their plans. "The beach, it is. There's plenty of time for more attractions, but a few breaths of the salty ocean air will do us all good."

Beth sighed, but she agreed, nonetheless. Flora met Jensen's eyes from across the table as the newlyweds started up a quiet conversation. *Thank you,* she mouthed. Warmth exploded in his chest. Whatever the reason, she dearly wanted a stop at the beach, and he'd been the one to ensure it would happen.

If that light in her eyes was the reward, he could get very used to guaranteeing Flora Montfort got what she wanted.

Chapter 8

Flora wasn't sure why she felt the need to push for a visit to the beach. But standing on the sand with that blue expanse stretching out endlessly always made her feel the smallness of her life in a comforting way. Her problems were not so big to a God who created something as vast as the ocean in one day.

And right now, she needed reassurance that her worries were under His control.

The last few weeks as they prepared and planned for the race, she'd been confident, sure that she was doing the right thing, that they would remain safe, and that she could win the tour. But now that they were here, ready to start in only two days, the reality of what she was about to embark upon had crashed down on Flora overnight. She wasn't certain she could handle this race, even though she'd tried to convince Jensen she was that very morning.

Now, as they wove around groups of visitors heading toward the bathing area, she was thankful for Jensen's quick support for her request at lunch. His tone had left no room for arguments, as much as she could see Beth wanted to. And whatever Beth wanted, Fred would fight to make happen. It was nice to have someone on her side this time. The only other person who'd ever shown such concern for her desires was Owen. Not Clement, not Henri. It was intoxicating to feel there was a man who cared that much about what was important to her.

They found an empty spot by the edge of the water, the waves lapping gently at the shore even as the sound of them crashing farther out filled the air. Children laughed and ran, splashing each other and anyone in their path. Many people had changed into bathing clothes to frolic in the water. But Flora was content to stand in the sand, close her eyes, and let the coastal atmosphere wash over her.

A movement at her side broke her out of the reverie. She looked up to see Jensen smiling at her, one of those genuine, charming ones that she didn't get to see often enough.

"Fred and Beth took a walk. I thought I'd stay with you and give them some time alone."

Flora returned his smile. "Would you like to sit in the sand? It gets everywhere, but to me, the feeling of it under my hands is worth the mess."

They were soon settled far enough from the wet, packed sand and the tide to stay dry, but close enough to admire the water. Flora let the tension ease from her shoulders as she stared out over the horizon. "It's easy to forget how insignificant we really are."

"You say that as if insignificance is a good

thing." Jensen's voice was filled with amusement.

She turned to face him. "Isn't it? I like remembering that the problems I face aren't bigger than anyone else's. And that God created much bigger things than my troubles. Don't you like knowing He's so much greater than what we go through?"

He didn't respond at first. Was he offended? Perhaps he didn't believe in God, in His goodness. Should she have asked before speaking about Him?

But Jensen's words calmed her fear. "Does that help you trust Him more? I believe in God, but trust Him to always do what's best for me? That's harder to do."

She let her eyes soak in the beauty of the rolling ocean again. "I don't know if shifting my perspective helps me trust better, but it does help me feel less panicked about the matters I'm facing."

Jensen's shoulder brushed hers again as he ran his fingers through the sand between them. "What has you feeling that way right now?"

The last thing she'd meant to do was reveal her uncertainties to Jensen. But what could it hurt to let him know how she was feeling? They needed to work together, after all. And being honest with each other would help that process. "The race."

The knowing way his eyebrows raised made her stomach flutter. "I had a feeling you weren't all confidence as you tried to let on this morning."

Flora held up one hand to stop him. "I'm not so worried about my ability to drive the car. But things happen in races. You clearly know that as well as anyone. There are things that I may not be able to control. I don't want to be responsible for any injuries."

To her relief, he didn't tease her as Henri would have. Jensen immediately sobered. "You don't have to handle this alone. I'll be there every step of the way. My whole purpose for being here is to make sure everyone is safe, and we get through the tour without problems."

Unfortunately, that did sound like Henri. It was the same attitude he had the last time they parted, filled with over-confidence that he alone was responsible for her, and he would do what she couldn't. And then he'd gone and let tragedy strike himself.

Pain started throbbing in Flora's temple. Would she ever be free of the idea that a woman couldn't get herself through life? She pushed up out of the sand, the calm moment ruined. "You can't keep anything bad from happening to us by will alone. No one can control what happens during a race. And not one of us is invincible."

It felt cowardly, but Flora escaped across the beach, heading toward where Jensen indicated Fred and Beth went on their walk. It had been a mistake to open up to Jensen. No matter how kind and understanding he sometimes seemed, he was still a man who had far too much confidence in his ability to control his world. And she couldn't let herself get caught up in that kind of thinking again.

Catching up with the other two, Flora thanked them for giving her some time on the beach. "Why don't we spend the rest of the day at Luna Park? Beth, I'm sure you know of some attractions there that we can't miss."

Jensen caught up to them only seconds behind her with a scowl fixed on his face. "Wouldn't you rather find somewhere to sit and enjoy a quiet afternoon? We'll have plenty of activity packed into every day once the race begins. I'd like to take another look at the car after the long drive here."

Beth shook her head, refusing to fall for his attempt to get them back to the hotel. Flora had seen his discomfort all morning, and after their conversation on the way into town yesterday, she could guess he didn't appreciate crowded tourist spots. But he was the one who promised Fred the chance to give Beth all the things she'd been dreaming of for her wedding trip. Now he would have to handle what came with that promise.

So they left the beach and crossed back through Dreamland to the exit, spilling out onto Surf Avenue with a throng of other tourists. As the group entered Luna Park, they admired how each park along the famous beach maintained a unique feel while showcasing distinct architecture and fascinating attractions.

Beth led the way straight to A Trip to the Moon. Flora found the idea of the cyclorama captivating. They joined other spectators in a seating area made to look like a winged ship. The show began with the ship rocking from one side to the other, the unexpected movement causing Flora to grab Jensen's arm. Blushing, she quickly pulled her hand away. She didn't need to give him any more reason to argue that she was too feeble to handle driving in the tour.

As the ship swayed, canvas panels showing different scenes shifted around them. It appeared they were lifting from the ground, then they watched the earth grow smaller and smaller while the moon's surface grew. Actual wind picked up around them. A sudden clap of thunder made Flora gasp, along with many of the other spectators.

Jensen leaned toward her. "Think I could protect you from a fake storm, at least?"

Flora glared at him and pointed her chin in the air. How dare he throw her words back in her face? And over such a silly thing as an amusement ride too. The stakes for the race were so much more serious. She refused to look at him again as the simulated storm calmed and the ship appeared to land in a crater on the lunar surface.

The passengers began to disembark and were

led through a magical tunnel to the City of the Moon by employees dressed in fantastical alien costumes. Beth took charge of leading their group around the space, exclaiming over every piece of scenery. But she drew the line when they reached a section where guests picked bits of green cheese from the walls to taste. Her nose wrinkled in disgust, and she pulled Fred away. Flora had to agree—the smell alone was enough to drive her from the room as quickly as possible.

But when she tried to turn and follow them, she found Jensen standing so close behind her that she couldn't walk away without pushing him aside. The heat of his body reached hers, awareness of him flaring from her head to her toes.

He spoke low and close to her ear, sending a shiver skittering up her spine. "I dare you to try a piece."

Jensen had no idea what possessed him to needle Flora this way. Maybe it was the sting he still felt from her words on the beach. Thinking back over the conversation, he could see where he'd gone wrong, the words he'd let out that must have upset her. But there was no reason she needed to lash out at him, accusing him of being unable to protect those he'd promised to look out for.

The cutting remark he'd made in the winged ship hadn't been kind. He couldn't deny that. But the way she'd reached out and grabbed his arm when the fake storm startled her—as if she wanted to lean on him for protection—stirred up a longing he didn't want to explore. And now he was in the mood to make her as uncomfortable as that had made him.

But it was backfiring. The feel of her body lined up against his was taking over all his senses. If he leaned forward the slightest bit, he'd be able to bury his face in her hair. She tensed as he whispered the challenge in her ear, and it felt as though a rock dropped into the pit of his stomach.

But he didn't step away. He couldn't. She turned a bit toward him, enough to look over her shoulder and meet his gaze. Her eyes were intense, flashing with temper over his dare and—at least, he hoped—the same awareness of their proximity that he was feeling.

And she didn't move away either. Instead, she reached out and plucked a piece of cheese from the wall, as outlandish as that action was. Looking back at him again, she kept her confident gaze locked with his as she deliberately raised the bite and put it in her mouth. He nearly lost his composure right there, the longing to pull her into his arms almost more than he could resist.

But the moment of desire was broken when her face twisted into an expression of horror. She twirled around to face him, covering her mouth with one hand as she spoke around the bite of cheese. "This is terrible. I need to get rid of it or I'll be sick."

Jensen immediately pulled the handkerchief from his pocket. "Here, use this." Then he pulled her forward to shield her from the other visitors as she spit the offending cheese into the cloth and balled it up.

Flora looked up at him once she was done, her expression vulnerable. "Thank you. I'm sorry, but that was awful. I doubt you'll want your handkerchief back."

"I have others. We'll get rid of it when we see a garbage can. Let's get you out of here."

He found himself putting one arm around her shoulders and leading the way through the crowd to pass over a narrow bridge built into a hallway. They emerged from the door at the end into the heat and sunlight of the July afternoon, and Jensen sighed in relief. Fred and Beth had claimed a bench near the building, so he took Flora over and gestured for her to sit with them.

Beth's eyes flicked back and forth between them as Flora sank onto the seat. "You look as green as that cheese, dear. Are you well?"

Jensen didn't want to explain what had led to Flora taking that bite, and he doubted she did either. "It must have been too much time with that smell, combined with the heat. Let's take a rest somewhere."

A groan came from Beth's direction. "I was so hoping we could do some of the rides, like the circle swing and Whirl the Whirl. They're right down there."

Flora shook her head. "I couldn't possibly stand to be tossed around that much, Beth. But why don't you and Fred go on? And Jensen, of course. If you'd rather?"

Did she mean for it to sound as though she'd prefer if he stayed with her? Because it sounded that way to him. "I'll stay and make sure Flora doesn't take a turn for the worse. You two go on. We'll meet you at the restaurant for dinner."

Fred and Beth traipsed off hand in hand to find more fun while Jensen lowered himself onto the bench next to Flora. "Do you want to sit here a while? Or find somewhere cooler?"

"Somewhere cooler sounds perfect. I heard Beth talking about a theatre. Maybe there will be a show we can watch."

Jensen found the theatre with little trouble, and they settled in to watch the variety of vaudeville acts that crossed the stage. They were entertaining enough. Jensen even found himself chuckling alongside Flora's lyrical laugh. He hated to admit how much he enjoyed looking over to see her smiling again. He could hardly remember now why he'd felt the need to push at her earlier. Watching her enjoy life was so much better than frustrating her.

By the time they left the theatre, evening was falling. Flora looked up in wonder as the electric lights outlining every rooftop in the park lit the whole place up. "Isn't it beautiful, Jensen?"

His heart skipped a beat or two as he watched her face, the glow from the lights making her look ethereal, highlighting her already beautiful features. Who cared about some strung-up lights when he could look at Flora?

And just like that, Jensen realized he'd gotten himself into a dangerous situation.

They continued walking, but his heart had dropped out of his chest. He was falling for Flora. He'd promised to watch out for everyone on this trip, and now his heart was betraying him, opening him up to making mistakes, ones that could have lethal consequences. Having an adventurous woman like this in his life was too much of a risk.

The mistakes were already happening. Since he'd met her, Jensen had gotten roped into being the mechanic for a ten-day automobile tour. He'd been put in charge of three people who not only didn't have the sense to stay out of such a dangerous event, but they sought it out. And now he found himself willing to risk both his and Flora's hearts, just because she was lovely and he enjoyed her company more than he'd ever expected.

No, letting that happen was a complication he

couldn't allow. Putting a little space between them, Jensen silently led the way to the restaurant. Thankfully, Fred and Beth were on time and already waiting for them by the door. He'd have to take care that he spent as little time alone with Flora as possible on the rest of this journey. She cluttered his brain in the worst way.

The supper went by in a blur, and they finally returned to the hotel. Jensen was exhausted and thrilled to be alone for the first time all day. Yet rest alluded him. He paced his room for a time, but then headed downstairs to sit in the lobby and read a newspaper, hoping it would be boring enough to quiet his roiling thoughts.

Instead, he found Fred, who saw him before he could sneak away to find a more secluded spot. Fred grinned and waved for Jensen to join him. How could he say no?

Jensen settled into a winged chair near the one Fred had claimed in an alcove away from the front desk. He might as well get a few minutes of small talk over with, then excuse himself. "What brings you down here this evening? I thought you'd spend every moment with Beth, this being your wedding trip and all."

Fred crossed his legs and looked up to examine the intricately designed ceiling. "Adjusting to married life is taking a little time. I find I occasionally need a moment of quiet to myself."

Jensen stifled a laugh. Beth did tend toward

constant talking. In comparison, time spent with Flora included frequent stretches of comfortable silence that were actually a balm to his spirit.

He shook his head. He had to stop thinking of Flora like that, imagining what a lifetime of moments spent with her might be like. "I suppose it's easier to find that time at home than on the road."

Fred nodded, looking cheered that Jensen understood his plight. "Yes, exactly. I get time alone when I'm studying or preparing sermons, and once we move into the parsonage the church will provide, I imagine there will be a little space to spread out and pursue our separate interests a bit."

The mention of Fred's job reminded Jensen of the situation awaiting him when he returned from this trip. "Are you looking forward to starting your ministry after this is over?"

"Very much. There's plenty to be anxious about when I think about being responsible for a congregation, but I'm glad I finally get the chance to do the Lord's work."

Jensen considered the term for a moment. He'd heard it before but never thought of what it might mean for him. Was there some work he should be doing for the Lord? He couldn't even figure out what he was good enough at to eke out a living. It was doubtful he would ever have the chance to do something that would benefit anyone else's spiritual life.

As if realizing there was more to the question than friendly interest, Fred fixed his gaze on Jensen. "Father told me about what's happening at the store. How do you feel about the fact that working at Harrison Goods has been such a struggle?"

"I've felt better about a lot of things."

Fred frowned. "You don't have to be glib with me, Jensen. I'm your friend, and I want to know what's changed in your life. You aren't the smiling, caring man you were when I was growing up and watched you and Gregory start your careers. Has working at Harrison Goods taken that out of you?"

No, Gregory did. Thank goodness Jensen hadn't spoken the words out loud. He appreciated the rest of the Harrison family's unspoken agreement not to talk about Gregory. They shied away from reference to his name or the accident. It was hard not to bring up the man who'd been such a big part of his life, but at least if no one mentioned him, Jensen's secrets were more likely to stay that way and not rip the family apart. "It's not as bad as that. It's a solid, secure job."

"That doesn't mean it provides any benefit to your life, though. Father said he intended to give you a position long enough to find something you enjoy more. Have you any thoughts about what that might be?"

How had he gotten wrapped up in this conversation instead of chatting about the weather or something else similarly innocuous? Jensen shook his head and pushed up from the chair. "I don't know, Fred, and I can't think about it when I'm tired. I'm going to get some rest now. I'll see you in the morning."

Fred wished him a good night, but Jensen could feel his friend's curious eyes drilling into his back until the stairs curved and hid him from view of the lobby. He prepared himself for a long night. He might not find much sleep in his room, but at least he wouldn't have to discuss his problems with anyone for a few hours.

Chapter 9

The first day of the tour dawned sunny and clear, and Flora should have been excited. Even though it had been two days since the Coney Island trip, the morning light brought all the conflicting moments from that day back to her. It had occurred to her in the hours she'd spent watching Jensen go over the car in meticulous detail in the hotel garage that when he turned into the gruffer version of himself, he was working through something in his mind. If only he would tell her what those things were. If he'd allow it, there was a good chance she could help him without their conversation devolving into a petty argument.

The end of that day in Coney Island—when she'd walked with Jensen under the amazing lights of Luna Park, before their dinner with Fred and Beth—had glued itself into Flora's mind as one of the most beautiful moments of her life. Even now, as she twisted her hair up and secured it with enough pins to keep it tightly under her hat, her heart thumped hard at the memory of his closeness, their hands brushing as they walked.

Of course, that led to remembering the intense moment before she'd tasted that horrible cheese. And then his kindness to her the rest of the day. Laughing together at the vaudeville show. So far, she'd enjoyed his company far more on this trip than she would ever have imagined a few weeks ago.

But what would the race bring? Would the sullen version of Jensen show up today, filled with worry about things he couldn't control?

Pressing a wide-brimmed hat onto her head, Flora secured it with a bow under her chin and gave herself one last appraisal in the mirror. Her favorite lightweight driving jacket was mostly wrinkle-free, and she appeared ready for a day of driving. If only she could calm her nerves so she might feel as put-together as she looked.

Joining the others in the lobby, Flora nodded to them all in greeting. She'd keep the weight of such an important event to herself. Jensen hardly met her eyes, while Beth and Fred filled in enough conversation for all four of them. It would be a very long race indeed if this continued for the entire ten days.

They loaded into the car, and Flora navigated through the busy city to the Automobile Club of America headquarters at 58th Street and Fifth Avenue, where the race would start. Spectators and team members were everywhere when they arrived. Flora eased the Decauville into a spot at the end of a line of cars that had already formed. While Beth and Fred wandered off to look at the other cars, Jensen opened the hood to check everything over one last time. Flora leaned against the driver's side door, taking in all the pre-race activity.

It had been so long since she'd experienced the thrill and tension of the moments before a race started. She counted more than thirty other cars. Hoping to ease the strangeness between them, she mentioned a few standouts to Jensen. "This is a solid field of competitors. There are at least three Pierce-Arrows, a few White Steamers, Packards, and Napiers. The Decauville can run right with any of those."

He offered a grunt while his face remained buried in the engine. Flora fought the urge to grab his shoulder and turn him to see the most beautiful automobile in the group. "You should see this stunning black Panhard et Levassor. The wood trim is so elegant compared to all the other cars. What a machine."

He didn't respond, clearly not sharing her passion for the fine collection of cars around them. She turned her attention to the people. Drivers, mechanics, and riders were all milling around, admiring each other's vehicles and answering questions from the gathered spectators. Flora watched it all from her spot, not sure whether to mingle with the other teams or not. In France, race teams hadn't always been friendly with each other. What would the atmosphere be like here?

A man with a badge marking him as an official for the race walked over and glanced at a page in his hand. He turned to Jensen. "This is the Decauville driven by an F. Montfort?"

F. Montfort? Flora straightened. Mr. Harrison hadn't put her full name on the application? Jensen kept his eyes on the official as he stepped between the man and Flora. "Yes, it is."

At least it wasn't a lie. But did the man think he was speaking to F. Montfort? He checked off a spot on the paper, then pulled a thick packet from the bag on his shoulder. "Included here is your car number. Affix it in a visible place, please. You'll also find maps, descriptions of the designated route, details about lodging, and other important information. Please don't lose these items. The race starts in twenty minutes."

Flora started to speak up, but Jensen grabbed the packet and thanked the official while he strode toward the next team. She speared Jensen with her gaze. "Why did you talk over me? Someone needs to correct the assumption that you're F. Montfort."

Jensen handed her the packet while shaking his head. "No, we don't. I don't know why Mr. Harrison made that choice, but look around. How many other women do you see?"

Without even glancing at the groups scattered among the cars, she knew what he meant. There were only a handful of women with the teams, and most of them were already sitting in the back seat of a car. They weren't the drivers. "It could turn out to be a benefit that he did it this way. A female driver might very well have been denied entry."

As much as Flora hated it, he was right. Hadn't she had the same issue in France? Henri had even gone so far as to sign up with his name as the driver, then switch seats with her at the last moment. "But everyone will realize soon enough."

Jensen shrugged. "Let's see if they're willing to take that stand here in front of these crowds with all the publicity that's on the line."

Another good point. Flora forced her neck and shoulders to relax. She had a long day of driving ahead and couldn't waste time on a headache from worrying about something she had no control over. What mattered now was proving that she had every right to drive with these men—and that she could keep up with the best of them.

Hopping into the car, she opened the packet and began studying the route descriptions, maps, and rules. There were windows of time for the cars to arrive at each stop. While Flora didn't know the northeast well, she could tell consistent speed—not a breakneck pace—would be essential. That would help the safety factor and ease Jensen's mind. But they still couldn't afford any mistakes if they were to meet the expected times every day.

It wasn't long before the teams started moving toward their vehicles and getting settled inside.

Fred and Beth returned and climbed into the back together. Jensen came to stand by Flora. "Are you ready?"

She swallowed the lump of doubt that formed in her throat. She hadn't started a race since the one before Henri died. Before their last fight. Before she discovered his debt and her world was turned upside down and shaken to pieces.

But there wasn't much choice now. Racing was all she had, and she needed to show she could still do it. She nodded with all the confidence she could muster.

Jensen looked grim as he patted the car's hood. "Then let's go."

He walked around to the passenger side of the car and climbed in. Flora didn't check to see if any of those around them were looking their way, commenting under their breaths about a female driver. It didn't matter what they thought right now. They'd see soon enough that she could drive as well as any of them. Better than a lot of them.

The air stilled as the teams all got into place. The crowds which now lined the street quieted. At the front of the line, a representative from the American Automobile Association raised a megaphone almost as tall as he was to make several announcements, outlining what the packet contained and a few important rules. Then he told the drivers to start their cars.

Flora went through the familiar procedure

along with the other drivers. The air vibrated with the sound of so many engines roaring to life at once.

After a few moments to ensure all the cars had started, the announcer once again put the megaphone to his lips and shouted, "Group one, let's race!"

At once, the sound changed as the front engines shifted into gear. The first cars in line took off while the rest moved up to the line to await their staggered start times, which only varied by a few minutes each. When her turn came, Flora eased into driving, watching the five cars around them to ensure they didn't hit anyone before they even left the starting line.

Clumps of wagons and carriages held up the drivers for some time on the city streets. Flora's fingers grew numb on the steering wheel from gripping it so tightly. Finally, after an hour or so of creeping along with cars getting shuffled around in the traffic, the Decauville emerged onto an open road with several other racers.

Flora drew a deep breath and forced her body to relax. They'd made it out of the city. Now there were ten days of racing in unknown conditions to contend with.

Nothing to worry about there.

As Flora navigated the road out of New York City, Jensen pored over the map for the first leg, trying to become as familiar as possible with the route they would be taking. His job as the mechanic also included watching out for other cars and hazards, and for a long race like this, keeping them on the right path. Thankfully, the first part of the route had been well marked with confetti by the tour officials. Flora hadn't needed one bit of direction yet, so he could focus on what they would face the rest of the day.

Once they got on a long stretch of open road and he was confident in the route, Jensen finally leaned back and let himself take in the scenery. He'd never made time to travel much and thus had never been to this part of New England. By mid-morning, when they crossed into Connecticut, he was enthralled with the glimpses of Long Island Sound from the winding coastal road. The tension that had built in his chest since they left Philadelphia drained a bit, leaving him more relaxed than he'd felt in a long time. As long as he kept a vigilant focus on their safety, he might enjoy the experience along the way.

Their current route was an easy enough drive. The hard-packed dirt was even and mostly free of ruts. They made good time all morning. As they entered a town called New Haven, confetti marked a turn from the coastal road to one that headed straight north.

Fred leaned forward and tapped Flora on the shoulder, holding up a basket of picnic food they'd purchased from the hotel. "Should we stop for a bite of lunch now?"

Emotions warred in Flora's eyes. She seemed torn between pushing on and making sure everyone was comfortable. But soon enough, comfort won out, and she slowed the car, turning off the road by an open pasture.

Fred swung himself out of the vehicle and helped Beth out, then lifted the basket from the back. As they all settled on a blanket Flora had pulled from under the seat, Beth exclaimed over the contents of the basket. "Oh, look at this food. There are even the most darling petit fours. I can't wait until the girls hear about this. Cakes from the Waldorf-Astoria."

They all seemed content enough setting up the picnic, so Jensen opened the car's hood to check everything inside. But it wasn't long before he felt Flora's presence at his side. Without looking at her, he asked, "How does the car feel when you're driving?"

A pause made him turn to look at her. She leaned against the front of the car, arms crossed over her waist, her gaze focused on the fluffy clouds overhead. "It's handling fine. Feels light enough to be fast while still holding the road well."

The way her chin tilted up and the far-off expression on her face brought to mind that moment under the lights at Luna Park when he realized how much he enjoyed having her at his side. It felt the same now, as they stood together by the open car.

If he didn't already know she was the type of woman he had to save from herself, he might slide over close to her right now. Even reach for her hand, if she seemed to welcome it.

The sound of a car horn split the peaceful country air, startling both of them. They leaned around the Decauville to see a White steam car race by, the three men inside waving. Jensen had been too focused on making sure the car was ready earlier to look for Sam Kelly at the starting line, but there he was, in the car careening past them.

That wasn't what caused the shock that jolted Jensen out of his relaxation, though. The all-too-familiar sneer of the driver did that. Archie Franklin. The rival he and Gregory had raced neck and neck with for years. The only person who knew why Jensen hadn't been in the race car with Gregory the day he died. The one man who could destroy the Harrison family's trust in Jensen.

Trying to stop his hands from shaking, Jensen stepped out into the road and watched the car disappear over a hill up ahead, a whoop from Sam echoing back to them. He turned to find Flora smiling at Sam's antics. "He's such a fun fellow. How can you look so miserable after that display of pure joy?"

"There's nothing joyful about being a fool. He's not taking the risks seriously. There are real consequences for mistakes out here. Lives can be changed—even lost. There's no room for silliness."

Flora threw up her hands. "That again. Jensen, you know as well as anyone that life is too short to live in fear of what's around the corner. I'm aware of the risks, as I'm certain the other teams are, including Sam. But every moment of our lives contains some element of risk. Why should that mean there can't be any fun in the midst of it?"

Jensen stalked toward her, ready to settle the matter once and for all. If he could get her to understand the importance of his effort to keep his friends safe, they might be able to work together for the rest of the tour rather than pulling in different directions. "We've had fun. I allowed plenty of fun in New York. But this is serious business. People die during these races, Flora."

Her eyes flashed, and her lips tightened into a hard line. All at once, Jensen remembered he wasn't the only one who'd lost someone dear because of a reckless racing choice. He started to reach for her hand, wishing he could pull the words back, but stopped himself before he touched her. He had no right to do so. "I'm so sorry. I shouldn't have let my words get ahead of my thoughts. I know you've experienced that loss firsthand too."

"Yes, I have." The chill in her voice told him the apology wasn't enough. "I'm more than aware of what happens when someone dies during a race. Don't you think I weighed all that before agreeing to this? Before ever stepping foot back in a car? It took months, Jensen, before I could even look at this machine. Henri bought it for me, and while we never raced it, I still felt the horror of the moment I heard about his accident every time I went near it. But I managed to get past that fear and discover joy in my life again. I don't know what made you feel you have to control everything to be safe, but it might be time for you to worry more about yourself and the pain you carry than about everyone else's choices."

She spun on the toe of one boot and marched back to the picnic blanket. Jensen stood rooted to the spot, unable to think what he could even say to her in response. She had been through a worse loss than his and yet, as she said, she'd found a way to dig out from under that pain. Was he more stuck in the memory of Gregory's death than he realized? Should he be more focused on healing and less on protecting those around him?

He thought about it all afternoon. The drive was long, but while the roads grew more rutted in spots, they were never dangerously so. The packed dirt smoothed out closer to towns, which they encountered often. But Jensen's thoughts made for rough going no matter how well-kept the route was.

He went over and over Flora's words. Somehow, although she didn't know the circumstances of the accident, she had put her finger on exactly what held Jensen back in every aspect of his life. Was it time to let the pain of Gregory's death go? Was it even possible for him to release the guilt over his part in the tragedy? He'd never thought it would be possible, but Flora had been able to move forward with her life.

Maybe he could too.

Chapter 10

Flora drove the car into Hartford, Connecticut, squarely within the time frame listed in the rule book. It was a relief to leave the car for the officials to inspect after she'd accomplished her goal for the day—getting there on time with no mechanical issues that would deduct points from their score. She could rest easy that night knowing at least she hadn't failed on the first day.

There were several who had. Word spread around the area marked off for the cars to park overnight that two competitors had gotten lost and missed the window for full points. Another team had broken off an entire wheel hitting a particularly deep rut while going too fast. They decided it wasn't worth continuing after the amount of time it would take to repair the car. So she could also take pride in not being the first team out of the race.

Once the car had been checked and parked, Flora looked around the area where many of the drivers and mechanics were standing around talking. Most of them pretended she wasn't there at all. Sam Kelly tipped his hat to her but then turned right back to his teammates. Unsure what else to do, she wandered through the rows of cars, taking her time heading toward the hotel. It was quite a relief to see Beth waving to get Flora's attention as she came out the door.

Looping her arm through Flora's, Beth steered them away from the building. "I've been told it's a short walk to the shops in town. Let's have some time to relax, just us ladies."

Flora glanced back at the hotel even as Beth pulled her away. "What about Fred and Jensen?"

Beth grinned. "Oh, Fred likes to have some time to himself now and then. He tries not to say it in as many words, to protect my feelings, I'm sure. But I need time apart occasionally too. So I arrange for errands to keep me busy. I haven't seen Jensen since we arrived, though. Do you think he'd want to come along?"

Flora's face must have shown complete disbelief that Beth would even ask, because the other woman took one look at her and dissolved into laughter. "No, you're quite right. Jensen would not want to come shopping with us."

With that settled, they followed the directions Beth had gotten to the nicest shopping district in Hartford. The evening flew by in a rush of admiring goods while Beth chattered about everything under the sun. It wasn't until they were in the last store on the main street, a milliner's shop, that Beth finally paused and met Flora's gaze. "You must tell me how you're feeling about today. Was it difficult getting in the car this morning to start a race without your husband?"

A sudden wave of emotion caught Flora off guard, closing her throat so she had to swallow several times.

Beth gasped and rested her hand on Flora's arm. "Oh, dear, I've hurt you by saying it so bluntly. I'm sorry. If you don't want to talk about it, of course, I can mind my own business."

Shaking her head, Flora offered the best smile she could muster to show Beth she wasn't upset at the question. "No, I don't mind talking about Henri and his death. It was hard, but I've come to terms with it. What made me emotional is realizing how long it's been since someone asked me how I feel about something."

"Not even Jensen?"

The tone Beth used made a flush start creeping up Flora's neck. She and Jensen had spent a good deal of time together since this whole thing started. How must that look to everyone around them? "No, especially not Jensen. He has moments of kindness and even charm, but then he goes right back to frowning at me."

Beth linked arms with Flora again as they left the shop. They strolled back along the street, heading in the direction of the hotel but in no hurry. Beth's voice was calmer and more serious than Flora had ever heard her. "Fred told me a little about Jensen's past, and it's hard, all of it.

He lost his parents at a young age. Thankfully, the Harrisons took him in, and they're as close as any family. But he was especially dear friends with Fred's brother, Gregory."

Flora had heard mentions of the eldest Harrison brother, but never details about what had happened to him. "That story feels rather like a closely held family secret."

Beth nodded. "It is. Most of the family doesn't talk about him much. As the youngest, Fred has fewer memories of Gregory, but also feels free to bring him up when the others don't."

"Do you know how Gregory died?"

Looking toward the hotel as it grew closer with each step, Beth hesitated. Then she glanced at Flora with a sad smile. "Only a bit. It was a racing accident five years ago. Jensen was his mechanic, but for some reason, he wasn't in the car when the accident occurred. That's all I know. Fred was fifteen, and the family tried to protect him by refusing to tell him any details. Now they don't talk about it at all."

Flora let the sadness of that revelation wash over her. Jensen lost his best friend to a racing accident, much like the way she lost Henri. Then the family refused to grieve properly, instead shrouding Gregory's life in silence. It was all so tragic.

And it gave Jensen's mood changes so much perspective. Their conversation at lunch jumped to the forefront of her mind. The way he'd said that she lost someone to racing, too—as if he was commiserating with her—made sense now. She'd been right when she told him he was stuck in his pain, although at the time, she hadn't known how similar his loss was to hers.

But one question lingered. Why hadn't Jensen been in the car helping his teammate as he should have been during a race?

The two women reached the hotel and found a crowd still gathered around the parked race cars. Many of the drivers and mechanics were milling around, talking with spectators about their cars and the first leg of the tour. Maybe it was time to join them and see if she could get to know any of the other team members a bit.

Bidding Beth goodnight, Flora headed for the first car that had arrived, the lovely White Model E Steamer that had blown past them while they stopped for lunch. Sam wasn't there anymore, but the driver was telling a group of onlookers what must have been a riveting tale, based on their rapt expressions. Flora paused to listen as he wrapped up his story. "And that's what got me here a full half hour before any other drivers—perfect control of a perfect automobile."

Flora turned away so no one would see her roll her eyes. The driver continued his pride-filled diatribe as she walked toward the next vehicle, and she did her best to ignore the loud boasts. His car was very nice to look at and must run well since he'd arrived first. But that didn't make it perfect. And it certainly didn't make him perfect, as he seemed to believe.

Moving on, she encountered many of the same conversations happening all around the parking area. Drivers boasting about their skills. Mechanics claiming any small adjustment they made was what brought their car in faster than so many others. And not one of them made any effort to acknowledge Flora's presence.

She passed the White Steamer again on the way back to the hotel, but this time, Sam was there and waved her over when he caught her eye. "Mrs. Montfort, come meet my crew. This is our driver, Archie Franklin, and Charles Ray riding along. Fellows, this is Mrs. Flora Montfort, driver of that fine Decauville straight from France."

The men all shook her hand, though Mr. Franklin's eyes traveled up and down her first in a disconcerting way. Flora pushed the discomfort away. She was used to all kinds of unwanted and unnecessary looks from men in races. If she continued to drive well, it wouldn't be the last unpleasant glance sent her way. "It's a pleasure to meet you both. Is this your first race?"

Charlie Ray, who seemed the friendlier of the two, answered before Mr. Franklin could even take a breath. "We've all been in racing for years and were handpicked by Mr. Ronald Dorman of the Dorman Sporting Equipment empire to lead his racing team."

Was he actually puffing out his chest with pride? Flora stifled a giggle, not wanting to offend the first men on this tour who even bothered to admit she existed. "He must trust all three of you, then. And he's supplied you with a very fine car."

This time, Mr. Franklin managed to respond before Mr. Ray, his words slow and deliberate. "I own the car, ma'am. Mr. Dorman is funding the team, but this is my automobile. Get used to seeing the back of it as I reach the finish in front of you every night."

What a pompous response to a friendly remark. Before Flora could return her own barb, Mr. Ray spoke again. "Did you hear the news, Mrs. Montfort? About the teams that got lost?"

Flora shook her head and Mr. Ray continued, looking quite pleased he had information to reveal. "Word is, the confetti marking the route got tampered with. Who would do such a thing to a group of people out enjoying a friendly competition? We're not hurting anyone."

With a scowl that never seemed to leave his face, Mr. Franklin waved off his teammate's concern. "Think, man. It's bits of paper. The wind was most likely responsible. Or the previous cars crushed it into the dirt. They were the last two teams, anyway, and hardly worth being concerned about. This would be a better competition if they didn't let anyone with access to a car join. Qualified drivers would make for a more competitive race."

A chill settled over Flora when Mr. Franklin looked her over deliberately again. Was he referring to her? Did he believe, as many people did, that she shouldn't compete because she was a woman?

With a change of the subject that saved her from snapping a retort she couldn't take back, Sam held out his arm to her with an easy smile. "Can I take you for a stroll around the grounds, Mrs. Montfort? I'd love to hear about your first day."

Grateful for his rescue, Flora nodded to the other two men and took Sam's arm. As they walked away, the tension drained from her body. "Thank you, Sam. I don't know how I offended Mr. Franklin, but he was quite disagreeable."

Shrugging, Sam continued ambling on through the cars and onlookers. "Ah, he's always that way. He's vying for a spot high up in Mr. Dorman's company, is what Charles says. I guess he'd do just about anything to get it. Dorman's worth a fortune, you know. Right up there with Mr. Harrison."

Oh, she knew plenty by now about the rivalry between Mr. Harrison and Mr. Dorman. "There's often money behind unhappy people, isn't there Sam?"

He nodded, his usual cheerfulness unaffected by the serious topic. "Sure is. Good thing I don't have a bit of it to turn me into a grump."

Flora laughed and continued doing so as Sam entertained her during their entire loop around the parking area. No matter how alienated she'd felt most of the day, she couldn't consider it a bad one if it ended with a laugh.

As he returned to the Decauville after freshening up, Jensen watched Flora and Sam promenade around the cars, arm in arm and laughing like old friends. The bite of jealousy at how comfortable they looked together was unexpected. And unpleasant.

Jensen turned to answer a few questions about the car for a local, who admired the vehicle before moving on and leaving Jensen to his thoughts. It was getting late into the evening, and the crowd of spectators began to thin out.

Fred emerged from the hotel and met Jensen by the car, scuffing the ground with the toe of his shoe. "How did the evening go, Jensen? Did the locals enjoy seeing Flora's fine automobile?"

"It seemed as though they did. Many appreciated discussing the differences between it and American cars."

Fred nodded and leaned against the Decauville,

settling in right beside Jensen. He released a deep sigh. If he wasn't going to get to retire for the night, Jensen might as well attempt to get to the bottom of whatever Fred came out to discuss. "Did Beth get to do all the shopping she wanted?"

Shrugging, Fred stuck his hands in his pockets. "For now, I suppose. At least it keeps her from stewing over having a baby."

There it was. The newlyweds must have been encountering some friction over starting a family, and that was why Fred had wandered outside looking as though he needed to talk. "So you'd rather let her spend all your money?"

Fred looked up at the darkening sky where clouds were beginning to gather. "It's an inheritance from her aunt who died last year. She was childless and left most of her money to Beth. It's not much, but I feel terrible that I haven't been able to give her what she wants most, so I figure she might as well use the money in any way that makes her happy."

Worry lines etched into Fred's forehead that had never been there before. Were Beth's hopes for a baby taking a bigger toll than Fred let on? The weight on a man who knew he was disappointing his wife had to be a heavy load to bear.

But Fred shifted to look at Jensen and changed the subject. "Have you come to any decisions on what you'll do when we get back?" He must've talked as much about his troubles as he'd needed to.

Pushing away from the car, Jensen grabbed a cloth from under the seat and started wiping the day's dirt from the smooth metal. "Nope."

"It isn't like you to not have a plan. I always thought you had everything figured out."

Across the lawn, Jensen again caught a glimpse of Flora and Sam, still with their arms linked, walking toward the hotel. A fist constricted around his heart. "That's a child's perspective talking. You're a man now. I'm sure you're beginning to understand that it's not worth trying to decide your entire life all at once. The plans we make rarely work out the way we hope."

To Jensen's horror, Fred's eyes followed his gaze, and he turned back to Jensen with the most knowing expression. "Flora and Sam make a nice pair."

"No, they don't." Jensen tossed the cloth back onto the seat of the car and stalked away. He was sure he heard Fred chuckling as he retreated, but he refused to look back and find out. Fred could think what he wanted about Jensen's relationship with Flora. Not that there was a relationship to speak of. As soon as this trip was over, he was going to figure out how to make his life as stable and quiet as possible. Flora could go take whatever reckless chances she wanted with hers. If Sam was one of those choices, so be it.

Getting as far as he could from Fred meant Jensen ended up at the front of the line of cars, where the day's leader was parked, ready to start the next morning with the first group. He let himself blend into the edge of a group still surrounding the second-place car, but he didn't bother listening to the stories the driver was going on about. They were all too far-fetched for any thinking person to believe, anyway.

An all-too-familiar voice nearby drew his mind away from Flora's present companion. "Hello, Jensen. It's been quite some time since I saw you around race cars."

So much for a few moments to think without anyone talking to him. And of all people, Archie Franklin. He stood at Jensen's left side, hands in his pockets, looking supremely relaxed. The exact opposite of Jensen's reaction to seeing his old racing competitor. "Hello, Archie. Nice run today. I ought to be going now."

"Oh, stay a minute, Jensen." He started to turn away, but something in Archie's voice held him back. "I have something to say."

Stopping in his tracks, Jensen turned without a word, bracing himself for whatever Archie had up his sleeve. "I never got to tell you how sorry I was about Gregory. It always seemed like a bad time to bring it up."

"It always was a bad time. You're the last person I'd accept condolences from."

Archie's face was smooth and unbothered, not filled with the remorse Jensen would have liked to see. "Now, you talk as if I had some part in what happened. It was a race. Things happen in races. We all knew it then, and we all know it now."

It was difficult, but Jensen managed to keep his fist from driving straight into Archie's nose. "You pushed him. You kept goading him until he made a mistake. That mistake cost him his life, Archie. Don't tell me it's just something that happens."

Archie's expression filled with a strong emotion Jensen was familiar with seeing on his face—deviousness. "I'm not the one who let him get in the car. Encouraged him to, I'd even say. That was all you, my friend. You're the one who told him to race me and then backed out at the last minute, leaving him without anyone to look out for him while he was driving. All I did was drive my best. And that was better than his best."

Jensen took a step forward. He didn't have the self-control to keep his hands off Archie now, but a young couple strolling past paused, obviously seeing that the situation was about to explode. Jensen's rage cooled enough for him to step back. He couldn't let his temper get the better of him again, especially not with so many people watching. He leaned back on his heels and let his hands clench and unclench several times, hoping to release his tension through them. "I'm not talking about this with you."

But Archie wasn't done. "Does your dear employer know what part you had to play in the crash that killed his son?"

Jensen's heart froze solid. He could tell from Archie's pleased look that the answer was written all over Jensen's face. Still, he had to try to cover his blunder. "What does it matter? Encouraging him to race you wasn't wrong."

Over the last five years, he'd told himself that time and again. Every time he looked at Mr. Harrison's grief-ravaged face or wondered if Mrs. Harrison's mental decline would have been slower if she hadn't lost her son, he repeated the same words in his mind. He should have confessed his part in the accident when it happened. Back then, they might have understood, might not have been upset over his cowardice.

But he'd hidden the fact that he'd been the one to convince Gregory to race Archie. Jensen had been more bothered by Archie's lies and taunts than Gregory, but Gregory was the one who lost his life over them. Jensen should have been in the car to watch for the dirty tricks Archie was famous for using in races at the time, but he'd changed his mind at the starting line. By then, Gregory refused to back out, and in the heat of an argument, Jensen had jumped out of the car mere moments before his friend drove off to his death.

Now, face-to-face with Archie once again, Jensen still didn't have the self-control to ignore the taunts. And he couldn't let his weakness hurt anyone else.

Archie watched him steadily, as if he could read every thought running through Jensen's mind. "I see you never mentioned that detail to Gregory's family. It would be a shame if they were to find out now, years later. It would open those painful wounds all over again."

How could he respond to that? He'd never been able to convince himself his part in the accident was unimportant. If it was as inconsequential as he'd tried to believe over the years, he would have explained it to them earlier. The truth was, he hadn't wanted his surrogate family to know what part he'd played in their tragedy. He longed for them to see him as a son, as much as Fred was and Gregory had been. But if they found out his secret, they would blame him, spurn him, perhaps even cut him from their lives. For five years, he'd done nothing but work to support the Harrison family. With one small revelation, he could lose everything he held dear.

Strolling a few steps closer to Jensen, Archie was the picture of absolute self-confidence. He knew he had something over Jensen. It remained to be seen what he was going to do with it. "Knowing what we both know now, here's what we'll do. Your team will lose this race. You're the mechanic for a female driver. She must rely on you to handle all the workings of the car that she doesn't understand. You can find a way to compromise the car that she'll never know about. Make a little something happen to knock off some points. Maybe then she'll even decide to quit the race and you can go right back to your safe little office job. Whatever you choose, stay out of my way, or your secret will be revealed to the Harrison family as painfully as I can manage to make it."

Jensen stood frozen, staring at Archie as the driver tipped his hat with a smirk, then wandered away whistling, looking quite pleased with his work. In a way, the demand wasn't the most terrible plan Jensen had imagined from Archie. The option of returning to a quiet, safe life with Flora, Fred, and Beth securely out of the race sounded perfect.

But did he have it in him to betray Flora that way? Or Fred and Beth? Or Mr. Harrison? They'd put their trust in him to give his best for the team. Could he destroy their dreams on purpose to protect himself from the repercussions of his cowardice?

Chapter 11

The next morning, Flora waved at Sam, who walked past as she climbed into the Decauville and settled in for the second day of driving. The walk with him the night before had been just the relaxing activity she needed. He was funny and straightforward, the opposite of Jensen. The entire tour would be so much easier if she was more drawn to Sam than to her mechanic.

Hands freezing in the middle of straightening her black skirt, Flora realized that was a truth she'd been trying to deny to herself for weeks. She was drawn to Jensen in a way different from any other man, including Henri. That had been a hot flash of infatuation. This felt like a deeper, more intriguing interest in discovering who he was deep down. If only Jensen would be more open, show more of the charming side that snuck out on occasion. If they weren't always at odds, she might be able to get somewhere in learning who Jensen was at his core.

As the man himself hopped into the car next to her, tendrils of awareness started creeping through Flora. And they were accompanied by an even more unpleasant truth—that maybe Jensen was standoffish with her because he wasn't interested in the way she was. Maybe he had no intention of getting to know her, and therefore didn't feel the need to open the deeper parts of his life to her.

As the morning went on, heavy clouds moved in overhead, matching the mood that overtook Flora. It was the kind of day she wished she could tuck her feet under her in a cozy chair and enjoy a book and a cup of the strong French coffee she'd come to enjoy in Paris. She'd been longing to read *The Call of the Wild* since Isabelle had raved about it the year before, but the motivation to read had eluded Flora since Henri's death and the discovery of his failure to provide for his family.

Instead of a comfortable day indoors, she would have to endure a damp one sitting in very close quarters with a man who would prefer to be anywhere but at her side.

The rain started after they took a break for lunch. In the backseat, Beth pulled out her parasol—not that a frilly thing like that would do much good against a full-blown storm in the open touring car. But the rain was light enough for an hour or so that Flora wished she had one of her own.

Soon enough, though, Beth nearly lost the parasol as the wind picked up, swirling around them. Fred helped her pull it down and stash it on the floorboards before it got blown away. Flora had to put one hand up to hold her hat in place, even with it tied securely under her chin. Still, she was determined to finish this leg of the tour as well as they had yesterday.

Unfortunately, the weather had other ideas. They came over a rise in the muddy road, and Flora had to stop the car. Where their path sloped downward on the other side of the hill, water rushed across, a current washing away the road itself as it passed. Flora looked at Jensen, unsure what the wisest course of action would be.

Without returning her look, Jensen swung himself out of the car and stepped down the hill a few feet, nearly sinking into the thick mud. He finally turned to meet her eyes and shook his head, words unneeded and likely to be drowned out in the din of the rain, rushing water, and running engine. They wouldn't be getting through this spot.

Returning to his seat, Jensen leaned close to her and raised his voice over the noise. "Turn around. We'll find shelter and figure out what to do."

It took a few tries, but Flora got the car turned around without getting stuck in the mud and began the trek to find a dry place. When Henri had purchased this car, she hadn't thought twice about not having an enclosed top like some manufacturers were fond of making. It had seemed like a lot of extra weight on a car she wanted to be as light and fast as possible. Most races didn't run in the rain. But now she could see it would have been worth at least considering.

After backtracking several miles, they found the last small town they'd passed through and parked on the main street outside a hotel with a restaurant next door. Fred and Beth dashed to the restaurant, but Flora took a few more minutes in the rain to pull a tarp over the Decauville. She prayed as she and Jensen tugged the tarp into place that this delay wouldn't cost them the chance of winning so early in the tour. There were so many days left.

Finally, they were all inside the nearly empty restaurant, wrapped in towels that the kind waitress had borrowed from the hotel while they watched the pouring rain through the large front window. Beth leaned against Fred, the two of them looking cozy and sweet. Flora turned away, trying to find anything less saccharine to look at.

Jensen didn't seem able to sit for long. He was soon up pacing the floor in front of their table, stopping to look up at the sky every few times he passed the window.

Unbearable tension built inside Flora's chest. "We need to get going. Jensen, is there another way on the map that we can use to go around? One that might not be flooded?"

He stopped pacing and brightened, as if having a task to occupy his mind helped the situation. "Let me see. I have the paperwork right here."

Jensen pulled the envelope full of maps and itineraries from inside his jacket and laid them out on an empty table nearby. Fred joined him, leaving the women together.

Beth, looking as comfortable as a person could be despite being drenched, looked over at Flora. "Maybe we should stay here until the rain lets up. Surely, it won't delay us too long."

Flora glanced at her pocket watch. "We still have to get the rest of the way to Boston. Judging from how long the waitress said it takes by carriage, we have at least three more hours to drive."

Beth patted Flora's hand. "The car is faster than that. We don't have to be there until six o'clock, correct?"

Struggling to keep from unleashing her frustration on Beth, Flora watched the men as they pored over the map, several locals joining them now. "With this weather making the road conditions worse, it's very likely even the Decauville will take longer than a carriage on a good day. We need to keep moving."

Beth fell silent. Had Flora's tone been harsher than she realized? But she couldn't help thinking of all the drivers who would press on through the weather undeterred. Any teams that had already crossed the flooded road would be continuing toward the next stop while the Harrison Goods team sat idle. They would lose points on the second day and be forced to run the rest of the tour knowing they had no chance of winning. Flora couldn't bear it.

Just then, Jensen straightened and turned to face them, holding the map up with a wide grin that made Flora's heart leap in her chest. "We have it. These gentlemen tell us there's a ferry that runs across the river on the other side of town. It should be passable. If we can keep moving from there, we'll have a chance at arriving in Boston on time."

Flora had an unexpected impulse to jump up and fling her arms around Jensen. He'd saved the day, and her rebellious heart was thrilled with that fact. Her mind knew better, though. There was nothing romantic about thinking she could depend on a man who despised the thing she loved most. No matter how she might be drawn to his softer, kinder side, he, too, often acted as though everyone around him ought to agree with his every opinion, much like Clement had.

Memories of her older brother made a shiver travel up Flora's spine. She had to start proving to herself and everyone around her that she was as capable as any of the male drivers or mechanics, including Jensen. What would be left for her after this race if she didn't?

When Flora pulled the car up at the river crossing, Jensen realized immediately that he'd made a mistake.

There was no well-built ferry with a permanent dock as he'd been expecting. Instead, a flat wagon drawn by matching white horses stood at the ready, ropes coiled on top. While the locals had assured him the car could be taken across, he wasn't sure how they would even get it onto that wagon, much less through the rushing, head-high water.

Glancing next to him, Jensen cleared his throat, ready to take responsibility for the mistake. "I'm sorry, Flora. I thought this would be a viable solution."

But she didn't even hesitate. Swinging herself down from the car, Flora tugged her jacket sleeves into place and grinned. "This will do fine. We'll get across and catch up in no time."

She started marching toward the rough-looking men waiting with the horses, but Jensen rushed to stop her. "Flora, wait. This isn't a good idea. The rain may have almost stopped, but everything is still soaked. That wet wood will be slippery, and the ropes won't hold well. If we put this car on there and the slightest shift happens during the crossing, the whole thing will go under."

Undeterred, she moved around him. "I'm sure they have a method for doing it, or the man at the restaurant wouldn't have suggested we come here. We can at least ask them."

Before he could stop himself, Jensen's hand shot out and grabbed her upper arm. She turned back toward him, standing close enough he could smell a floral scent coming from her hair. Distracted by her closeness, he stared at her until she swallowed hard. But that didn't discourage her one bit.

"We're crossing here, Jensen. It's the only way."

Frustrated, he threw up his hands. "No, it isn't. The rain is clearing off. We can go back to the other crossing and wait until the water slows. Or keep driving until we get to the next one. Anything is better than the foolish, dangerous notion that we could get the car across this way."

At that moment, the sounds of an approaching engine drowned out further discussion. Before they could react, another team drove straight up to the wagon. Waving to Jensen and Flora, the driver chatted with the locals, then they began working together, setting up wide wooden planks to form a ramp. Getting back into his car, the driver guided it up the bending, heaving planks. The car was soon tied into place, and the team members each took up a spot around the vehicle to brace it while the wagon driver urged his horses into the raging river.

Jensen didn't want to watch the whole contraption be swallowed by the river, but he couldn't look away. To his shock, after several nerve-wracking minutes, the horses strained enough to pull the heavy wagon to the opposite bank.

They'd done it. Finally freeing his gaze from the debacle, Jensen felt Flora fuming before he even looked at her.

"I told you it would be fine. And now we've wasted twenty minutes, and another team is in front of us."

Without giving him time to apologize, Flora stomped over to talk to the local man waiting for the wagon to return, arranging for them to go next.

Jensen dropped back to lean against the car while they waited. Sure, one team had made it safely to the other side. But this still seemed like a terrible idea.

Fred leaned over the side of the car from the back, where he still sat with Beth. "Let me guess. You don't want to do this, and she's set on it."

Wiping a few errant raindrops from his face, Jensen nodded. It wasn't as though he could deny what had happened right in front of them. "Seems to be the way our relationship will always be."

Beth offered a sweet smile. "She wants to know you trust and respect her as an equal. It shouldn't be so hard to prove to her if you try."

Wrapping an arm around his wife, Fred nodded. "That's true. You do respect her ability, don't you? And trust her to drive this car?"

"Of course I do." But Jensen could see how his instinct to protect all of them might make it seem otherwise. "How do I show her that when she always wants to buck safety in favor of unnecessary risks, though?"

He watched Flora walking back toward them as Fred responded. "Start by asking her opinion and listening to it. Try to see things from her perspective."

Stopping in front of them, Flora looked triumphant. "As soon as the wagon returns, we'll load the car on. Beth, you're welcome to stay seated. The rest of us will help keep the car from shifting. Jensen, do you want to get in before I drive over to the loading area?"

Her brown eyes held pensiveness as she waited for his answer. Listen to her perspective, Fred said. Jensen already knew what she wanted. Could he stand by and help her, even if he didn't agree? "Sure. Let's get to the other side."

The relieved smile that graced her features at his response was worth the effort of biting his tongue. She radiated confidence as she hopped back into the car while he returned to his seat. He did his best not to show the way his stomach churned, much like the roiling water facing them.

Before he was ready, the wagon returned, and Flora eased the car up the make-shift ramps onto what they called a ferry. Jensen joined Fred at the back of the car while one of the ferrymen took the spot opposite Flora at the front. And then the driver urged the horses into motion.

It was the shifting of the wagon Jensen hadn't

anticipated that made the trip worse. With so much weight on it, he'd assumed the water wouldn't do much to move the wagon, but the entire contraption tilted and jerked back and forth. By the time they reached the shore, Jensen wasn't sure he could keep down the contents of his stomach for one more minute.

As soon as the wagon stopped on dry land, he jumped down and dropped into the mud, unable to care if it added to the mess already covering him. Fred did the same, breathing hard as he sat next to Jensen. They were all dripping wet again, including Beth, who looked rather nauseous herself in the back seat of the car. Flora was the only one who appeared to have come through the experience unscathed. She was charmingly damp, with only a few tendrils of hair out of place. Jensen had a hard time not staring at her as she backed the car down the ramp and pulled it up an incline to the road.

Energetic and ready to get back to racing, Flora gestured for the men to join her and Beth. Fred jumped right up, but Jensen groaned as muscles he hadn't worked in a long time protested the strain of the crossing.

Fred grinned and offered a hand to help. "Come on, you can make it, old friend."

They returned to their seats and waved to the ferry operators as Flora put the car into motion and they pulled away from the river. It wasn't more than a few minutes before she sent a smile toward Jensen. "It turned out fine, didn't it? You saved the day, after all."

Her words lifted his heart, even through a stab of guilt that he'd fought her so hard. "I did? You're the one who saw it would work. I would have turned us straight around, and we'd still be sitting by a crossing waiting for the water to calm."

Her gaze held him captive, and another smile curved her lips upward. The sore muscles, frayed nerves, and irritated feelings all faded in light of her approval. Jensen could see now why Fred would do anything to give Beth the trip of her dreams. Seeing Flora smile like that as a result of his actions was intoxicating.

And a dangerous distraction.

For the next few hours, Jensen did his best to focus on the now-damp map he pulled out instead of on the woman beside him and they made it to the stop in Boston without any problems bigger than rutted, muddy roads. Flora parked the car with the others in the designated spot, and they all disembarked to allow the officials to inspect the car and record their points.

The newlyweds wandered off to get settled in the hotel while Jensen and Flora remained with the car, waiting for the officials to finish. Should he apologize to Flora for doubting her earlier? He still thought the river crossing had been a huge risk, but she was right enough that they had made it across. He didn't gather his thoughts quickly enough, though, as Sam headed toward them from where his team's car was parked, quite a few spots in front of the Harrison Goods team.

Sam stopped next to Flora, rather closer than necessary. Looking over the muddy Decauville, the young mechanic let out a whistle. "Looks as though you had a rough day. You didn't start too far behind us this morning. Did you have trouble with the storm?"

Flora sighed. "We came to an impassable spot and had to find a way around. Mr. Franklin must have been going quite fast to cross there before it flooded."

"Ah, yes, he was speeding along. The car ran quite well today." Was Jensen imagining things, or did Sam's eyes shift away from Flora, as if he didn't want to hold her gaze when he answered?

Not seeming to notice, Flora shrugged. "Well, I'm glad for you, even if it didn't go as well for us."

Sam nudged her with his elbow, grinning in the silliest way, trying to amuse her. "Cheer up, now. Tomorrow's a new day, and you have every possibility of taking the lead."

To Jensen's disbelief, Flora responded to Sam's obvious flirtation with a giggle. "Give me the chance and I'll take it from you without a problem."

Jensen had heard enough. Turning away from the pair, he marched across the yard to the hotel. If she wanted to flirt instead of focusing on the tour, so be it. But he didn't have to stand around and watch it happen.

Chapter 12

Flora's heart dropped as Jensen trudged toward the hotel. His broad shoulders were rigid, his hands clenched into fists at his side.

What had she done to upset him? She thought back over the conversation with Sam. Had their light-hearted teasing about how badly the Harrison Goods team had done that day bothered him that much? He'd seemed to accept her decision, but was he still angry over her insistence that they take the makeshift ferry earlier?

Sam, on the other hand, had acknowledged her driving skill and made her smile. He didn't question her ability to make informed decisions. While she'd agreed to let Mr. Harrison's racing crew work on her car at the shop, she'd hoped once they were on the road, Jensen would work together with her to keep the car running well. But he made no effort to include her when he checked over the car each evening, and now he'd stomped off without a word.

The officials finished with their inspection, and Sam joined her when she climbed into the car, needing a few minutes of peace even if it meant enduring the humid heat of the summer evening. Flora pulled at a loose button on her white shirtwaist. The little irritation made her miss Isabelle, who always took care of the mending tasks Flora would never get to if left to herself. How was Isabelle faring as a guest of the Harrisons? Flora resolved to write a letter to her that night updating her on their progress.

Sam stretched his legs out and put both hands behind his head, looking as comfortable as a person could be. "Jensen seemed mad. What's he got to be upset about? You made it in time."

"Who knows what makes that man feel anything."

Sam laughed, a hearty, loud guffaw that brought an unintended smile to Flora's lips. He was enjoyable company. But something about seeing him in the passenger seat made her miss Jensen. A larger part of her than she would have expected wished it was him enjoying the evening with her instead of Sam.

The thought forced all lightheartedness from her mind. She was coming to rely on Jensen's presence far too much. She would need to be able to do this on her own if she wanted to continue racing when he was no longer being forced to ride along. "Sam, I'm going to take a quick look at the engine."

Sam fixed his gaze on her. "Is there something wrong with it?"

"No, but Jensen usually does all the maintenance, and I haven't had my hands in the engine in too long."

Sam sat up with a nod. "So I was right to guess that you know what you're doing with an engine."

Warmth settled over Flora at Sam's easy confidence in her, a nice feeling after all the doubt she faced with Jensen. "It's good to be around someone who accepts that I'm capable of handling myself."

Sam swung down out of the car and came to stand by Flora as she pulled back the hood. She spent a few blissful moments checking the oil and fittings before closing the cover again. She'd grabbed a cloth to wipe the grease off when Sam reached out and put his hand over hers, stilling her work. "While it's just the two of us, there's something I came over here to tell you. I keep trying to talk myself out of saying it, but I'd hate to see anything bad happen to you because I didn't."

A chill washed away the nice feeling of finally having a friend. Sam was never this serious. "Something bad? What does that mean?"

Reaching out absently, Sam twisted the radiator cap back and forth, as though he was searching for the right words. "Archie told me something he overheard at the stop last night, a conversation between Jensen and one of the other drivers. I hate to believe what he heard because I've known Jensen for so long, but Archie doesn't have a reason to lie about it."

Flora tried to keep up with what Sam was saying, but it didn't make any sense yet. "What did Mr. Franklin overhear?"

"He heard them talking about ways a car might be damaged without it being obvious. Letting the oil tank run dry, pouring dirt in the radiator, all kinds of things that would disable a car enough to need major repairs while looking natural."

A ringing started in Flora's ears. She let her hip press against the side of the Decauville for support. If only she could erase the doubts about Jensen that now filled her mind. "And why does that lead you to think something bad is going to happen to me?"

Sam rubbed the back of his neck. "Archie said when he talked to Jensen himself earlier, Jensen kept saying how he didn't want to be racing, how he wished there was a way it could be over already. Flora, I don't want to believe it, but could he be planning to damage your car so your team can't finish the race?"

She didn't want to believe it either. But didn't the idea fit with Jensen's frustration about being talked into joining the tour? Didn't it seem possible that he would try to find a way to eliminate them before there was any chance of injury?

To her horror, tears started gathering in her eyes. Her heart ached at the mere thought that he would do something like this when it meant so much to her. And the reality that he could hurt her so easily was terrifying. "What am I supposed to do now, Sam? He's our mechanic, with full access to the car any time he wants. How can I keep going with doubts about his integrity?"

Seeing her tears, Sam reached out and pulled her into an embrace. It was nothing but friendly and reassuring. Exactly what she needed. With Sam, there were no worries about unpredictable emotions or losing control of her heart.

With one arm still comfortably around her, Sam met her gaze. "I don't know if what Archie said is true. I've known Jensen for years and would never have believed he could do something like this. Maybe that other driver is the one who moved the markers so teams got lost and he's looking for ways to sabotage others. But I thought you should know so you can keep an eye on things."

His words brought a bit of relief that washed away some of her worries. Archie Franklin wasn't the most reliable source, and Jensen's hesitancy to race didn't mean he would destroy her dream to get out of it.

Forcing herself to relax, she finally pulled away from Sam and tried to smile so he wouldn't worry about her. But then, she saw Jensen. He stood far enough away that he couldn't hear them but close enough to see their embrace. His jaw was tight and his expression blank. What must he think after seeing such a display of affection? Should she go explain?

Following the path of her gaze, Sam waved at Jensen, then looked at Flora when Jensen turned and walked away again. "Seems as though there's something between you two. Maybe I shouldn't have told you what Archie said."

Flora shook her head. Her silly, unrequited interest in Jensen wasn't anything to talk about. "No, there isn't. I'm glad you told me, even if it turns out to be conjecture."

"I hope it does. Jensen's always been kind to me. And even if you deny it, I can see it would hurt you if he turns out to be the bad guy here."

Sam gave Flora one last squeeze around the shoulders, then turned and headed toward the hotel. Flora stood by herself, trying to make sense of all he'd said. Jensen claimed he hated racing, but she'd seen his natural ability and passion when he worked on the engine. She knew him to be a good man, although a bit too convinced he knew better than those around him. She could understand the pain of loss changing a person, but could it have transformed him so much that he would sabotage his friends to keep from racing?

Flora straightened and checked that everything was in place in the car before heading to the hotel herself. She believed Jensen was trustworthy. Now she had to prove it to herself. And she had an idea how she could arrange to do just that. It would require her to humble herself more than she liked and use his assumptions about females in the racing world, but it might be the only way Flora could prove whether or not Jensen was on her side.

Jensen retreated to the hotel, wishing he'd walked out the door later. If he hadn't seen Flora and Sam embracing by the car, he wouldn't be aware that such a thing was even possible. But now that he'd seen it, he couldn't convince himself it wasn't true.

Why did it matter so much? Why did seeing Sam's arms wrapped around her shoulders feel like a knife cutting through his chest? He had no claim on her, and she was an independent widow, free to make her own choices about who she spent her time with.

If only he could get rid of the niggling little part of his heart that wished she'd chosen to spend it with him.

It was a long night, and the next day didn't start any better. A heavy fog settled around Boston by the time they were ready to leave, and it seemed to put everyone in a foul mood. Flora barely looked at Jensen as they got into their seats to wait for Fred and Beth.

Jensen glanced at the map he'd studied the night before during the many hours he couldn't sleep. "We'll start by heading north out of town."

"I'm aware of that, Jensen. You may be in charge of the maps, but I know enough about directions to understand we'll go north every day until the midpoint, then south back to New York."

Flora's words were clipped and sharp. Had she and Sam had a falling out already? Jensen refused to acknowledge how much his heart lifted at that thought. "We don't go straight north every time. I'm not telling you what to do—I'm trying to help you get a good start on this leg. That's what you dragged me along for, isn't it?"

Time froze as Flora's frosty eyes met his. That last comment must have gone too far.

"Flora, I apologize for being terse with you. It isn't your fault I'm here. But you argue with me about every change to the car and how to handle any challenges that come up. Now you don't want me directing you along the route. I need you to let me do what Mr. Harrison hired me to do."

Her icy expression might have thawed the slightest bit as she responded. "I'm sorry for my behavior too. I didn't consider that I could have been making it more difficult for you to do your job. But you must understand, I spend much of my life having my competence questioned by men. As a woman in a man's sport, every action I take is scrutinized, and I'm always found to be lacking. So I've made a habit of projecting confidence to cover my weaknesses."

The words struck Jensen in the heart. Hadn't he spent the last five years covering up one moment of tremendous weakness? Couldn't he show her as much grace as he would want to receive if he were ever to admit what happened with Gregory?

Turning so he faced her, Jensen pushed away thoughts of his mistakes. That was a topic for another time. "You're an excellent driver and a quick thinker. Anyone who wouldn't admit that is trying not to see it."

Flora's cheeks turned pink, a look Jensen very much enjoyed. "You believe that?"

"I do." While he might not have said so if asked, Jensen did believe in her. Her methods weren't always what he would choose, but she was the best driver he'd ever raced with.

They were sitting closer than usual, his knee pressed against her leg, their hands a mere breath apart on the seat. But while his heartbeat picked up a notch, her nearness reminded him of the scene he'd come across the night before. A question about it almost slipped off his tongue, but Jensen held it back. He'd look like a jealous fool if he questioned their relationship.

Instead, he examined her face, wishing for the right words to explain exactly how highly he thought of her driving skills and her strength as a person. Her determination caused friction when they faced off over safety, but it was still a quality that drew him inexorably to her.

Those words weren't his to say, unfortunately. He was only there to return her alive and well to her brother and then move on with whatever awaited him after this race. He couldn't make the kinds of promises a woman would expect from a man who cared about her . . . because he had no idea what future he might be able to give her.

And for the first time, that knowledge hurt.

Fred and Beth finally emerged from the hotel and made their way to their seats. The damp, murky weather must have affected them, as well, because Beth looked downright ill and Fred spent an inordinate amount of time assuring she was comfortable before settling into his usual spot.

By the time the officials restarted the race, the fog was thinning slightly, enough that it wouldn't be too much of a hazard. But the relief over that was short-lived. As Flora tried to start the car, a loud sputtering filled the air, drawing the attention of everyone in the area. Her gaze flew to meet his. "What was that?"

A lump formed in Jensen's stomach as his mind raced through the possibilities. "Maybe it was the result of some dampness from yesterday."

Flora faced the road, her forehead drawn tight with worry. "If there's a mechanical problem, we'll lose points at tonight's stop."

What could he say to encourage her when that

was the truth? "Let's not worry about that now. We'll see how it runs once we get going."

But it didn't get better on the open road. Flora let out several frustrated groans when the Decauville hesitated on the way up every hill. Jensen's practiced ear could hear the engine struggling to produce the necessary power when she tried to push it. They made slow progress through the day, driving through lunch to try to keep up a pace that would get them to the third stop in the required time frame.

Finally, the town of Portsmouth, New Hampshire, came into view. Jensen had been comparing strategies with other mechanics in the evenings and knew what he could do to fix the problem before the inspectors deducted points.

Checking the map, he found a spot two streets away from that day's finish line. He glanced at his pocket watch. Plenty of time to spare, despite the slow pace. "Pull over here, Flora. Give me a minute to check the car and see what I can do."

She steered the car to the side of the dirt road in front of a building labeled *First Bank of Portsmouth*, but her face showed exactly what she thought of his request. "Are you sure this is the time to stop? We can't miss the arrival window."

Jensen pulled the cover off the engine and leaned over to examine all the lines and attachment points, taking care to avoid the spots that were hot from hours of driving. He straightened, ready to dig his tools out from under the seat when Flora joined him. "I'm going to check all the connections and make sure nothing has come loose. It could be a problem getting fuel to the engine. It won't take long to find out, so you can sit and wait with Fred and Beth."

The words had no more left his mouth when Jensen realized he shouldn't have added that last part. He'd only meant she could relax instead of worrying, but her expression clearly stated it hadn't sounded that way.

To his surprise, the frustration in her eyes cleared, and she took a deep breath. "I was hoping to watch you fix it. If you don't mind."

Was she intending to hover and make sure he did everything how she wanted, as she had at the shop before the tour started? A small part of him wanted to believe she might want to spend time with him, but he quieted that errant longing immediately. "What for?"

She chewed her bottom lip for several seconds before answering, her eyes earnest when she finally turned them toward him. "I'd like to improve my mechanical knowledge. What better time than when we're out here driving and working on the car for days on end?"

That wasn't at all what he expected. "You seem plenty knowledgeable about how the car runs. Enough to know your mind on how it should be set up to race, anyway."

Her lips quirked in a rueful smile at his reminder of the hours they spent debating how to prepare the car for the tour. "Knowledge and actual experience are two different things. I want to know that I can repair the car on my own when needed. I was hoping you'd let me practice under your supervision for the remainder of the tour. You're very skilled with the mechanics, so there's no doubt I'd be learning from the best."

Jensen assessed her as he considered the request. It was appealing to imagine having her at his side, working together on the car instead of facing off over ideas about it. He could envision hours of watching her delight in accomplishing something hard, of seeing her grow and knowing he got to be part of it. It sounded like a dream.

But perhaps that was the very reason he should say no.

Chapter 13

Flora stopped herself from fidgeting with that loose button again while she waited for Jensen to answer her request. Did he see through the ruse? It wasn't a lie. She did believe there was always something to learn, and that applied to her experience with engines as well as it did anything else.

Yes, she had more ability to work on the car herself than she was letting on. But if he hadn't bothered to notice she was capable of it before now, that wasn't her fault.

She'd waited all day for the right moment to put her plan into action, and while she never would have wanted the car to need a repair before reaching the day's stop, it was convenient for her purpose. If he agreed, she would have a good excuse to keep an eye on Jensen's work on the car and prove beyond a doubt that he wouldn't sabotage their trip.

But would he agree?

She watched his face as he considered her request, but it was unreadable. She fought the urge to tap her foot as she waited. As important as it was for her to know he was trustworthy, they were still in the middle of a leg and had a stop to get to in the next hour.

Finally, he nodded once. "I'll show you what I can. Let me get my tools, and we'll see if we can figure out this problem."

Delight spread through Flora. She refused to believe it was anything more than relief that she'd get to discover what he was up to, but there was a tiny part of her mind that was giddy at the thought of spending time working alongside him as she'd imagined.

That part of her needed to keep to itself.

Setting her attention on the car, Flora let Jensen explain how to check the lines connecting various parts of the engine, even though that was something she already knew quite well how to do. Finally, he handed her a wrench, and they got started, one on each side of the car. Flora tried not to look too deft at handling the wrench or knowing which way to turn it to tighten the connections.

They'd worked through most of the lines before Jensen finally stood and pointed at the metal clamp holding a rubber tube on his side. "Here's the culprit. This fuel line is worn out, and a leak formed around the clamp. We have time to fix it if we work fast. Let me grab an extra line and a new clamp."

Flora went around to his side of the car and followed his instructions to hold the new line. She watched him remove the cracked rubber tube and handed him the new one when he was ready. Their hands brushed, and their bodies were close enough that she could smell his soap mixed with sweat from the day when he reached forward. Spending time close together like this was necessary if she was going to determine his motives, but it was also likely a terrible idea for her heart.

Soon enough, he stepped back from the car and wiped his hands on a rag tucked into his waistband. "Why don't you try to start it, and we'll see if we were successful?"

Flora returned to her seat, feeling Fred and Beth watching as she reached to start the engine. To her relief, it turned over immediately and started running as smoothly as ever. Jensen grinned as he replaced the cover and gathered his tools. Glancing toward the back seat, Flora found Beth and Fred weren't celebrating as much as she'd expected. She turned to face them. "We should make it in time. Isn't that a relief?"

Fred nodded without comment, and Beth offered a smile that didn't quite seem genuine. Neither response was characteristic of the couple. Fred straightened Beth's light jacket in a protective gesture that caught Flora's curiosity. But it didn't seem like the time to ask if they were all right. Not when the clock was still ticking.

Once everything was cleaned up, Jensen climbed into the passenger seat and offered her a half smile. "Thanks for your help. Having extra hands made it a simple fix. Now, let's get to the check-in."

But neither of them moved. Jensen's eyes held such admiration that she couldn't look away. Flora's breath turned shallow, and she swallowed around the emotion rising in her chest. Henri had never looked at her like that, with an honest, real appreciation for what she'd contributed to their racing career. He'd tended to push her to do more and drive better, critiquing instead of encouraging.

A shout of greeting from a team racing past them on the dirt street pulled Flora from her daze. They had a leg to finish. She pushed the pedal forward and set the car into motion, thankful it seemed to be completely back to normal, and with a little time still to spare before the arrival window passed.

It was a relief to finally drive the car to the inspection area and get their official check-in time. Fred and Beth immediately went to find their rooms and then likely take an evening walk as they were fond of doing. Considering the difference in their behavior that day from the beginning of the trip, Flora resolved to find Beth when there was time to talk and ask how they were doing. It was possible she'd been so focused on the race that she'd missed something going on in the couple's life.

Or maybe Jensen was the distraction. Flora

found her eyes drawn to him even now, as they waited for the mechanical inspection that would determine their points for the day. He stood leaning against the Decauville with his legs crossed at the ankles, looking as though he didn't have a care in the world. Was he that good at hiding his feelings? Flora was an anxious mess, ready to burst into tears over the events of the first few legs of the tour.

But growing up with Clement had taught her tears wouldn't solve anything and often made the situation worse.

The inspector finally got to their car. He nodded in greeting to her, then addressed Jensen, as most of the officials did, even though she was the car owner and driver. "Good evening. How'd your car run today?"

Jensen skipped over their trouble on the road. "Well enough to get us here. These conditions are as grueling as we were told, that's for sure."

The inspector poked around the engine for a few minutes, checking off items on the paper he held as he went. Finally, he signed the bottom with a flourish. "Full points for today. Well done and good luck tomorrow."

Flora let out a sigh as soon as the official moved on to the car behind them.

Jensen responded with one of his half smiles, which were becoming more common the farther they traveled. "We made it, Flora. Still with full points, and we're almost halfway through. I didn't expect it to go this well when I saw all the obstacles we'd face."

Giving herself a moment to stare up at the darkening sky, where a star was starting to peek out here and there, Flora leaned against the car next to him. She didn't look but rather felt Jensen join her, their shoulders nearly touching. "And what do you think about our chances for the rest of the tour?"

"If you keep driving as you have been and we stop running into trouble, we'll gain spots in no time. We're still holding strong in the middle, so there's no reason to count us out yet."

"Driving as I have been?"

Jensen tilted his head, looking pleased. "Yes. You've been driving responsibly. Slow and careful enough to stay safe and arrive at the finish line on time."

There it was. He must have been distracted by all the problems plaguing their drive that day because he hadn't complained about staying safe for several whole hours. "Why does safe have to be slow? You keep saying you believe in my ability to drive a race car, but then you turn around and try to hold me back."

He pushed away from the car, the companionable moment ruined. "Why do you have to see it as holding you back? I'm only reminding you that this is an endurance race, not one focused on speed."

She stepped forward to face him head-on, not deterred by the fact that she had to tilt her head back quite far to do so. "But speed is still a necessary element if we hope to win."

"The winner will be chosen by points, not the first to cross the finish line."

"And we don't get the full points if we don't keep a solid pace to make up for the conditions and obstacles."

They finally ran out of arguments for their sides and stood facing each other, closer than Flora had realized. Would they forever repeat the same fight? In her mind, decades passed and she could see them standing on the porch of a little house, gray and wrinkled and still going back and forth about speed versus safety.

Oh my. She actually wanted to see that come to pass. She wanted Jensen to be in her life thirty, forty, or fifty years in the future. Her emotions were in such a whirl that she was longing for the most absurd things, such as spending the rest of her life quarreling with this man in a fight they would never resolve.

And then a giggle slipped from her lips before she could stop it. Jensen's face scrunched in confusion, making her laugh even more. Without warning, a wide grin turned his lips up, and he released a responding chuckle. His eyes sparkled with amusement. And in the midst of it all, she couldn't stop noticing that if he bent only a little, his lips would be remarkably near to hers.

Then someone nearby gave a deliberate cough and shuffled their feet. Thoughts of his lips disappeared.

Once again, she'd allowed herself to lose control, thanks to Jensen's obsession with safety. If they'd been seen kissing, she risked her reputation being damaged and the men in the racing community respecting her even less than they already did. She had to get ahold of herself and stop responding to Jensen, both his baiting comments and his tempting nearness.

Jensen tore his gaze away from Flora to find Sam and Archie watching them, Sam with a knowing grin and Archie looking irritated by their display.

And what a display it was. Jensen found himself so close to Flora that he would only have to breathe and she would be in his arms. How could he help himself when her eyes had filled with delight and that sweet, lyrical laughter spilled out of her right in the middle of a fight?

Straightening, Jensen shook off the effect of her nearness and faced the other two men. "You had another good run today, Archie. I suppose I should offer congratulations."

Shrugging, Archie ran one hand over the

Decauville's hood. "I won't hold my breath."

Sam ducked between them and addressed Flora, much to Jensen's dislike. "Most of the teams will be offering rides to the public tomorrow night once we arrive at the midway point. Will you join us, Flora? I'm sure many locals would love the chance to say they've been driven around by a female race car driver."

Jensen waited for her to respond in irritation at the reminder that she was treated differently. Instead, she nodded, cheerful and genuine. "I don't see why not. It might be fun to socialize with the spectators more."

Sam glanced back at Archie. "I'm glad you agree with me, Flora. Archie is annoyed with the locals at best."

Finally coming around the car to join their group, Archie's mouth drew into a tight line. "They're welcome to exist. I just want them to stay out of my way."

"You should have seen him today," Sam confessed. "A farmer leading a flock of sheep wouldn't get them out of the road. Archie blew the horn so loud it sent them running in all directions."

Jensen glanced at Flora. Were they supposed to be amused by the story?

Flora frowned. "That poor man was working to feed his family. You made his day so much harder than it needed to be."

Archie chuckled, although the sound held haughtiness rather than warmth. "You should have seen how fast those creatures scattered. It was his own fault, anyway. All he had to do was get them off the road before I got there. These people will have to learn that roads are for driving now, not walking animals."

A sour feeling started in Jensen's stomach. There had been much talk amongst the teams about the mischief going on during the tour. Small things, such as missing route markers and rumors that teams were cutting through fields to get ahead, damaging property along the way. The attitude Archie displayed now, combined with what Jensen had seen of his tactics in the past, made it all too easy to imagine Archie doing those very things.

But what could he do about it? Archie already had him in an impossible position. He was expected to sabotage his team. Was that why Archie had sought them out now, to find out if Jensen was following through? He'd hoped for more time to figure out how he was going to get around Archie's demands while keeping his friends safe.

Flora appeared as sickened by Archie's behavior as Jensen felt. She stood with her arms crossed, wearing that expression of indignation he'd become familiar with back at the shop. "It's people like you who give driving a bad name and cause the locals to be so skeptical of us. I hope you don't intend to take guests out for a drive at Bretton Woods tomorrow."

Archie stared at Flora for long enough that Jensen raised one foot, ready to step between them. But finally, a slimy grin settled on Archie's face, and he looked away. "Oh, that was just racing. I'll be civil to the spectators tomorrow. I don't want to damage Mr. Dorman's good name, after all."

Flora's posture relaxed, but Jensen had seen enough of Archie's antics in the past to know better. The man had something else up his sleeve, something he was holding close. And it didn't seem to be his blackmail of Jensen. More than ever, Jensen was convinced Archie was behind the shenanigans that were following the tour around. But he wouldn't be able to say so until he figured out how to protect himself from Archie's wrath.

It took a great effort, but Jensen managed to force Archie out of his mind long enough to get some rest that night and prepare for the drive to the midpoint. They would stay five nights at the Mount Washington Hotel in Bretton Woods, New Hampshire. Since he planned to avoid all the pre-arranged social events he could, Jensen would use the long stop to figure out a solution to his problem. Sooner or later, Archie would expect Jensen to comply or he would follow through on his threats. Jensen would need to be ready for that moment.

In the morning, Jensen beat the rest of the Harrison Goods team to the car, giving him time to sit and watch a beautiful sunrise scorch the sky with red, orange, and yellow streaks. It reminded him of a verse he'd learned from Mrs. Harrison as a child. Something about the sky proclaiming God's glory. It had been years since he'd thought about the days when he sat alongside Gregory and Aggie while Mrs. Harrison read to them from the Bible with baby Fred in her lap.

He remembered the way she used to pray, so comfortable about approaching the Creator of everything with even the smallest problem. An unexpected urge hit him, one that said maybe the struggles of the tour wouldn't be so difficult if he turned them over to God as Mrs. Harrison would have.

But it had been so long since he'd bothered to pray. Would God even want to hear from him?

Before he could figure out an answer, Fred, Beth, and Flora emerged from the hotel together and made their way to the car. A bout of chivalry hit Jensen, urging him to jump out and give Flora a hand to climb up into the driver's seat, but he quelled it. If he did, she would likely respond with a snide remark about how he felt she wasn't capable of getting into the car herself.

Or would she?

Jensen had to admit, the more he got to know her, the more he saw a caring, intelligent, talented woman who fascinated him, rather than the self-centered one he'd assumed she was at first. She'd been responding warmly to his efforts to be more supportive, to listen better as Fred had said he should. Even last night, when they'd fallen back into arguing their viewpoints on the best way to run the tour, it had ended with camaraderie instead of animosity.

Those thoughts carried Jensen through their first uneventful leg. Flora drove with the perfect amount of intensity, focused rather than impetuous. They came up on the first team in front of them outside the limits of Portsmouth.

The road was clear and wide enough to pass, so Jensen turned to check behind them. Then he leaned close so Flora wouldn't miss any of his words. "You're clear all around. I suggest passing this team at a steady pace. I don't think they have the power in that car to keep up with us, so no need to push."

Flora didn't need to respond or even look at him. A slight smile played on her lips, and she immediately increased their speed—but only the necessary amount to pass. They moved around the other team with shared smiles and friendly waves. Jensen found himself leaning back against the seat, more relaxed than he'd felt since the first moment Mr. Harrison had mentioned racing.

The rest of the day flew by in a similar fashion. When they encountered other cars, he gave Flora tips about possible speed and the likelihood the driver would try to race or block her attempt to pass. There was only one moment when she looked over at him and disagreed. "Jensen, I've been watching the teams just as you have. This driver will try to race me, I know it. I'm going to have to go faster this time."

Fred had been right about listening to her opinion so far. Jensen looked behind them one more time, found it clear, and nodded once.

That was all she needed. Flora eased the car to a faster speed and passed before the other team knew what was happening. The other car's engine roared, confirming Flora's words as the driver tried to race back around them.

But she anticipated his move. Jensen's grin echoed the delight that filled his chest when he looked back and saw they were already pulling away. He glanced at Flora to find her chin held high and her eyes gleaming. Building her confidence was far more fun than pushing her to the point of anger. If he could find more ways to do so, it was possible they would make it through the tour with a friendship intact at the end.

And Jensen very much wanted that to happen.

Chapter 14

For the first time in the tour, the Harrison Goods team ended the day in a higher position than they started. Flora floated around her room at the grand Mount Washington Hotel, as pleased as if they'd ended in first. The way Jensen had worked with her that day instead of against her was all she'd been dreaming of since they left Philadelphia. The rest of the tour was bound to continue improving if they kept communicating and supporting each other as they had that day.

After an early supper and a few minutes spent relaxing and freshening up, Flora met Jensen in front of the sprawling hotel, where the cars were parked in order of their finishing positions. The white building with its distinctive red roof was built into the side of a hill overlooking an expansive lawn that sloped down toward a pasture, giving it an impressive view of the mountain-ringed valley. Locals and hotel guests were everywhere, taking in the spectacle of so many automobiles in one place. Some of the drivers had already started giving people rides, evidenced by the sputter and roar of engines and the smell of gasoline in the air.

Flora found Jensen waiting with several strangers by the Decauville, which was lined up in the ninth spot. Ninth. A thrill ran through Flora as she looked ahead of them and saw only eight teams they would have to pass once they got back on the road. That delight surely came through in her smile as she approached Jensen, who stood with an older couple.

When she reached the group, Jensen stepped close to Flora and introduced her to his companions. "This is Mrs. Montfort, our driver. Flora, this is Mr. and Mrs. Grady. They'd like a ride, whenever you're ready."

Mr. Grady's eyes narrowed as he took her in. "My wife told me this car was driven by a female, but you're quite small and delicate. Are you certain you can handle this machine?"

Flora gritted her teeth, reining in her emotions before answering as kindly as she could. "I've driven us all the way here from Philadelphia without a bit of trouble. I'm sure you'll find a ride with me enjoyable and safe."

The irony of uttering Jensen's favorite word to describe her driving was not lost on Flora, but she was no longer in any mood to laugh about it. Jensen helped the couple get situated in the Decauville while Flora started it up. They took a slow turn around the hotel grounds, then returned to their parking spot where Jensen waited.

Before the couple had even finished thanking her for the ride, a group of older men approached, one addressing Jensen with boisterous volume.

"Did I see what I think I saw? You let your wife drive this contraption?"

Mr. Grady had at least tried to be decent while voicing his doubts about a female driving a car. This man didn't even look at Flora, as if she wasn't worth being acknowledged.

Jensen's jaw tightened as the crowd snickered, and he shot a sideways glance at Flora before responding for her. "Mrs. Montfort owns this car, and while she's not my wife, she is an excellent driver. Today her skill gained five spots for our team in the tour."

"Ha!" The man's exclamation—louder still than his first comments—drew the attention of everyone in the parking area. "She's a pretty little thing. Suppose I climb on in here and show her how an automobile should be driven."

Jensen stepped between the man and Flora's car, but that only intensified the crowd's interest. Flora's face burned with all those eyes trained on her while she could do nothing about this buffoon's scoffing.

It seemed as if everyone in attendance held their breath while Jensen stared down the local men, silently daring them to approach the car. Flora noticed out of the corner of her eye that several of the other drivers and mechanics were working their way over to stand by Jensen, and her heart swelled. Were they there to defend her too?

But as the group of locals backed down, Flora had to admit that the other teams most likely intended to stand up for Jensen, not her. He was one of them. Despite her driving skill, she would always be an outsider in this man's sport. She'd felt it too many times after races with Henri when the men would crowd around to congratulate those who did well and offer good-natured teasing to those who didn't. Flora had always been on the outskirts of those gatherings, and Henri would laugh in her face and wave her off if she tried to join.

With that memory fresh in her mind, Flora watched the group of men back away. From a distance, she examined Jensen as he glanced around. When his gaze found hers, there was not one hint of the derision she'd expected to find. No anger or laughter at her expense. Rather, admiration.

He looked as he had when they'd been in A Trip to the Moon at Coney Island, his lips inches from hers, his expression heated.

Her heart stirred, and her breath caught in her chest. After the way her faults had been exposed by those men, could he actually be feeling appreciation instead of disdain?

She stopped in her tracks. Anger she could face. That would have been Clement's response if her presence caused him public embarrassment. Even him joining in the mocking she'd expected or tearing her down in front of the onlookers. But a look of desire . . . that was beyond her ability to understand.

Jensen started walking, meeting her where she stood blocked from view of the spectators by one of the massive rocks that dotted the lawn. For the longest moment, he stared, his eyes roaming her face. His voice was rough when he finally spoke. "Are you all right, Flora? That was unpleasant, I know."

The kindness in his words almost broke the tenuous grip she held over her emotions. The last few days had been taxing in too many ways, and tears threatened. Of all things, she couldn't allow herself to cry in front of these men. They would never see her as an equal if she did.

Flora turned and started a brisk walk toward the hotel. A small part of her hoped Jensen might follow, but she didn't dare ask him to or even turn back to see if he did. To her relief, she didn't make it far before his arm slid around her shoulders, the weight comforting and warm. She let herself lean into him a little, enough to show she didn't mind the contact. But she kept moving, aiming for a deserted stretch of the wide veranda that ran around the majority of the hotel.

When they finally reached a more private spot, Flora dropped into a wicker chair, regretting the loss of Jensen's arm around her immediately. But he took hold of another chair and dragged it around to face hers, close enough that their knees pressed together when he sat down.

He leaned forward, getting even closer. "Please tell me why you're about to cry. That scene was unfortunate, but I've seen you stand up to worse without batting an eye."

Letting herself examine his expression again, Flora saw more concern there than anything. Not a hint of scorn over her emotional display. Which made it all the harder to keep herself under control. "You're not embarrassed by having to defend me? Or angry? Or ready to hold it over me as proof that I'll never make my way without you?"

Jensen's head jerked back. "Of course not. Those men are backward and ignorant. Your grace and composure in the face of their rant put us all to shame. Believe me, I was ready to take a fist to them if it meant they would shut their mouths. You didn't deserve one word they said. And didn't you see the other drivers and mechanics gather around to stand with us?"

She'd been wrong—not only about this situation, but the entire time she'd known Jensen. All along, she'd been expecting him to respond as Clement or Henri would have. She'd closed her mind to his helpful efforts lest they be followed by belittling comments or controlling actions. She tossed aside Jensen's advice and expertise because she was living as if she were still stuck with the men who'd run her life before.

Leaning toward him, Flora searched his face, finding only sincere caring written there. "I'm sorry, Jensen. I've been treating you as if you've done something wrong when it was . . . others who did. You don't deserve to be treated the way you have been."

Too late, Flora realized her words had brought more questions to his mind than she'd intended. She could see them forming but couldn't think of a way to distract him before he asked one. "Who hurt you, Flora? Who did something wrong toward you?"

The tears were burning behind her eyes again. Flora tried to blink them away, willing herself not to cry over Clement. She didn't want to discuss him, but maybe giving Jensen a glimpse into her childhood would help him see she hadn't meant to dismiss him so often. "My brother."

When his eyes widened, she rushed to correct his assumption. "Oh, not Owen. He's always been a darling. We had an older brother, Clement. Our father died when Owen and I were young, but Clement was already an adult, so he took over the household. We had old family money, so he only had to use it wisely and our family would have been secure for a long time." Flora couldn't hold back a sniffle as the tears still threatened to fall.

Jensen reached out and slid his rough, warm

hand over hers. Her mind stuttered to a stop as the feeling of his skin on hers took over her senses. "Let me guess. He didn't manage to do that simple task."

"No. He took to frequent gambling. He ruined quite a few young women for his pleasure, as well. Our family reputation was in tatters and our assets were almost depleted by the time our mother died." Flora struggled to find the words to continue. She hadn't revealed the worst of it yet.

But Jensen's kind voice soothed her humiliation. "That must have felt so hopeless."

Meeting his gaze again, Flora could see understanding written there. "I nearly forgot you also lost your parents at a young age."

"Yes, younger than you must have been. I was fortunate that the Harrison family was so kind to me."

Flora took an odd comfort in the connection of their similar losses.

Jensen seemed to, as well. "How was it living with Clement after that? I can't imagine it was easy."

His earnest concern bolstered her courage to continue. "No, it wasn't. Clement grew angrier with every dollar he lost. Once I reached an appropriate age, he started threatening to marry me off to one of his gambling partners to pay his debts. He reminded me of that possibility any time I tried to do something on my own or said something he didn't like."

"What about Owen? Did he stand up for you?"

Flora couldn't help smiling a little when she thought of Owen's kindness as a youth, although it was quickly followed by unpleasant memories. "He tried a few times. He was so young, but he would step in front of me when Clement got his angriest. He often took the brunt of Clement's physical retaliation."

Silence fell between them as Jensen processed her story.

Flora couldn't meet his eyes. What must he think of her for allowing her brother to control her that way? Did he now see her as weak, incapable of defending herself and her younger brother?

And why did it matter so much if he did?

Jensen was struck speechless for a long time. Anger burned in his chest. He couldn't believe kind, strong, always-hopeful Flora had grown up in such a nightmare. And he wished her older brother was still living so he could go tell the man what he thought of anyone who would treat a young woman and a boy like that.

It was all he could do to put aside visions of a grown man's hand connecting with Flora's beautiful face and focus on what she needed right now. After much searching, he found the words he wanted to say. "Flora, I'm glad you told me. And I hope you can see the differences between me and him. I hope you'll learn to trust me."

Her eyes flew up to meet his, and Jensen gulped at the vulnerable, unsure look on her face. He'd never seen her so insecure. He longed to wrap his arms around her and replace that expression with a more enthusiastic one.

She responded so softly, he had to lean even closer to hear her. Not that he minded reducing the inches between them in the least. "I'm so sorry I treated you as if you might be like him. It's been years. I thought I'd moved past the hurt he caused."

"You're not the one who needs to apologize." Jensen skimmed his fingers over her cheek, wiping a falling tear with his thumb. There was no stopping his instincts now. Sliding his hand to her neck, he gently urged her to lean forward and meet him, leaving room for her to refuse. To his relief, she completed the movement without hesitation, and their lips met.

The soft heat of her mouth was enough to drown in. Jensen let his fingers twine in the loose tendrils of chestnut hair that teased her neck, amazed at the silkiness of it. And when she shifted her knees so she could scoot to the edge of her chair and press closer to him, he nearly lost himself in the kiss.

He wrapped his free arm around her but still

couldn't get her close enough. The single shred of reason remaining in his mind warned him they were on a public veranda, where at any moment they could be observed by men whose respect she was trying her best to earn. He couldn't be the reason they dismissed her as a serious competitor.

Even though it meant losing the most important connection of his life, Jensen ended the kiss and rested his forehead against hers. His hands refused to break contact with her skin. A little sigh escaped her lips, the breath brushing his cheek, and he froze for a minute as he harnessed the desire to start the kiss all over again.

After a few moments that weren't nearly long enough, Jensen leaned back, the loss of her touch leaving behind a chill. The world felt different, as if everything had tilted in a way no one else would even notice but Jensen wasn't sure he could ever forget.

Flora's eyes fluttered open to reveal a depth of warring emotions. But she didn't look unhappy anymore, and that—he was pretty sure—had been his goal the moment he'd started leaning toward her.

Her mind seemed to clear all at once. She jumped up out of her chair, knocking it backward so that it almost fell over. "I should go. Retiring early sounds like the wisest choice after such a day."

Amused at how flustered she was, Jensen stood

along with her. "What about your interest in spending more time working on the car together? I planned to do it tomorrow, but it's a fine evening to give the engine a more thorough going-over."

As he'd expected, she shook her head, backing away while waving her hands in an obvious display of nervous energy. "No, I need some time to myself tonight. It can wait until tomorrow. When there are more people around."

Without another word, she turned and hurried across the veranda to the nearest door leading into the building. Jensen dropped back into his chair. He'd kissed her. His amusement over her reaction faded with that realization. What had he been thinking, to kiss her when she'd shown few signs of caring for him in any way other than as her teammate?

All their previous fighting had paled in comparison to the vulnerable expression on her face when she'd told him about her brother. But a kiss? Was that all his mind could come up with to replace her pain with something good?

Jensen let his head rest against the high back of the chair, his eyes on the beadboard ceiling of the veranda. Now he was going to have to spend the next several days gallivanting around Bretton Woods with Flora in awkward denial that anything had happened between them. Because there was no promise behind that kiss. It had been purely impulse.

A rush of worries hit him hard. What if she thought it meant more than comfort? She'd been flustered just now, but if she went to bed and thought it through and came to the conclusion that he must have intentions toward her . . . what could he do then? And how could he tell her he'd meant nothing by it without hurting her?

He had nothing to offer her after this tour was over. His career at Harrison Goods was as good as done. He refused to continue working for Mr. Harrison's racing crew after his debt to Fred was paid. If Archie had his way, Jensen would be thrown out of the Harrison family forever, anyway.

His life was stalling like the Decauville trying to run with a fuel leak.

For years, he'd tried to control everything. He'd avoided risky decisions and anything his emotions led him to do. Until he met Flora.

Now he was racing again. His hands reveled in the feel of cool engine metal, and his heart beat a little easier when the wind was blowing through his hair. The thrill of speeding past another car was settling back into his spirit, leaving normal day-to-day activities feeling empty.

And he was impulsively kissing a woman he was coming to care far too much about.

Jumping up from the chair—and almost repeating the way Flora had knocked hers backward—Jensen stalked around the corner of the hotel and leaned against the railing where he could see the cars lined up along the front of the property. Without speaking a word, he let his heart cry out a prayer to the Lord, the only one who could help him out of this mess. The desire to pray again had been building in him for days. So he uttered a prayer for guidance, for an opportunity to show itself clearly enough that his dense mind would get the point.

He spent a long time like that, letting God's presence soothe his battered spirit for the first time he could remember. And when he finished, he felt better—more hopeful and less worried—than he'd ever felt before.

His life might still be a mess. And he'd likely made it worse by kissing Flora with that urge to rescue her.

But he had to hold on to the truth that with the Lord's help, something good could come out of the mess he'd made.

Chapter 15

Straightening her hat in the small mirror on the wall of her room for the fifth time, Flora paused and rested her fingertips on her lips. Three days later, she could still feel Jensen's mouth on hers as they sat on the veranda that first night, could feel his hand buried in her hair and his arm around her. She couldn't shake the desire to run downstairs, find him, and continue what they'd started.

Flora squared her shoulders and headed for the door. Time to leave her room and find the others whether she was ready to face Jensen again or not. The last three days had been excruciating, working on the car alongside him while they both refused to acknowledge that their entire relationship had changed. Yes, she'd loved every minute as he guided her through the steps of filling the oil tank, cleaning and replacing lines, checking connections, and tightening bolts. He'd never once been condescending as she'd thought he would be. It had been lovely enough that dreams of a lifetime doing that very thing started creeping into her mind.

Neither of them had mentioned that kiss. It had seemed too intimate to bring up the next morning. But as the days passed, the moments when their hands brushed as they exchanged a tool, or when he moved close behind her to lean over and watch her work, or when his face ended up so very near hers as they peered at the engine together . . . those moments would have been so much easier if there was some definition to what had happened between them.

Leaving her room, Flora tried not to think about how long it had taken her to get ready that morning, or how much extra care she'd put into choosing an outfit for the day. She told herself it was because she wanted to appear professional and competent, not because she wanted Jensen to notice. Despite Jensen's hesitation, he hadn't argued when she brought up joining many of the other teams in a local hill climb that had been established the year before. Climb to the Clouds, they called it. She needed to represent the Harrison Goods racing team well.

That was definitely the only reason she pinched her cheeks to add a little color on the way down the stairs.

Flora was conflicted when she found Fred and Beth waiting in the lobby with no sign of Jensen anywhere. Fred stepped forward and greeted Flora with a nod. "Jensen is already outside. He said he needed to see to something on the car before you race it again."

Nodding, Flora swallowed a surge of disappointment. Some part of her must have been hoping Jensen would be there to greet her, as anxious to spend more time together as she was.

How ridiculous. One kiss didn't have to mean anything. It didn't have to change the way they'd been working together. After all, she was the one who'd rushed off right after, as if she regretted it. She could have stayed and worked on the car as he'd suggested. Had that given him the wrong idea? Did he think she had spurned his kiss?

Nothing could be farther from the truth.

Sliding her arm around Beth's waist, Flora examined her face. "Beth, you don't look well. Are you sure you want to attend today? You and Fred could stay here and rest. We'll have to get back on the road tomorrow whether we're up to it or not."

A slight smile broke through Beth's pallor. "I can't deny I'm not feeling my best. But I want to go. The excursion will be a nice way to celebrate a surprise we've been wanting to tell you about."

"A surprise?"

Fred and Beth exchanged a meaningful look, hesitating to answer her. For the first time, Flora noticed Beth's hand resting on her stomach in a significant way. The paleness, the quieter demeanor, Fred's increased concern for her comfort on the last leg . . .

"Beth, are you expecting?"

Beth nodded and Fred grinned. Delighted, Flora

hugged them both. "Oh, how exciting. Have you told anyone else?"

Beth shook her head. "We plan to tell Jensen when we find him. We wrote to our families when we arrived here, so you're likely the first to know."

Flora embraced Beth again, so pleased for the sweet couple. She ignored the pang of emptiness in her own body that always accompanied another woman's happy announcement. There was nothing to be done about what hadn't happened when Henri was alive.

Except this time, a tendril of hope stirred. She'd assumed she wouldn't feel the desire to marry again after things had been so disastrous with Henri. It hadn't seemed worth the risk of being tied to someone she couldn't get along with, this time likely for much longer.

But when Jensen kissed her . . . imagining their relationship deepening into marriage didn't seem so outrageous anymore. If only he'd been there next to her to share in Fred and Beth's happy news. When he heard, would he imagine a family with her? Would such an idea excite or terrify him?

Fred and Beth led the way outside with Flora trailing behind. Her heart pounded most ridiculously as if she was nervous about coming face to face with Jensen when she'd spent more than a week with him at her side. They'd even been together most of the last several days since the kiss happened. It was silly to be so anxious.

Be that as it may, she still had to work not to straighten her hat again, or tug at her skirt, making sure it hung in perfect folds. What should she do with her hands? Finally, she clasped them behind her back, just to keep from worrying about it anymore.

Jensen was taller than most of the other men, and she could pick him out from the crowd of teams clear across the expansive hotel lawn. Fred and Beth reached him first, and Flora hung back a moment to let them reveal their news how they wanted to. Fred was talking, waving his hands in animated accompaniment to his words. Then Jensen broke into a rare grin and pulled his friend into an exuberant embrace. As he released Fred, Jensen's eyes scanned the lawn, stopping when they found Flora.

Every nerve in her body started to tingle. She couldn't look away even as his grin faded into an intense, searching expression. What did that mean? Was he unhappy to see her? Or was he thinking the same kind of life-changing, forever-centered thoughts that she'd been having that morning?

Several drivers started their engines, and everyone else headed for their cars so they could get to the mountain where the race would take place.

It was now or never to join Jensen in the front seat of the Decauville. Flora forced her feet into motion, wondering with every step if she should turn back and spend the day in her room. No. She'd gotten through the last few days working with him and it had been fine. But her heart still argued that if Jensen regretted kissing her or was upset by her reaction, it would be miserable to finish the tour sitting next to him every day.

Unlike the days since their kiss, his expression was easier to read as she grew closer. There was heat in the depths of his eyes. His fingers twitched as if he wanted to reach for her. At least, she hoped that's what it meant, because she wanted to reach for him. Fred and Beth were already settling in when Flora reached the car and stood in front of Jensen, her mouth going dry.

His voice was low and rough, meant for her ears only. "I hope you had a better night's rest than I did. Are you ready for this excursion?"

She blinked up at him. Did he mean he hadn't slept well for thinking of her? One corner of his mouth lifted in a slight smile. He must have read the question on her face because he leaned closer as he walked her to her side of the car. "Yes, I dreamed about that kiss all night. About you. Every night since."

Heat rushed over her, making her lightheaded. What on earth did one say in response to that? Thankfully, she was saved by the commotion of the first few cars pulling out of the drive, and soon enough, they were on the road, where the noise made it hard to hold any private conversation.

But that didn't mean she was unaware of his closeness. Was he sitting farther toward the center of the seat than usual? She didn't remember his knee bumping hers so often before when the car jostled on rough roads. Flora did her best to keep her eyes on the road ahead, but all too often she found them wandering to look his way. Every time, he met her gaze with that same roguish half smile.

And every time, her heart raced with a speed that would win this hill climb in record time.

It was going to be a long day surrounded by others until they could find a few moments alone again.

Jensen didn't know what he was doing anymore. He'd managed to be a gentleman for three days while longing to wrap her in his arms again. The way she bit her lower lip and darted a glance his way when she talked about joining the hill climb had destroyed all his arguments about safety before he could utter them.

It hadn't been his intention to ever bring up their kiss. When she'd walked across that lawn looking so beautiful and so unsure, his heart had burst all over again. Turning her vulnerability into passion was becoming a dangerous habit.

It hadn't helped to learn about Beth's happy condition. The way Fred had been fretting over her for the last few days made more sense in light of it. But their announcement turned Jensen's mind in an unexpected direction. He'd considered marriage in the past, but the risks of opening his heart seemed insurmountable. Now, with Flora, it had just happened, without him intending it to. And here he was, thinking about what it would be like to care for and protect her the way Fred did with Beth.

Having a distraction in the form of this excursion up the mountain was a blessing, even if it was also more dangerous than any other day of the tour. After the time he spent reconnecting with God on their first night in Bretton Woods, Jensen had come to a realization. The only way he would get through the rest of the tour without the weight of worry for everyone's safety destroying him would be to let God take it off his shoulders.

So he'd started every morning praying for God to protect them and letting every one of his fears rest in God's peace. This morning, he'd even prayed over the car, which felt silly but eased the immense dread that would have otherwise gripped him in the face of this high-speed trek up the side of a mountain.

Arriving at the base of Mount Washington,

they parked with the other Glidden Tour cars alongside racers who had come in for this event. About three-quarters of the tour teams had come, but there were more than just race cars gathered. Jensen saw several heavy-looking trucks and even a few motorcycles. The air was filled with palpable excitement, but many of the new drivers displayed an extra intensity that the Glidden Tour teams didn't share.

The race participants were still arriving, so Fred and Beth took a walk while Jensen and Flora remained with the Decauville. Flora shuffled from one foot to the other as they waited for the start time. "At least the weather is lovely today."

Jensen arched an eyebrow. Flora, who was rarely at a loss for words, was talking about the weather? Could she be attempting to avoid talking about those private moments together? "Sure is. Did you notice that fine Indian motorcycle over there? That'll zip right up the mountain."

Flora looked over the competition. Had her thoughts been going the same direction as his that morning, or was she focused on the race ahead? Truly, he should refrain from bringing up their kiss until they had time to discuss what was going on between them. But that didn't stop him from wishing he had a right to sneak another one right there at the starting line.

As a few of the drivers started lining up, Fred and Beth returned from their walk around the staging area, Fred with his arm wrapped protectively around Beth's waist. Flora turned to Beth, keeping her voice low. "How are you feeling, Beth? Have you had much sickness?"

Beth nodded, pressing one hand to her stomach. "A bit. It's not too bad right now, but it isn't pleasant either. I've found it gets worse in the evenings."

Fred spoke up, his eyes never leaving Beth's face. "We've decided it might be wiser to wait here for you to finish the race. There's no need to have passengers along on such a dangerous drive in the first place, and we'd hate to be a distraction that might keep you from winning."

Flora shook her head. "You're not a distraction. Are you sure you want to miss this adventure? This is the very thing you were looking for in your honeymoon."

The couple exchanged uneasy glances. Was impending parenthood already changing them?

"It looks as though there's a spectator area set up over there." Jensen pointed to their left. "Why don't you take shelter from the sun and see if there's a place Beth can sit for the duration? It shouldn't be a long race. Last year's winner completed it in less than half an hour."

The couple wished them luck and turned toward the row of canopies without hesitation. Flora bit her lip as she watched them go. "What do you think has gotten into them? This is sure to be a highlight of the tour, and they're willing to miss it?"

She seemed quite hurt by their wise choice.

"Flora, I don't think it has anything to do with you. Parenthood is a life-changing event, even before reaching the birth, it seems. I think they're finding there are things more important to them than adventure now."

Flora rounded on him, her eyes flashing. "Does it have to be one or the other? Does being a parent have to exclude adventure and excitement? Can't a woman have children and also continue living?"

"Of course. But maybe Beth doesn't want to take unnecessary risks with their child's safety."

"So you're saying I'm dangerous, that they're going to risk the baby's life riding with me?"

She was all fire and fervor now. How was he going to get her calmed down enough before this race started to drive sensibly? "It doesn't have anything to do with you. This race is inherently dangerous. One look at the road snaking up that mountain and anyone could see it. All those tight turns, narrow stretches, and sheer drop-offs are asking for trouble."

Jensen stepped closer to Flora and took her hand in his. Her soft skin almost undid him, but he retained enough self-control to remember her reputation among these men was important. He couldn't go kissing her senseless in front of them without damaging the way they saw her.

But then she looked up at him with wide, conflicted eyes, and he sucked in a deep breath. It was much easier to know he should keep his distance than to actually do so. Meeting her gaze, he tried to impart confidence through his words. "This is a short race, but it's not easy. You need to focus on safe driving to reach the top."

"If it takes less than an hour, there's no time to waste on safety. I'll have to push hard to pass cars on that road."

There she was, back to her usual reckless self, but at least she didn't appear to be on the verge of tears as she had a few moments before. Jensen let go of her hand and threw his response out as he headed around the car to climb into his seat. "Attempt to use both, if you would."

She clearly took his comment as a challenge. Settling in her seat, Flora started the car and drove to the starting spot they'd been assigned, not too far back in the field, but not at the front either. Jensen glimpsed Archie and Sam much farther ahead of them. How had they managed to snag that position? Knowing Archie, it hadn't been anything good.

Jensen put Archie out of his mind, determined to focus on helping Flora during this fiasco. While they waited for the starting signal, Flora adjusted everything possible—her hat, her skirt, her foot on the pedal, her hands on the steering wheel. Finally, she looked over at him. "Do you think we can win this?"

If he said no, would she back out and stay safely here at ground level? Or would it spur her on and cause more recklessness? Either way, it didn't matter. He couldn't even try to lie to her. "You're an excellent driver, Flora. You have every chance of winning."

The smile that brightened her face was worth the chances they were about to undertake. More focused than ever, she turned her eyes to the front as the race officials shouted instructions. And then the gunshot signal spurred cars into motion for the most dangerous race Jensen had ever heard of.

Chapter 16

Flora let the warmth of Jensen's faith in her driving ability push her through the nervousness that accompanied the start of every race. Those few moments sitting in readiness while waiting for the signal were always the worst. But knowing he was expecting her to drive them to victory made it infinitely less tense.

At the signal, the cars in front of her took off, and Flora pushed the gas pedal forward, trying to keep an even pace of acceleration. It didn't do any good to lurch around as some of the drivers were doing. She had more control, more finesse than that. She knew from experience that the best course of action was to let the starting rush settle before trying to fight for positions. In a race this short, everything would be concentrated into a quicker time frame, but she still didn't want to get caught up in a starting line wreck.

They began on a wide stretch of dirt road that sloped upward at a gentle rate. Easing around some of the heavier, slower-moving cars, Flora focused on looking ahead for spots to pass. Once they were on the winding part of the mountain road, there wouldn't be many, from the way Jensen described the course. The road would be narrow with many sharp turns and steep drops.

She would have to take his advice and use both wise driving and speed if she wanted to get through the entire course.

As the cars reached the part of the road that started to narrow, she could see what they were up against. Rather than curving around a tall spire as she'd imagined, the road began a steep incline as it cut through the long mountain range. It was marked with sharp turns and sudden rises that required quick acceleration to get up. In many places, the rutted dirt path clung to the side of the rock with a sheer drop mere feet from where the cars drove through. For a moment, her stomach clenched. How was she going to find enough places to pass all the vehicles in front of them?

Then Jensen nudged her arm and pointed ahead. "Watch those front cars. They've done this before."

Without losing her focus on the road, Flora watched one of the leading cars come up on the outside of another as they approached a turn. The car trying to pass forced the inside car to either slow down or be crushed against the rock wall. She could do that. As long as she didn't misjudge the space and get run off the road instead.

Easing closer to the car in front of her, Flora waited for the next spot wide enough for two vehicles. Then she swung to the outside—not too far, so that the other driver felt pinched, while she was in no danger of going off the side of the mountain. As they came out of the turn, she pressed the gas, sending them flying ahead of the other car.

She shot a grin toward Jensen, who looked rather tense but gave a good effort at a smile in return. She returned her focus to the road and repeated the maneuver, this time managing to pass two cars. With determination and intense concentration—along with a few drivers making mistakes that caused them to get stuck on the side of the road or spin around in the dirt—Flora moved up enough spots over the next fifteen minutes to get them into third place. They even passed Mr. Franklin and Sam with no trouble when the pair had to slow down to avoid an incapacitated motorcycle.

But the road grew narrower and steeper as it ascended, and the Decauville was not responding as easily, thanks to the increasing incline. There were fewer places to pass, and the drivers at the front knew what they were doing. The second-place car was able to block Flora's advances through several turns.

Unclenching her now-sore jaw, she glanced at Jensen to see if he had any other tips. But his eyes remained locked on the car in front of them. She stamped down a rush of disappointment.

Despite the heat below, it had grown much colder as they approached the summit, and Flora's fingers struggled to maintain a solid grip on the steering wheel. Now she understood why many of the other drivers had donned gloves before starting. No matter how she tried, there wasn't a way to get around that car.

It wasn't nearly long enough before the finish line appeared up ahead. A brisk wind had picked up, which the officials had warned the drivers about beforehand. In preparation for the tour, the Harrison Goods crew had lightened the Decauville as much as possible, usually a good way to increase speed. But up here, the lighter car was a detriment. Flora felt as if they would be blown straight down the side of the mountain if a strong gust hit.

That wasn't her biggest worry, though. It was clear now that there wouldn't be time to pass both cars ahead of her. Flora flexed her cold fingers and tightened her grip on the steering wheel. Maybe she could at least get around one and come in second.

Seeing her last chance on a short straightaway, Flora started moving the Decauville into position on the outside line. Without warning, Jensen's hand shot out and grabbed the steering wheel, pulling them back into line behind the other car. Shocked, Flora steered them across the painted finish line in third place.

As soon as the car was parked in the marked area away from the road, Flora jumped out and rounded the vehicle, marching straight up to

Jensen. "What was that? I had a chance to pass him, and you ruined it."

Jensen took off the goggles he'd chosen to wear for the race and placed them on the passenger seat with deliberate slowness before meeting her eyes. His tone was infuriatingly calm. "I saved us from a certain crash. Didn't you see him swinging out?"

Throwing up her hands, Flora let the adrenaline from the race take over. "How could I have missed it? Don't you think I was taking that into consideration? I had room."

Jensen winced, but Flora couldn't believe he felt bad about his choice. "You didn't, Flora. We would be careening down those sharp rocks right now if I hadn't done it."

Fury almost blinded her. "Did you do that on purpose?"

"I just told you I did."

"No, did you make me lose the race? Did you think a failure here would make me stop racing altogether? That I would quit the tour and we could go home? That's what you've been wanting all along, isn't it?"

Once the words were out, Flora realized she'd been harboring that thought in the back of her mind since Sam mentioned Mr. Franklin's accusation. She didn't want to believe Jensen would do such a thing, but it seemed a little part of her did believe it.

His response wasn't at all what she expected, though. She'd hoped for a quick, genuine denial, convincing her he would never hinder her chance at victory. Instead, his voice turned cold, and his posture went rigid. "You weren't going to win it, anyway."

Pain speared through her. It was true, of course. She'd been racing for second place with no way to get to the leader in time. But that didn't stop the words from stinging her pride. "You're right. With such an unsupportive teammate, I won't be winning anything."

Unable to face him after the words they'd both said, Flora walked away, forcing her spine to remain straight and strong when all she wanted was to crumble. But what good would that do anyone?

The scenery from the top of Mount Washington was awe-inspiring. But Flora couldn't enjoy it like many of the others who'd completed the trek above the clouds. Despite the jacket she'd had the sense to put on before the race, the cold was seeping into Flora's bones, and the impossibly strong wind was giving her a headache. She couldn't stay up here all day. She would have to go back and face Jensen long enough to get them off the mountain and back to the hotel.

Driving back down in a cloud of shame and anger, with Jensen silent next to her, was the worst amount of time Flora had ever spent in an automobile. She couldn't stop replaying that moment in her mind, seeing over and over the second-place car swinging out—but only slightly. There had been enough room, she was sure of it.

But what if there hadn't been?

The reality was that the other car could have kept moving to the outside, as he'd done on every other turn. If the Decauville had been too close, he very well might have clipped the front end, sending Flora and Jensen into a spin on a dangerously narrow road with the very real possibility of falling hundreds of feet.

But Jensen hadn't let her make that choice. He'd assumed he knew better than she did and took the chance to do something great away from her. It was too much like Clement and Henri, always making decisions for her. She'd been so sure Jensen was different, but in reality, was he?

Jensen had no idea what had caused him to grab the wheel and stop Flora from making that last pass. It hadn't been voluntary. One minute, he'd been watching the car ahead of them, noticing signs that the driver was going to swing out in the final turn. His mind had raced through the realization that the driver was focused on looking for a way around the leader and he didn't have anyone riding along to check behind him. He didn't know the Decauville was approaching.

The next thing Jensen knew, his hand had shot out and stopped Flora.

He snuck a glance at her face as they retraced the winding road back down, with much less intensity this time. Her jawline was tight, and she stared ahead without wavering. Even if she was aware of his scrutiny, she wouldn't give him the satisfaction of meeting his gaze.

But had there been any choice? He analyzed every memory of those brief moments—the way that car had started moving toward the outer line, narrowing the way through until he was sure the Decauvillle would be pushed off the side if they got any closer. Maintaining their third-place position was better than a fiery death at the bottom of the mountain.

Would Flora ever be able to see that? More importantly, would she forgive him?

Why did getting an answer to that question feel so vital to his very existence? Jensen couldn't help but remember the feel of her soft skin when he'd held her hand before the race, the joyful confidence in her eyes when they'd started the race, working as a team who trusted each other. Making her happy had been a rewarding experience. Even if she might never forgive him, could he find a way to make her look that content again?

The trip down the mountain felt like forever, but finally, they came to a stop by the spectator area where Fred and Beth waited. The couple rushed over, clearly expecting excellent news. But Flora jumped out of the car and marched straight past them toward the tent, where she got a drink of water from a table set up in the shade. The extreme rise in temperature compared to the top of the mountain made Jensen wish he could join her and guzzle down a cup, too, but she clearly needed time to herself.

Stopping in his tracks in surprise over Flora's abrupt departure, Fred turned to Jensen. "It didn't go as well as we hoped?"

Taking off his hat to wipe the sweat from his forehead, Jensen watched Flora drink with her back toward them, spine ramrod straight. "No. And it's my fault, so now she's angry."

Beth tilted her head in confusion. "How is it your fault?"

"I stopped her from making a dangerous pass at the end. She maintains there was room to get around, but I know there wasn't. I couldn't let her put us in danger to get one car ahead."

Fred clapped him on the shoulder. "My friend, you might have been right up there, but it's hard for anyone to accept that when they don't feel supported, much less when you physically take the choice out of their hands. You ought to try giving her the benefit of the doubt more often. Maybe knowing she has your trust and confidence would allow her to work *with* you.

The two of you would make better partners than enemies."

Next to him, Beth grinned. "Now that's decent advice. She's smart and capable. Show her you know it, and I'm sure she'll be more willing to admit when you're right."

Jensen shook his head but didn't respond as the two climbed into the car and got settled in the back. He'd tried. He'd been as supportive and encouraging as he could be before and during the hill climb. And still, she'd ended up angry, accusing him of doing the very thing he was fighting so hard to keep from doing.

And what about his feelings? He could admit grabbing the wheel likely wasn't the best reaction. He knew how smart she was and that she was an outstanding driver . . . when she wasn't overcome with recklessness. But why did he always have to be the one to push aside his concerns to encourage her?

Fred and Beth could give all the advice they wanted, but they were still newlyweds who hadn't faced much of life together. Mr. and Mrs. Harrison were the most happily married couple Jensen knew. Growing up in their home, he'd seen plenty of arguments between them over the years, and they'd always worked them out with conversation and compromise.

But now, Mr. Harrison was putting aside the business he loved and had poured his life into so he could care for his wife. Despite knowing that, soon enough, she would likely forget who he even was, he was choosing to love his wife well, in whatever way she needed him to now.

Jensen didn't know if he loved Flora, but he cared about her and longed for her happiness. Maybe he should follow Mr. Harrison's example and sacrifice what he preferred for her.

Now was as good as any time to try, so Jensen made his way toward the refreshment table where Flora still had her back toward him. He spoke before reaching her so she wouldn't be startled. "Flora?"

Whirling around, she speared him with eyes that flashed in familiar angry heat. "What, have you come to humiliate me further? I shared my family's secrets with you, I let you kiss me, and then I find out you're no different from Clement. You don't trust me to handle myself, and you think you should control me simply because you're a man."

Tears were gathering in her eyes, on top of all the flashing anger.

Moving a step closer, Jensen tried to keep his voice even. "That's not at all true. I didn't intend to grab the wheel from you. I should have told you what I saw instead of taking matters into my own hands. But please believe there was no thought of controlling you. It was all instinct to protect you. I saw the other driver moving over without looking, and all I could imagine was watching you get injured in a crash, bleeding and hurt, and I couldn't stand it. I—that would be the end of me, Flora."

He hadn't intended to say all that, but the words stopped Flora's temper short. She looked at him, blinking as it all sank in. "You weren't trying to prove you were right? Or that you know better than I do?"

"All I could think . . ." Unintended hoarseness crept into Jensen's voice, and he had to clear his throat to continue. "All I could think about was protecting you."

Stillness came over Flora and their eyes locked. She swallowed hard.

The raw emotion hanging between them was about to choke him with its intensity. He had to change the subject, and quickly. "Fred and Beth are waiting to return to the hotel. I could drive us back if you need a break."

Blinking as the moment passed, Flora nodded, much to his surprise. "I would appreciate that. Let's get back to the hotel. A restful evening will do us all good before we begin the return trip tomorrow."

Jensen offered her his arm. "I agree."

It was strange to have Flora sitting on the other side of him in the car, and even stranger to get into the driver's seat. He had to take a moment as the engine rumbled to life to force back memories of the last time he'd driven a car, the day that had forever changed him. He closed his eyes and let a deep breath work through his lungs and back out before setting his hands on the steering wheel.

He could do this for Flora. She needed him, and he wasn't going to let her down.

While he hesitated, Fred leaned forward and clapped Jensen on the shoulder. "Jensen, I haven't seen you drive in years. It suits you almost as well as it does Flora."

Mentally begging Fred to stay quiet, Jensen eased the car into motion. There was no way to forget the movement required to operate the car. Although the Decauville was much larger and more advanced than the hand-built race cars he used to drive, Jensen knew without thinking how to perform every action to get them on the road and back to the hotel. But he wouldn't claim that he enjoyed the experience anywhere near like he used to.

Fred, however, didn't take Jensen's silence as the hint it was and kept talking. "How long's it been since you drove, anyway? Since the racing days, I suppose? Gregory always said you had the makings of a great driver to go along with those mechanical skills."

Without looking, Jensen could tell the comment caught Flora's attention. That was exactly what he didn't want, but there was no way to tell Fred to keep his mouth shut without making it worse. "I'd say so."

Flora finally chimed in. "Perhaps we should take turns driving on the way back to New York, then."

Even over the noise of the car and the wind in their faces, the tartness in her voice was audible. Jensen may have calmed her immediate anger over his mistake on the mountain, but there was no way she'd recover so quickly from the hurt he'd caused. When the sting passed, she was probably going to be curious about his racing career. He would have to decide between confessing his part in what happened with Gregory or lying to Flora about it.

Neither of those options felt like something he could live with.

Chapter 17

Flora had to drag herself out of her room the next morning. As she drove the Decauville out of the Mount Washington Hotel driveway in order with the other tour competitors, she tried to force her mind to focus, to watch the road, and think about what needed to happen that day. But that was as impossible as it had been the entire sleepless night.

Beth had told Flora earlier about the racing crash that killed Fred's brother, but hearing Fred talk about Jensen's racing days had sparked so many questions. Why did Jensen never speak of it? He must realize that she knew he was connected to the sport. The instincts that told him the best way to set up the car and how to inform her of what was happening around them while she was focused on driving could only have come from years of experience.

Yet he chose to withhold any mention of his racing life from her.

The memory of his impassioned expression at Mount Washington the day before when he admitted to being consumed with her safety made her wonder if Gregory's death had made a bigger impact on Jensen than she'd realized. Of course, losing his best friend in a tragic accident would have affected him. He must have felt the grief as strongly as if he lost his own sibling. But was that where his consuming instinct to avoid risk at all costs originated? Rather than working through his grief, had it become the impetus for a life centered around remaining safe and risk-free, no matter the cost?

Flora glanced at him out of the corner of her eye as they reached the open road, heading south for the first time. He'd hardly spoken a word to any of them since they returned from the hill climb the day before. Fred's mere mention of Jensen's previous racing had caused him to close himself off from everyone around him.

By the time they stopped for lunch after an uneventful morning, Flora had thought of something even more devastating than young Jensen losing his best friend. He must have also been affected by the older Harrisons' unwillingness to talk about Gregory's death. Beth had told her it was treated as a family secret that no one would bring up. Jensen must have internalized the pain for so long, he was unable to bear the mention of that time.

And the thought broke Flora's heart.

Yes, he'd hurt her at the mountain summit. But she still cared about him enough that the situation he was in made her sad. After some time to think, she could see that her rash assumption that he was the same as Clement or Henri would never be true. Anyone forced to bear such an immense hurt without speaking of it would find it difficult to live a free, joyful life. Flora had endured heartache growing up but had Owen at her side. When he was gone and she lost Henri, Isabelle had been a constant companion, insisting that they not stifle their pain but let it out so they could find healing.

Jensen had never faced his pain, and it forced its way out in the form of an obsession with always picking the safest option—for himself and those around him. In a way, it seemed to show that he cared.

But what should Flora do with that realization? She watched him during their quick lunch at a local restaurant. If only he would tell her about it and thus open the communication between them. After all, she'd confessed her entire past to him. And it felt more freeing than she'd ever imagined. Especially now, with his harsh responses viewed in the light of his past hurt, their connection was stronger than it had ever been.

Beth was quiet during lunch, picking at her food and looking as if she wasn't feeling well. Fred fussed over her every few minutes while Jensen sulked, and Flora searched for a way to convince him he could let his pain out with her.

The quiet at their table set Flora on edge until one of the local patrons at the next table speared them with a glare, his voice loud enough to draw the attention of everyone in the room. "I don't know what this world is coming to when you motorists come driving through here like the devil himself's at your tails. I don't like it, I tell you. People aren't meant to move that fast."

The four of them turned in unison to stare at the two men. What had caused that outburst? Flora tried to clear up what was happening. "Excuse me?"

The other man at the table pointed a finger at them. "John's right. Nothing good comes of having that kind of power. What you folks did over at Kelly's farm proves it."

Jensen's eyebrows scrunched together as he frowned. "We haven't done anything except drive into town on the road. What happened at Kelly's farm?"

John sat up straighter. "You ruffians drove right through three of their fields, tore them all up. That wasn't any accident. Someone took time to go back and forth through the crop and spin circles in it. I spoke to Hershel Kelly myself right before I came in here. He's mighty upset."

His companion nodded. "Has every right to be too. After last year's harvest, we all need a good year. Now his crop's a mess."

Jensen's expression mirrored Flora's feeling that something very wrong was going on. She turned back to the two men. "I'm sorry that happened, but it wasn't the four of us. I hate to admit it, but not everyone participating in the

Glidden Tour has concern for those around them, and I apologize for that. It doesn't mean we're all that way, though."

The two men stood, dropped money on the table for their food, and left the restaurant, muttering together all the while. Flora tried not to let their anger get to her, but she couldn't forget all the things that had happened earlier in the race. Would a participant in the tour really damage a farmer's field on purpose without regard for his livelihood?

They finished their meal, all lost in their thoughts about what they'd learned. Jensen was the first to push away from the table and stand. "Guess we better get going if we're going to make it in the time limit today."

Back in the car, Flora steered them out of town. A pall had settled over the Harrison Goods team. Fred and Beth were uncharacteristically quiet while Jensen didn't even get out the map as he usually did. Recognizing they all needed a moment to think, Flora didn't ask him to direct her, instead keeping her eyes open for the colorful confetti the tour officials used to mark turns along the route.

As the afternoon wore on, Fred and Beth dozed off in the backseat. Maybe now was a good time to try to get Jensen to share with her. Flora nudged him with her elbow and kept her voice low so she wouldn't wake the couple. "I don't know how they can sleep with all this bumping around."

Jensen glanced back, and a half smile lifted one corner of his lips. "Fred could sleep anywhere as a child, so I'm not surprised. His favorite place to nap was Sunday church service, no matter how hard those pews were."

Flora chuckled along with him, hope lifting her heart. "What about you? Did you enjoy church or sleep through it?"

"Oh, I listened well enough. I guess I got a lot out of it back then, before . . . well, before I realized church attendance doesn't guarantee an easy life. My faith's been a bit stagnant since then. But it might be time to change that."

Flora could finally read between his words. He meant before Gregory died. She didn't want to push, but perhaps he would someday feel free to bring it up with her. "I always spent church services wondering what life was like in private for everyone else there. Clement was a stickler for putting on a façade of being the perfect family when we were in public. I often wished I could peek inside other homes and see if they were all as miserable as we were."

There was silence for long enough that Flora looked over at Jensen. But instead of contemplating her words or forming his response, he was leaning forward, squinting at a sign ahead of them on the road. "Flora, stop the car."

Startled, she did as he said, pulling over to the side of the road. By the time she stopped, the cast iron sign was close enough to read clearly. *Vermont—8 miles.*

"Vermont? We don't have any stops in Vermont, do we?"

Jensen was riffling through their tour packet, finally pulling out a map and spreading it on the dashboard in front of him. "No. The route doesn't go into Vermont at all."

Flora's heart sank. They'd gotten off course. It had been three hours since lunch. Had she missed a turn right away, or more recently? How long would it take to get back to their route? Why hadn't she asked Jensen for directions instead of trying to pry into his past?

Whatever the outcome of this mistake, it was entirely her fault.

Jensen kicked himself for not paying more attention. He'd been so wrapped up in his worries that he hadn't even bothered to glance at the map that day, relying on Flora to guide them using the route markers.

If this ended their chances of winning, it would be entirely his fault.

Flora took quick action and turned the car around in the road. "At least we only went straight and didn't make any turns since lunch. It can't be that difficult to find where we made the mistake. Especially now that you have the map out again."

Remorse coursed through him. Since driving the Decauville yesterday, he'd been consumed by memories of racing. Riding alongside Gregory in the first car, one they'd built by hand in the little shed they'd claimed as their own. The day when Mr. Harrison had bought Gregory his first new car—the lightest, leanest one they could find. That car had won them many a race.

But, as always, his thoughts had turned darker. He saw Archie leering at them, taunting that they'd never beaten him and they never would. He heard the sound of shouting voices as young Sam ran toward Jensen, gasping for breath with tears coursing down his cheeks. He felt the stitch in his side when he finally reached the accident scene and saw the end of Gregory's life for himself.

Forcing those memories back into the corner of his mind, Jensen refocused on the map in his lap. He couldn't let that moment continue to hurt people. The Harrisons would be devastated all over again if they had to learn new facts about that day. And if Flora found out the truth of what happened with Gregory—of Jensen's part in it—her opinion of him would be forever tainted by the way he'd abandoned his friend.

And it was starting to become very important to Jensen that she had a high opinion of him.

Fred and Beth woke as they picked up speed, with Flora driving faster than they had been earlier. Her tension was palpable. Fred scooted forward to address Jensen. "What's going on? Did we turn around?"

"Yes. Somehow, we missed a route marker, and we're rather far in the wrong direction."

"I'm certain there haven't been any turns for miles. How did I miss it?" Flora muttered, but it was loud enough that Jensen could catch most of it.

Was she blaming herself? Jensen hated for her to feel the same hard knot of frustration that was currently forming in his stomach. "Flora, I'm sure there's an explanation. I found where we are on the map. It looks as though we turned east instead of continuing south back by where we stopped for lunch. Maybe it was the traffic. There were a lot of wagons coming and going. Or the distraction of that scene at the diner."

She bit her lower lip, a gesture that made Jensen's heart lurch. She was still not convinced. "That confetti is usually everywhere. I don't know how I could have overlooked it."

He wasn't going to change her mind right now, so Jensen leaned back and scanned the map, making sure he knew where they needed to go to return to the tour route. The drive back to the small town seemed to take forever, even though they were traveling faster than on the way out.

Finally, buildings that looked familiar appeared on the horizon.

Jensen broke the long silence. "We're almost there. The turn is before you get into the town itself."

Flora slowed the car as they neared the buildings. To Jensen's surprise, the intersection where they needed to turn was completely clean and unmarked. Flora remarked on it first. "There's not a shred of confetti. I'd think it blew away, but this has been the calmest day of the entire tour, no hint of a breeze at all."

Flora turned the car around the corner at a crawl, all of them scouring the roadside for signs of the markers. But there wasn't a thing.

Beth leaned out over the edge of the car to look closer. "Perhaps the officials missed this turn. They could make mistakes like the rest of us."

It was a kind and generous sentiment, but Jensen's thought went in another direction. "Or it's another instance of someone connected to the race trying to stop others from succeeding."

Flora's eyes were sad when they turned to meet his gaze. "Damage to private property, removing markers, underhanded tactics. I hate to think someone on the tour would hurt their fellow teams and the reputation of motorists like this."

No matter his opinion on racing in general, Jensen could agree that it was bad sportsmanship, at best. Dangerous at worst. "We better get to the next stop as soon as possible and pray nothing else goes wrong."

Taking his cue, Flora accelerated, and they completed the leg in decent time, considering the hours they'd lost. But the day wasn't without its failures. They arrived at the hotel in Concord to learn that they had lost two positions.

Looking discouraged, Flora dropped onto the Decauville's running board, her face in her hands.

She needed comfort. But what words did he have that could take away the sting of failure? Yes, they had a few legs left in the tour to make up some ground. But with most teams still having the full points for every stop, the Harrison Goods team couldn't seem to advance from the middle of the pack.

Instead of trying to say the right thing, Jensen sat down and squeezed into the narrow space, pressed against her. There were several moments of silence, then, without warning, she leaned into him and let her head rest on his shoulder.

It was a nice feeling, reminding him of the warm contentment that washed over him when he held her hand before the Mount Washington race. Despite the care the Harrisons had shown him over the years, Jensen couldn't remember a time when someone had touched him with this kind of complete trust.

He could get used to it.

All too soon, an official came to check the Decauville, and Flora stood to greet him.

Jensen wandered along the line of cars, letting the pleasure of her closeness roll around in his mind. Unfortunately, Archie would choose that moment to find him, ruining Jensen's peaceful mood.

"Ah, Jensen. Dropping a spot again? You must have had another slow day. You'll notice that my team maintained third place with little effort. Poised to make a run for the win in the last few days, I'd say."

As always, when Archie opened his mouth, Jensen wished he could put his fist in it. But starting a fistfight might very well get the Harrison Goods team docked points by an official, and they couldn't afford that. "Good for you, Archie. Now leave me alone."

Jensen picked up his pace, but Archie fell into step beside him. "I see Mrs. Montfort's car is still running. I presume you haven't chosen to accept my generous offer, then."

Jensen shook his head. "And I never will. I may have to face dire consequences, but I can't stop you from doing what you want with the information you have."

After days of worrying over what he would do when Archie confronted him again, the response slipped out without warning, and Jensen found he meant it. It was time to face the choices he'd made in the past. If only he could do it the way he'd prefer.

Archie looked thoughtful, which was never a good thing. "That's very true. You can't. But since you don't see fit to help me, I suppose I'll have to take more drastic measures."

"Fine. Send a letter to the Harrisons. Or better yet, call them on the telephone in the hotel so they'll know right away. Just get it done."

"Oh, my friend, this is far from over, even if I reveal your little secret."

Jensen's heart plummeted, its pulsing almost drowning out Archie's words. "What do you mean?"

Deadly serious now, Archie leaned in close. "Mr. Dorman isn't just interested in me winning this tour. You know he has a personal issue with Mr. Harrison. He wants your team eliminated, with no hope of even finishing. That's what will satisfy him. That's what he's paying me for. And that's what he's going to get."

The truth was loud and clear in Archie's words. Mr. Dorman was set on completely humiliating Mr. Harrison, most likely to stop him from pursuing racing ever again. "How far are you going to go to appease another man's thirst for revenge, Archie? Sure, we never got along well, but you don't hate me enough to do real harm, do you?"

Archie rounded on Jensen, his eyes flashing with an intensity Jensen had never seen in him before. "Of course I do. You didn't have to endure what I did as a child, always under the thumb of a father who was never content that I'd done enough. You were Mr. Harrison's pride and joy right alongside his own children. And for no reason. It's not as though you showed any passion to succeed, any skill or talent worthy of his doting."

Swallowing hard, Jensen heard loud and clear all the things he had never spoken but had certainly thought about himself.

But Archie was far from done, and all Jensen could do was stand and listen. "Do you know what happened to me after Gregory died?"

Jensen had to shake his head, ashamed to admit he'd completely put Archie out of his mind when the reality of Gregory's death sank in and grief took over. He'd hardly thought about the man until the first day of the tour.

Archie ran his hand over his hair to smooth it and straightened his spine, visually pulling himself together. "I was ostracized by the racing world. No one wanted to race against a man that supposedly caused a deadly crash. No one would believe that precious Gregory Harrison could have been at fault. And then I realized something. They were right. He wasn't, but neither was I. It was your fault. Every driver needs a lookout to see what's going on behind and around them while he focuses on what's ahead. Gregory didn't do anything dangerous. You did. I had to claw my way back into this sport because of you, just as I had to struggle for everything in life."

There was nothing he could say in the face of the hard truth. He had left Gregory without anyone to watch for him, to help spot potential danger. Gregory had been a skilled driver and probably hadn't done a thing wrong.

It all came down to the fact that Jensen hadn't been where he should have been.

Archie must have seen his words hit home. His shoulders relaxed, and the grating, self-satisfied expression returned to his face. "All that to say, it's time I showed you what it's like to have to fight for what you want. Watch out, Jensen. I'm earning Ronald Dorman's approval one way or another."

With that, Archie shoved past, hitting Jensen's shoulder with his hard enough to make a point but still look as though he hadn't meant to for anyone watching. Then he stomped off, leaving the parking area and disappearing around the corner of the hotel. Jensen stood for a long time, staring after him and thinking over everything that Archie had said and accused him of.

All the things he had right.

But also, everything he had wrong. Jensen had fought more than Archie knew, and he was capable of standing up to the man. He just had to figure out how he was going to keep his friends from becoming victims in this feud first.

Chapter 18

Breakfast in the hotel dining room was a chaotic affair. The staff at each hotel would lay out a variety of scrumptious items for the tour teams to enjoy, but most of the participants were in a rush to get to their cars. There was too much jostling and grabbing for Flora's preference, so she liked to get there before everyone else, select a few items, and retreat to a quiet corner in the lobby.

But the entire hotel was crowded on this morning, and there was no peaceful spot to be found. Flora reluctantly sat down at one of the large tables in the dining room with Sam on one side of her and Fred and Beth on the other. Boisterous conversation surrounded them, and while her companions seemed unbothered by it, it was too much for Flora.

Seeming to notice her mood, Sam leaned over. "Not a morning person?"

Grimacing at a particularly loud burst of raucous laughter, Flora shook her head. "Not when I have to spend it in a room full of people who are far too chipper for the hour."

Sam chuckled, but the humor didn't reach his eyes. "Maybe a strong cup of coffee would improve your mood. I find it does mine."

Flora sighed. "No one here makes it as well as

they do in France. I've been spoiled. American coffee is hardly worth the effort."

After chewing a bite of biscuit slathered with jam, Sam glanced at her. "It appears your first day on the return trip didn't go so well."

There was no use in trying to make excuses. "No, it didn't. But we're still holding on in the middle. I won't give up hope of moving up in the standings until we drive into New York City."

Rather than describing the good day his team must have had, Sam went quiet. His lack of enthusiasm was unusual. She watched for a moment as he picked at his food before trying to start the conversation again. "How is your team doing? I know you finish in a good position every leg, but are you working well together? Enjoying the tour?"

Sam's gaze flitted around the room before returning to his plate. A prickle on the back of her neck set Flora on edge. Something wasn't right.

"Charlie left last night, if that tells you anything about how we're getting along. What matters is that we're in a position to win. That's what I have to focus on."

The comment was so unlike Sam that Flora opened her mouth to ask what on earth was going on with him. And why had their passenger left suddenly when they were headed back to New York, anyway. But a snippet of conversation from one end of the table stopped her before she could get answers. A man she recognized as a fellow driver was complaining about the time he lost the previous day due to a missed turn.

Flora turned to interject. "Excuse me, did you say you missed the turn in Plymouth?"

The man nodded, along with several others at the table. Conversations stilled as most of the room started listening. "We did. It took an hour before we found where we went wrong. There were no markers at the turn."

Flora straightened. At least they weren't the only ones who'd experienced trouble the day before. "Do you have any idea what happened?"

Another participant from across the room chimed in. "There was another one like that on the second day. Only caught a few teams, though, as far as I've been able to tell. Other teams know they saw confetti there, so it wasn't missed. Someone took great care to remove it."

The room buzzed again as people talked to those around them in hushed voices.

From the food table, a man standing with a half-filled plate spoke up. "For those who don't know me, I'm one of the tour officials. We're aware of the issue. Unfortunately, locals unhappy with our presence have been removing markers."

The room erupted as the hushed conversations turned louder.

The official set down his plate and raised

both hands in an effort to get the attention of the room's occupants. "Please, the best way to combat this is to be respectful. We've had locals complain to us about teams damaging their property, driving unsafely, and becoming a nuisance on the roads. We're here to show people that automobiles are an improved way to travel. Please don't be discourteous and harm the good name of the American Automobile Association."

The official was immediately swamped with participants asking questions and demanding answers on various matters.

Flora turned to Beth and Fred. "It's like those farmers at lunch yesterday who complained about one of our teams destroying that field. Who's doing such hurtful things?"

Fred sighed, watching the continuing commotion. "Competition sometimes brings out the worst in people. We'll have to keep our eyes and ears open. If we can isolate who's causing trouble, we can help keep the tour in the public's good graces."

Flora faced Sam, who'd turned a shade of gray that looked unhealthy. "Sam, are you ill?"

He jumped up, pushing his chair back from the table with enough force to rattle every glass upon it. "I'll be fine. I need to check the car over before the drive today."

He rushed from the dining room, leaving Flora, Fred, and Beth staring after him.

Flora turned to her companions. "What on earth has gotten into him?"

Fred's gaze lingered on the doorway. "You don't suppose he knows who's been doing these things? He might be afraid to name a team and make an enemy."

Flora rolled the thought over in her mind. "I'll talk to him later. Perhaps after today's leg, he'll feel more inclined to explain what's going on."

After they finished their meal, Jensen was already waiting by the Decauville. He still looked weighed down, more like the irritable man who started the tour with them than the kind, warm man she'd come to know since. Fred filled him in on what they'd learned over breakfast while they all got settled in their seats.

Jensen's jaw tightened when Fred outlined their concerns about Sam. "I've known Sam a long time. He's a good fellow but too anxious to make a name for himself. I'm worried about what he might have gotten involved with."

Flora looked at Jensen in surprise. "You think his team might be part of the problem? Why would he stand for that?"

For the first time that morning, Jensen met her eyes. "Ambition does strange things to a man."

But kind, funny Sam? "You said yourself, Sam is a good man. I can't believe he would participate in cheating and the destruction of property. If they're trespassing and harming others to get ahead, I have to believe Sam would put his foot down."

Jensen shrugged and looked away. "Well, I know his team's driver, and I don't believe Sam is strong enough to stand up to a bully like him. Not many men are."

The cars ahead of them roared to life, and Flora had to focus for the time being on starting the day's drive well. But she couldn't help wondering if Jensen was right. Could darling Sam be helping his team cheat while knowing it was hurting others?

Flora was glad for the good weather and easier roads on the day's drive. Half her mind was trying to decide what she believed about Mr. Franklin and Sam, while the other half thought about passing cars and making the turns Jensen pointed out. After starting the day in tenth, they were sitting in sixth place by afternoon.

This time, Jensen kept the map in one hand, checking it often so they didn't miss anything. Despite his gruff demeanor first thing that morning, he seemed more willing than ever to help Flora race around other cars.

As the outskirts of Worchester, Massachusetts, came into view, he leaned close, his muscular shoulder pressing against her arm. "You don't have any more turns until we get into town, and it looks like a decent stretch of road. Think we can pass that team up ahead before we get to the check-in?"

Throwing a grin toward him, Flora pushed the gas pedal in and started increasing their speed. "Do you even need to ask?"

As the town grew closer, Flora caught up to the car. Jensen had been right. The road ahead was clear and straight, and Flora executed a perfect pass. The other team waved and smiled as they did, making Flora smile as much as Jensen's encouragement. Those were the kind of competitors that made the tour an event that would last.

Very soon after, they entered Worchester. Flora navigated the city streets with no trouble, bringing them into the parking area near the hotel in fifth place, their highest finish in the tour.

Flora hopped out of the car, more energetic than after any of the other legs. She stood close to Jensen, speaking for his ears alone. "That was a wonderful day. Thank you for all the support you gave me. If we can repeat this the next two days, don't you think we have a chance to finish at the top?"

Staring into her bright, trusting eyes at that moment, Jensen wanted to promise her everything. Since his conversation with Archie the night before, Jensen's mind had been consumed with trying to figure out how he could protect those he cared about until he was able to find the right way to tell them everything.

But sitting next to Flora while they'd enjoyed a successful drive had refreshed his spirit. When she was confident and careful, she became the excellent driver Mr. Harrison claimed her to be. It had been a delight to work alongside her, giving her reference points for how far she was clear of other cars or rough stretches of road, finding ways they could match what she intended to do with the reality of what Jensen saw in the landscape.

Anytime he thought about returning to New York, though, a pressure built up inside him. When they finished this tour, he was going to have to face the fact that if Archie hadn't already exacted his revenge along the way, the first thing he would do would be to tell everyone who mattered about Jensen's long-held secret.

The truth of his involvement in Gregory's death was going to come out, one way or the other. Unless he kept Flora from driving the Decauville over that finish line.

Jensen shook that thought away and forced himself to smile down at Flora, standing so comfortably close to his side. He couldn't do that. Not to Flora and not to Mr. Harrison.

Even if it was the only way to protect himself.

Bringing his mind back to the moment, Jensen nodded. He could at least be honest in this. "I know you can bring us to the end in front, Flora. You're one of the best drivers I've ever seen."

Before his eyes, Flora straightened, confidence drawing her upright and brightening her beautiful features. His heart ached at the thought that he would have to disappoint her soon. Would she be angry when she found out he'd been keeping a secret? Disappointed? Hurt?

Fred and Beth waved goodbye as they left for their evening stroll, while Flora engaged the tour official who stepped over to check their car in polite conversation.

Jensen's heart was torn in two directions. He couldn't do anything about the feelings churning inside him, so for now, he pushed the issue to the back of his mind.

Once the official checked the car in and moved on, Jensen returned to Flora's side and pulled the cover off the engine. "I agreed to help you learn more about the car, so let's get back to it."

A wide, slow smile spread across Flora's face. She pushed the sleeves of her white shirtwaist up a bit from her wrists and ran one hand over her hair, smoothing a few loose strands. "I would love that."

For the next hour, Jensen walked her through his usual process for making small repairs that could be done on the road. Things such as patching a tire, flushing the radiator, and replacing spark plugs. Finally, she used the cloth he'd handed her to wipe off the layer of grime that accumulated on the dirt roads.

Now was as good a time as any to bring up the question he'd been considering since the moment she first asked to help him. "Flora, what was the real reason you wanted to work on the car with me?"

Her gaze flew to meet his, and her hand stilled in mid-swipe on the back fender. "What do you mean?"

He was getting better at reading her. That expression was not genuine ignorance. "You know as much about this engine as I do. That's clear as can be."

A pink flush started up her neck, and he couldn't stop a grin. She knew she was caught. "I'm sorry, I didn't mean to lie. I do believe there's plenty I can learn from you about the mechanics of the car. But I did try to use men's usual assumption that a woman wouldn't have any interest in cars to my advantage."

"There's no way I could have missed your knowledge after all those hours we spent arguing over the car's setup before the tour." Jensen examined her face, waiting for the explanation.

She finally spoke again. "I hope you're not angry with me for believing you would think that way, or for the deception. To be honest, I was a little worried that you were the one causing trouble for the tour."

Jensen's heart dropped, all warmth seeping from him. "Why would you think that?"

She rushed to explain. "I didn't fully believe it. But Sam told me some things Mr. Franklin said that made me doubt you. Only for a bit, but I thought if I could spend more time with you, I'd discover if it was true or not."

Of course, Archie was behind it. She looked so anguished Jensen couldn't be angry. "And did you?"

"I discovered you are kind and care so deeply for others that you can't help but want to keep them from any harm. You might make mistakes in trying to do so, but I don't believe you ever do it with wrong motives."

Her eyes spoke volumes, imploring him to believe her. And he did. He found he trusted her without question. Memories flooded Jensen's mind of all the time they'd spent together over her car. The hours sitting close as they drove. She'd come to be an integral part of his day.

And those times were almost at an end. The realization started tearing a hole in his heart. There were only a few days left of this, of spending time with Flora and participating in her life's passion. Then they would return to Philadelphia, where she would presumably continue driving for the Harrison Goods team and he would have to face the consequences of his choices.

As they gathered under the wide roof of the hotel porch later with Fred and Beth, Beth sighed as she leaned back in one of the comfortable chairs arranged along the railing. "It's hard to believe the trip will be over in two days. It feels as if it's just begun."

Fred took her hand in his, and she smiled at her husband. The action served to remind Jensen that no matter how much he longed to, he had no reason to take Flora's hand again, no right to harbor feelings beyond professional friendship. They would be going their separate ways as soon as they returned to the real world.

From his side, Flora spoke up. "We'll still have a day to drive back to Philadelphia from New York. So that's three more days to enjoy each other's company."

Fred nodded. "Thank you both for giving us the chance to experience this adventure. I couldn't imagine a better wedding trip."

Beth let her free hand rest across her belly, looking very motherly, although Jensen couldn't yet see any signs of the child within. "And now we can prepare for the years of building our family, knowing we've had a marvelous adventure together."

The sweetness of their joyful expressions as they gazed at each other was overpowering. Jensen had to hold himself back from jumping up and rushing to a less saccharine spot. But then he caught sight of Flora. She watched the two with such a wistful look. Was she thinking of her husband? She hardly ever spoke of him, come to think of it. Had theirs been the kind of love that Fred and Beth shared? And would Jensen ever have the right to ask her about such personal matters?

Jensen was saved from his romantic introspection by Beth rising from the chair. "I'm quite hungry. Fred, dear, will you get my wrap from our room before you join us for supper? I forgot it, and I always get a chill in the evening."

Nodding, Fred headed to oblige his wife while Jensen escorted the ladies inside. They found seats at a table, and Jensen had a few moments to compose himself while Flora and Beth talked about baby-related things. He was starting to wonder what was taking Fred so long when a commotion across the room caught everyone's attention.

Fred stormed through the door, pushing past the hotel staff waiting to help guests find seats. His face was red, and his eyes immediately locked on Jensen. Jensen's heart plunged and his teeth clenched together again as he rose to meet his friend. But more chill-inducing than Fred's obvious anger was Archie, who followed Fred in and lounged against the doorframe while watching the entire scene unfold. What had he done?

Stopping a mere foot in front of Jensen, Fred pushed his finger into Jensen's chest. "Why didn't you tell me what happened? All these years, all the questions I asked about Gregory, and you never told me the whole story. You lied to me, Jensen, all while pretending to be like a brother."

Helplessness washed over Jensen. "No, Fred. I never lied. I . . . couldn't tell you everything. You were so young. I didn't want to destroy the trust you had in me."

"More like, you didn't want to admit you'd done anything wrong. Archie may not be the nicest person, but at least he was willing to tell me the part you played in Gregory's death. You always said Gregory was your best friend. Well, that's hard to believe when you would tarnish his memory with half-truths."

With that, Fred turned and marched from the dining room. Jensen felt every eye on him, even when Beth stood and rushed after her husband, her face white with shock. The last thing anyone needed was for him to come face-to-face with Fred again right now, so Jensen sank back into his chair. As awful as being in this room was, it was the safest place for the moment.

He hung his head, refusing to look up to see if Archie was still watching him until the room returned to a somewhat more subdued level of conversation. Finally, he peeked at the doorway.

Blessedly empty. Then he glanced across the table at Flora, prepared for anything except the compassionate, determined face he found watching him.

Chapter 19

The anguish on Jensen's face tore at Flora's heart.

It had been devastating to watch Fred confront Jensen in such obvious pain. She could only imagine how much worse it felt to be Jensen, knowing what Fred had been referring to. And it was clear that he knew exactly what Fred had learned. There was guilt etched in every line of his body.

Keeping her voice firm while trying to convey her support, Flora refused to look away from his pain-filled eyes. "When you're ready to talk, you ought to explain what that outburst was all about."

Jensen glanced around the dining room, now mostly empty. "You've already heard bits about Fred's brother, Gregory."

The statement sounded more like a question, so Flora nodded, encouraging him to go on.

He rubbed one hand across the back of his neck as he leaned back in his chair. "He and I were inseparable growing up. As much like brothers as two boys could be. We started tinkering with engines when I was eighteen. Mr. Harrison brought a velocipede home from Germany to keep us from getting into trouble. We started building our own engines and attaching them to bicycles, looking for more speed. That turned into making race cars out of whatever automobile parts we could get our hands on and joining informal races outside town. I drove sometimes, but we found that we made a better team with me strategizing and Gregory driving." A tight smile crossed his face, dimmed by grief but there, nonetheless.

Flora sipped her water before speaking, giving him a moment to relive happier memories. "Was he a good driver?"

The smile brightened. "He was the best. He beat Archie every time."

Silence fell. Flora didn't try to break it but gave Jensen whatever time he needed to continue his story.

Finally, he spoke again, his eyes fixed on his fingers as they fiddled with the tablecloth. "That day, we had just finished preparing a new car, one Mr. Harrison bought us. Gregory was so excited to be the first to race it. He went on and on about how it would fly past everyone else and leave them in the dust. Archie didn't like Gregory's bragging and challenged him to a one-on-one race before the others arrived. I knew deep down it was a bad idea. Archie had always been more ruthless and intense than the rest of us."

Flora imagined a younger, more adventurous Jensen with his best friend at his side. Two months ago, it would have been hard to envision.

Now, she'd seen hints of that speed-chasing, race-loving younger man, and it was an easy image to conjure. "What did you do, then?"

His head dropped again. She had to strain to hear his response. "I let Archie get to me. He pushed and goaded without mercy, and I finally had enough. I convinced Gregory he had to beat Archie one more time to make him stop. It didn't take long to realize what a terrible idea it was. I tried to convince Gregory to back out, but he wouldn't. We fought about it. He even threw a punch at me when I told him only an idiot would go through with it. Then he went ahead without me."

A lump rose in Flora's throat. Thankfully, he didn't seem to expect her to speak. She could already see how he'd been blaming himself for whatever happened next, how his firm stance on protecting others stemmed from this one moment when he felt he'd failed his friend.

He swallowed hard a few times, then continued. "The new car was as fast as we thought it would be. Gregory pulled ahead right away. But without anyone riding along to watch for him, Gregory had to keep looking back to see where Archie was. Archie said that at some point, Gregory was looking behind him, and his wheel hit a rock or hole or something that caused him to lose control. I always wondered if Archie was telling the truth about that, but however it happened, the car flew headlong into a tree. Gregory was thrown pretty far from the car. The doctor who examined his body later said he was killed as soon as he hit the ground."

Looking around, Flora was glad the room had emptied. She slid over to sit in the chair they'd left open for Fred, right next to Jensen. She reached out and took his hand, causing him to finally look up at her. "You must have blamed yourself for so long." Tears gathered in his eyes, and he sniffed, confirming that she was right. "Oh, Jensen. The choices you made don't mean you were responsible for his death. He made choices, too, as did Mr. Franklin."

"But my anger and pride blinded me and made me careless. If I hadn't let Archie get into my head, I would never have told Gregory he should do anything so foolish. I convinced him, then abandoned him to die alone. Flora, everyone blamed Archie, and I let them. My terrible mistakes hurt so many people."

If only she knew what to say to take the guilt from his shoulders. Would hearing her story help ease his burden? "I believe you know my husband died two years ago." At his nod, she continued. "He also died in a racing crash."

Jensen's hand squeezed hers, sending a tingle up her arm. How strange to be talking about Henri while having such a response to Jensen. Flora ignored that thought and went on. "I should have been the one driving. But much like you and Gregory, we quarreled the morning of the race. We had been trying to start a family, and he was convinced that participating would be unhealthy for me. Those races were getting so competitive, it was very possible things could get out of hand. But it felt so much like Clement's controlling behavior that I pushed back."

Now she felt Jensen's rough fingers gliding over the skin of her hand, lightly rubbing. Heat pooled in her stomach, and she sucked in a breath. His eyes held hers as she finished her story. "I went to the race, anyway, but when he found me there, he refused to let me in the car. He drove in the race instead, to keep me from doing it. There was a problem with the engine, and he stalled going down a hill. Another competitor didn't see him until it was too late and crashed right into the back of his car. The car flipped and pinned him under it. I'm sorry to say it wasn't instant like Gregory."

Thank goodness, her eyes didn't fill with tears. She wanted to help Jensen see the truth, not wallow in her own emotions. "For so long, I wouldn't leave Isabelle's house, convinced I could have saved him, that it would have been different if I'd been driving. But the truth is, I'm not in control of my own life, let alone Henri's. The Lord took him then, and I cling to the truth that His will would have been accomplished no matter what I chose to do. It wasn't my fault, and Gregory's death wasn't yours."

A tear slid down Jensen's cheek, breaking Flora's heart the rest of the way. "Can you believe that, Jensen? Yes, you made mistakes, and there are consequences for that. But can you forgive yourself and move forward knowing you aren't guilty of causing Gregory's death?"

His hands rose to grip her upper arms. Flora's breath caught and held as he leaned forward. A heartbeat away from her lips, he paused. "With your confidence in me and the Lord's grace, I can."

Then he covered her mouth with his.

Flora lost herself for an amount of time she couldn't be sure of. She was only aware of the warmth of his lips, the sound of his quickening breaths, the feel of his hands sliding around to stroke her back. He reached up and buried one hand in her hair, tilting her head to meet his kiss at a different angle, and she was tempted to crawl out of her seat to be closer to him.

Just when she thought she might never catch her breath again, he pulled back. The world immediately felt colder and emptier without his body against hers. But he took her hand again, and she was grateful for the contact.

"Thank you for sharing your past, Flora. I'm sorry you've felt the same way I have for all these years. I wouldn't wish that shame on anyone."

"The best way to combat shame is to talk about it. Of course, you should speak to Fred before we leave. He deserves the same explanation you gave me. And you know you'll have to face the rest of the Harrisons when we return. You have to bring it into the open if you want to find any peace in your life."

Jensen knew she was right. He'd thought of little else since Archie first threatened him. If the Harrison Goods team somehow reached the finish line of the tour unscathed, Archie would find a way to exact his revenge, likely in a similar fashion to what he'd just done with Fred. The satisfaction and anticipation on Archie's face as he'd lounged in the doorway made Jensen fear that this was only the first in a line of moves he had planned to hurt the Harrison Goods team.

But looking into Flora's beautiful face, Jensen couldn't stand to worry her further. Archie was his problem. This entire situation existed because Jensen hadn't done the right thing five years ago. "That's my plan, as soon as we set foot in Philadelphia. As for Fred, I'll let him cool off for a bit. But I intend to sort the truth out of whatever Archie said as soon as Fred is ready to hear it."

Jensen stood and held out his arm for Flora. Once she joined him, they strolled together to the door of her room, both lost in their thoughts on the way.

She paused before entering and looked up at him. "Talking to Fred sooner is better than later. Otherwise, he'll take Mr. Franklin's spin on the truth to heart, and I'm sure that will lead to more confusion and hurt. Don't delay."

He leaned against the wall next to her, their bodies separated by mere inches. This close, he could see a smear of dirt across her neck, a remnant of a day on the road. Her hair was starting to fall from the loose arrangement she always wore, although that may have been due to his hand shifting it when they'd kissed in the dining room.

The memory of that kiss would be burned into his mind forever. Jensen couldn't imagine what the future might hold for them, but he felt for the first time that it could involve them being together, after all. They might be able to work through his messes and come out on the other side stronger—and together.

There was just so much heartbreak to get through first.

Reaching out, he stroked one finger across her cheek. As it had before their kiss, desire darkened her eyes, sending a jolt of longing through Jensen. She knew what kisses like this could lead to, and her expression showed she had more than a little interest in it.

But as much as he could see a future with her becoming possible someday, he still wasn't in a place to make promises. He didn't have a career to return to. He was embroiled in a mess of his own making that threatened her safety. Jensen dropped his hand and stepped back. He would have to sort out his past mistakes before making plans for their future.

Flora's face fell, but she reached out to touch his arm. "Don't forget, you've done nothing to be ashamed of. Regret, yes. But shame will destroy you and your relationship with the Harrisons. Get it all out in the open and healing can start."

Then she leaned forward and planted a light kiss on his cheek before spinning around and disappearing into her room. Jensen let the sensation of her lips on his skin linger for as long as possible. Then he went to his room, though he certainly wouldn't sleep well with the next day's responsibility hanging over him.

He was up and ready in the morning before the light started to break on the horizon. He situated himself at the dining room table closest to the door in a seat that let him see into the lobby Fred would have to pass through if he came to breakfast. Before long, Beth appeared by herself, her face gaunt. Jensen's heart clenched. Had his terrible choices unintentionally hurt her too?

She lowered herself into the chair opposite him and spoke without hesitation. "He's not coming to breakfast, so you might as well stop looking so hopeful."

Jensen sank back against his chair. "Was I that obvious?"

Nodding, she helped herself to a biscuit from his untouched plate. "He's on the porch in the back. It was otherwise deserted when I left him there, so this is as good a time as you're going to get to discuss what happened."

Jensen immediately rose, even as his heart clenched at the reality of the conversation to come.

She looked up as he stepped away from the table. "He wants to reconcile with you. Archie told him quite a few things, and I don't believe many of them. But he's confused. Try to remember, he cares about you and wants to remain close. You're the only brother he has left."

Those words propelled Jensen out of the dining room and toward the back entrance of the hotel. There he did indeed find Fred sitting alone, no one else around to overhear more of their private business. He claimed a creaky wooden chair next to Fred, praying his friend wouldn't leave in anger again.

And thankfully, he didn't. Fred kept his eyes trained on the small stretch of lawn behind the hotel, bringing up the subject hanging between them without resorting to small talk. "What do you have to say for yourself?"

Jensen weighed his words carefully. Fred might

bolt if he started wrong. "I have no defense to offer for keeping details about Gregory's death from your family for all this time. I only hope you can understand how the weight of it has burdened me since that day. I felt I was doing you all a favor, letting Archie take the blame so you'd have someone to put it on. But I knew all along it was wrong."

Somehow, the words he managed to utter must have been the right ones. When he glanced up, Fred was staring at him, unshed tears gathering in his eyes. "Is this why you never wanted to talk with me about my brother?"

Jensen could only nod.

Fred let out his breath in a rush. "I never understood why everyone went silent when his name came up. I was young and idolized him, and when he was gone, I longed for someone to share memories of my brother with me. But no one would."

The pain was so clear in Fred's voice that Jensen felt the physical blow of it. "I'm so sorry, Fred. I hate that I never did that for you."

Fred sighed. "I suppose we ought to sort through everything Archie told me. Beth kept saying how outlandish most of it was, but I suppose there are grains of truth hidden in his lies."

For the next half hour, they talked about the things Archie had said—many of which were outlandish, indeed. Jensen told Fred about the amazing mind Gregory had for engines and how he would figure things out all on his own and then teach them to Jensen. He told Fred how proud Gregory had been to have a younger brother. "He always claimed you'd replace me as his racing partner as soon as you were old enough to."

Fred smiled at that. "Thank you for your honesty, Jensen. I can tell you've finally told me everything. And it feels good to be talking about Gregory. I hope it's healing for you too."

Jensen had to admit that it was. There was a lightness filling his chest that he hadn't experienced in years. Even the thought of the coming confession to Fred's parents brought less fear than any other time he'd imagined it.

Once again, Jensen's heart turned to silent prayer. *Lord, I hate that it had to come to this, but I guess I should thank You for the push to get this out in the open. Please protect us as we finish this tour. Keep Archie from achieving his plans to harm us.*

What a relief to entrust his worries to someone else, for the first time in a long time . . . the only one who could do something about them. After a little more time spent in the quiet of the morning, he and Fred went to join the ladies at the car. It was time to run the penultimate leg of the tour and face whatever Archie would throw at them next.

Chapter 20

Standing with Beth by the Decauville, Flora had never been so relieved as the moment when she saw Jensen and Fred exit the hotel together, grinning like old friends again. She smiled at Beth. "It looks as though you were right. They managed to talk through the situation, after all."

Beth's shoulders relaxed and her smile returned. "I so hoped they would. They're both good men, and they care about each other. Now that it's all coming out into the open, the whole family can start to heal."

Flora's heart beat a little faster as the two men approached. Grumpy Jensen had been quite attractive in his own way. But smiling, relaxed Jensen took her breath away. Shyness enveloped her. What would they talk about today with last night's kisses hanging in the back of her mind—and presumably his too? The first kiss at Bretton Woods could have been played off as an accident, a moment they got caught up in. But last night . . .

Flora's face burned at the brazen way she'd planted her lips on his cheek before retreating to her room. What must he think of her?

As if privy to her introspection, Jensen glanced straight at her, and his peaceful expression turned into a warm smirk. It reminded her of the day after their first kiss when everything he said made her think of what came after a kiss like that, and how much she longed to experience that with him.

Heat flamed to life, fanning through her entire body. There would be no repeat of yesterday's excellent driving if she didn't get her mind back where it belonged—on the day ahead. Climbing into her seat, Flora busied herself with securing her hat to withstand the wind and arranging her skirts so they were out of the way of all the handles and the pedal.

The car shifted as Jensen settled in next to her. So close, yet also farther than her traitorous heart wanted him to be. He leaned close to speak for her ears alone. "Good morning. You'll be happy to know we're starting this part of the journey with less anger and fewer secrets. Largely thanks to your excellent advice last night that I should talk to Fred right away."

Flora forced herself not to get lost in those intense hazel eyes. "I'm glad you two were able to talk. Now that you know how much better it feels to reach out and include people who care about you in your pain, I hope you'll do the same with Mr. and Mrs. Harrison when we return."

"As long as you'll be there to support me, I intend to." He leaned back against the plush seat, settling one arm along the top so that it was almost wrapped around her, his fingers grazing her shoulder.

Another rush of desire hit her unbidden. She immediately turned her attention to the line of cars in front of them. Only four teams stood between her and a first-place finish on this leg.

Then there was no more time for Flora to think about the feel of Jensen's fingers lightly catching the fabric covering her shoulder. The lead cars lurched into motion, and the smell of gasoline filled the air. Flora's body hummed in anticipation of the rush that accompanied moving up in the race field. This was not the time to let a man distract her. She had a job to do, and nothing would keep her from doing it well.

At least, that was the thought that sustained her for the first few hours of the day. Not long into the drive, they passed Mr. Franklin and Sam, who were stopped on the side of the road changing a tire. Flora and Jensen exchanged a look, and she knew what he was thinking—that if they could stay ahead of those two, they wouldn't risk a fight to pass them later on. There was no doubt Mr. Franklin would make it difficult for them if he was in front.

They decided not to stop for lunch, and soon enough, another car was in Flora's sight. But the team ahead was fast, and the roads in the area were filled with sharp curves and deep ruts that made passing difficult. Despite being forced to follow them for at least another hour, it bolstered Flora's confidence that the Decauville was fast enough to keep up with the front-runners.

Finally, Jensen looked up from the map and pointed ahead. "It looks as though there's a nice straight stretch coming up, and the road conditions here are as good as we've seen. If you can stay close to this team until the bend by those trees, you'll be in a good position to pass them on the other side."

Adrenaline poured through Flora's body. The beginning of the tour had been so difficult, and they were due for some good luck. This felt like the solid run she'd been waiting for.

Flora accelerated until they were only a car's length behind the other team. One of their passengers looked back and waved with a grin. Flora returned the gesture, optimism permeating the atmosphere. This was racing. Not dealing with teams who cheated and destroyed property or angry locals or mechanical problems that could be prevented if the team communicated better. Just two skilled drivers ready to see whose car was the best.

As the bend approached, Flora readied herself for a quick pass, knowing the other driver was aware of their presence and preparing himself to block her. What she didn't expect was for him to slam on his brakes the second they rounded the blind curve.

As both cars came to an abrupt stop, Flora couldn't believe her eyes. The road ahead was completely blocked by cows.

"Cows?" Jensen must have been as stunned as she was. "Why are there cows on the road?"

The other team members had disembarked from their car and were walking around, trying to figure out how to get through. The closest cows stared at them for a moment, then returned to chewing at the grass growing between the ruts in the dirt surface. One lifted its head and mooed mournfully. They didn't seem interested in moving one bit for the cars to get through.

Fred and Jensen were staring at the scene with wide eyes, as if trying to sort out if what they were seeing was real. Beth had covered her mouth with one hand, mirth evident in her glowing eyes and the upturn of her lips. Before Flora could say a word, a snorting laugh burst from Beth, drawing the men's attention.

An answering laugh bubbled up in Flora's chest. She turned away to try to stem it, but it wouldn't be contained. Once she started, she could hardly catch her breath, the laughter came on so fast. After a fight to get herself back under control, Flora made the mistake of looking up. Next to her, Jensen's eyes were watering, and his face was red as he, too, tried not to lose control. Which made Flora's giggles start up all over again.

It wasn't long before the other team was watching them guffaw like mad while stranded and helpless in the blocked roadway. But Flora didn't care in the least if they looked as though they were losing their minds. After so much heartache on the tour and the emotional revelations of the previous day, all four of them needed a moment of pure levity.

Eventually, they pulled themselves together. Fred was the first to hop out of the car and start trying to help the other team encourage the cows to move by waving their arms and shouting. As Flora climbed out to see what could be done, another car approached from behind them, and her heart sank. They would have to work so hard to avoid losing positions when they got back on the road.

If they got back on the road before time ran out for the day.

When Jensen groaned, Flora looked closer. The car coming around the bend belonged to none other than Mr. Franklin and Sam. She offered a friendly wave to Sam, but Mr. Franklin only glared at them all.

He held out one arm, blocking Sam from getting out of the car. "What's the holdup here?"

Jensen gestured toward the roadblock. "I would think it's obvious."

Archie's scowl deepened, and he dropped back in his seat, obviously unwilling to help the rest of them. He looked so much like a petulant child who was angry over being told to wait, it was surprising he didn't launch into a full pout.

They turned their attention back to the problem at hand. The stubborn animals refused to move a muscle, no matter what the frustrated humans tried. After far too long spent coercing and waving their arms, one of the men from the front team hit both hands on the hood of his car in exasperation.

Unexpectedly, several of the cows that hadn't moved the entire time jumped into motion and sauntered away. "Maybe that will do it. They don't care about humans walking around, but they're not used to noise from cars. Everyone, get back in the cars, and we'll slowly move forward and see if they figure out to get out of the way."

One of the men grew excited as he jumped into the front car. "They didn't move a muscle when we first pulled up here. We have a horn. I bet if we honk, they'll move faster."

"No!" Jensen got the group's attention with his firm—but not too loud—exclamation. "A noise that foreign and sudden could make them panic and run into the cars. They're huge. They could injure themselves or do damage to us. We'll have to take our time. Let's start with Flora's more cautious suggestion."

Flora's heart warmed as they all got in place

and started up their cars again. The cows shifted from foot to foot at the increased noise.

Jensen smiled at her while they waited on the first car to start moving forward. "Very well-thought-out solution."

Easing the floor pedal forward to give the car a bit of gas, Flora let the satisfaction of his confidence envelope her. It was a satisfying sensation, knowing the man she cared about believed in her and trusted her to make decisions for them all.

The man I care about?

The thought caught Flora unaware. She peeked at Jensen, who watched the team in front of them and the slowly shifting cows as they followed Flora's suggestion. When had she come to care about him as more than a friend and her partner in the tour?

Now that the realization had come to her, Flora couldn't deny the truth of it. She cared for Jensen with more intensity than she'd ever imagined she would feel again. Could she go so far as to say she loved him? The flutter in her heart when he caught her watching him and responded with a broad smile confirmed it.

Somewhere along the road, she'd fallen in love with Jensen Gable.

Jensen couldn't help noticing the mysterious smile that graced Flora's lips. Why had he ever been confused about how to support her? He once again reveled in the pleasure of knowing that he'd put that smile on her face and that confidence in her movements. He'd given her what she needed in that moment, and he would do anything to continue doing so.

But right now, they had a job to do. The close proximity of three cars was a concern. They all knew they'd lost time and there might be more teams coming behind them quite soon. The front two cars presumably had gained time on them. Plus, they'd all be aware of the opportunity to either get ahead or lose positions when they resumed racing. It all came down to whether Flora's idea would get the cows to move, and who would get the jump on the others as soon as the creatures were out of the way.

And in the middle of it all, Flora was distracting him with that glowing countenance.

Shaking off the direction his thoughts wanted to follow, Jensen forced himself to look past the cows to the straightaway he'd noticed on the map earlier. In reality, the road here was hardly wide enough for one car to speed along. Passing wasn't as safe an option as it had been in other locations. But with the three cars all bunched together, did they have a choice?

It was time to prove that he knew Flora was the best driver in the tour.

Keeping his voice only loud enough for

Flora to hear over the engine, Jensen laid out his plan. "I know I've made it difficult for you to take risks to gain positions, but this time, I think you should try to pass despite how narrow the road is. You'll have to use the edge of the pasture."

Jensen held Flora's gaze as he watched her process his instructions. He prayed she could feel his confidence coming through.

After a moment, she nodded and turned her attention back to the road, where the team in front of them was inching forward. "Then let's get around this team and hold off Mr. Franklin and Sam."

As he'd been sure they would, the cows heaved into motion when the running engines drew close to them. They took their time, but that was better than having them stampede all around. Finally, the first car reached the last several cows standing in the way, with all the others cleared far enough off the road that the teams had a clear path to drive.

Without warning, loud honking split the air from behind them.

Jensen gripped the top of the car door, jerking around to see Archie squeezing the air horn attached next to his windshield. Panicked *moos* filled the air as the previously calm cows responded to the noise as Jensen had thought they would, with fear.

The driver in front of them stomped on the accelerator, and his car jerked forward and took off down the straight section of road, leaving a trail of scattering, wild-eyed cows. The temptation rose to curse Archie, but Jensen was in a better place now. He would respond graciously, as God would want him to.

Several cows bumped the Decauville as they loped past, and Flora gasped, her lips parted as she watched the massive beasts tramping around in every direction.

He put a soothing hand on her shoulder. "Don't worry about the team in front of us. Just keep driving. I'll watch for cows. Let's see if we can stay in front of Archie."

The Decauville lurched back into motion as Flora pushed the gas pedal in, and they moved forward. Thankfully, the rest of the cows ran away from the cars rather than toward them.

Jensen glanced back. "Archie will do exactly what I suggested you do, so be on the lookout for him to come around the side. They're catching up."

Jensen almost told Flora to slow down and let them pass. But showing her how much he trusted her to make these choices for them was too important. So he kept watch behind them as Archie approached, occasionally glancing ahead to see what was coming at them up the road.

Flora's hands gripped the steering wheel until

they turned white. "Jensen, it gets very narrow up there. Is that a bridge?"

Nodding, he looked back at Archie again. "Yes, one of those open bridges with no railing, so it's hard to see. If you can beat them to it, they'll have to back off a bit. The road winds around after that for several miles."

The engine growled as Flora pushed the accelerator harder. Jensen kept his eyes trained behind them, trying to ignore Archie's smug expression. "You're going to make it. He doesn't have enough room to pass now. Be careful to aim for the center of the bridge so none of the wheels drop off and pull us over the side."

Flora nodded but kept all her attention on the road ahead. Jensen glanced back. Archie's car was right on the back of Decauville, a mere foot from their bumper. With a wild grin, Archie jerked his steering wheel to the side, sending his car racing around the Decauville.

Too late, Jensen shouted a warning.

Flora glanced at the car coming up beside them and cried out. "The bridge is too close!"

They all gasped at the sound of metal crunching, and Flora slammed her foot on the brake, bringing the Decauville to a sudden stop in the middle of the bridge. Immediately, Jensen jumped out, followed by Flora and Fred. They ran to the edge of the bridge. Archie's car lay overturned in the deep ravine below, precariously propped up by young trees that grew along the shallow creek.

Jensen's hands shook as he wiped them on his trousers.

Flora whispered what they were all thinking. "Did they survive?"

A groan from below confirmed that at least one of the men was alive. Spurred into action, Jensen and Fred picked their way down the embankment, careful to secure footholds before each step so they wouldn't slide too far and end up in the water. They reached the toppled car and dropped to the ground to look for the occupants.

They were able to help Sam out without trouble, Jensen almost faint with relief to find that his friend was only scratched from the fall. One larger cut on his forehead dripped blood onto his cheek, but he was otherwise unharmed. Scrambling to the other side, Fred and Jensen worked at pulling back the brush, squeezing as far under the car as they could to try to see Archie.

From the top where she stood clutching hands with Beth, Flora called down, "What about Mr. Franklin? Where is he?"

Jensen returned to the passenger side and pushed his face under the car, catching a glimpse of cloth-covered limbs tangled in the wreckage. But he couldn't reach Archie. "Fred, Sam, lift that side as much as you can."

The car shifted, but it wasn't even close to far

enough. The sound of crunching grass told him Flora had joined the effort, but to no avail. The large car wouldn't move any farther.

"It's too heavy." Fred's voice sounded strained. "We can't hold it up."

Wriggling out from underneath, Jensen let his body flop back against a thin tree trunk as the others let the car rest on the ground again. "We aren't going to be able to get him out. He's pinned under the seat back. It . . . might already be too late."

Flora released a sob as his words settled into the silence surrounding them. "There has to be something we can do, Jensen. Can we go for help? We might be able to move it with more people to lift."

It was a thin thread of hope, but Fred jumped into action. "We're close to the next overnight stop, aren't we, Jensen? Beth and I will drive into town and get whatever help we can. Sam, come along and you can find a doctor who can be on hand when we get Archie out. I'm sure he'll need one."

But Sam didn't move, his eyes on the ground. "Are you sure you want to give up your chance to win in order to help us?"

They all stopped to look at him. Beth was the first to respond, her voice filled with kindness. "We can't leave you here. Why wouldn't we help?"

Sam finally looked up, and tears streamed down his cheeks. "We've been cheating the entire time. Cutting through fields to stay in front. Archie even paid some locals to move those markers you missed a couple of days ago. And I knew all along he convinced you to sabotage your car at the beginning, Jensen, but I didn't say anything to stop him."

Shock kept everyone from responding for the longest minutes of Jensen's life. His eyes were glued to Flora, who stared at the upended car with emotions flitting across her face. Sam was wrong, but weren't there more important things at stake than Jensen defending himself?

Praying Flora didn't take Sam's claim seriously, Jensen pushed up from the ground to go to her, but she held out a hand to stop him. "We need to get Mr. Franklin out. Then we can face the consequences of everyone's choices. Sam, we won't leave the two of you in this state, regardless of what either of you might have done. You go with Fred and Beth. Hurry."

Chapter 21

Flora prayed no one else noticed the way her hands were shaking as she directed everyone into action. She wasn't sure how much longer she could remain upright, her legs threatening to buckle under her. If she could make it through until the group left in the Decauville, she could take a moment to get herself pulled together.

If only she could jump into the car with them, she could get away from the terrible sight of the overturned car. But the hot sun brought a sheen of perspiration to Beth's skin, and the strain of worry visibly weighed the other woman down. Sam looked as if he was about to cry, his eyes locked on the car with Mr. Franklin somewhere underneath. They both needed to get some space from the accident to recover from the shock of it.

While Fred climbed up the bank to Beth's side, Sam finally pushed up from the ground and stood in front of Flora. He grabbed her arm, his voice low so no one would overhear but intense in a way she'd never heard from him. "You don't have to give up the tour, Flora. All of you can go. Just stop and inform the doctor in Pittsfield of our location. Then get to the check-in. Show Archie his way of going about winning was the wrong way."

It was such a tempting plan. Flora glanced at Jensen, whose eyes hadn't left her since Sam's admission. He'd gone pale and shoved his hands deep into his pockets. Was it possible that what Sam said was true? Could Jensen be as guilty as he looked?

Flora pulled her gaze away from him to focus on Sam. "No, we need to show him the right way by proving that others are more important than ourselves. Jensen and I will stay here and try to get Mr. Franklin out. As much as he's done wrong, his life is still worth more than winning a race."

Sam started climbing up the embankment as Flora gathered her strength to stay with Jensen. Her mind refused to stop hearing Sam's admission over and over. He'd said Jensen had sabotaged their team. What did that mean? Had Jensen intentionally damaged the Decauville the day they had to stop before the check-in point? Or could he have made them miss that turn after Bretton Woods?

Sam had planted the seed of doubt about Jensen in her mind at the beginning of the tour. But even though she'd contrived to keep an eye on him, she'd never believed he would hurt their team. Now Sam's revelation had her questioning every moment of the tour, everything Jensen had said or done. He'd been so unhappy about racing to begin with. Had he hoped a few mishaps would convince her to drop out of the tour early?

Her stomach heaved even considering the possibility in light of their closeness now. But last week, before all the time they'd spent together, all the growth she believed they'd both experienced, would he have done it? Jensen had told her all about Mr. Franklin's dislike of him and how the other man had been blamed for Gregory's death. Had Mr. Franklin used the guilt Jensen carried to convince him to force the Harrison Goods team out of the tour? Perhaps told him they would be safer back in Philadelphia?

There were so many questions swirling in her mind alongside worry for Sam and even Mr. Franklin that Flora could only sink to the ground in confused exhaustion as soon as the Decauville was out of sight. The skittling of loose rocks signaled Jensen's approach, and his hand tentatively slid over hers. She wanted to push him away, but also to turn and bury her face in his chest. "I don't know what to think, Jensen. What to believe."

"I hope you'll believe me when I tell you I didn't sabotage the car or our run." He sounded as broken as he looked. But could she trust him? Or was he only upset over being found out?

She let him continue stroking the back of her hand but tried in vain not to enjoy it. "Why would Sam lie?"

"I think Archie is the one who lied. Sam probably doesn't know I chose not to take Archie up on his offer. Archie likes to twist the truth to make people do what he wants. If he saw a way to get Sam to keep helping him cheat by saying I was part of it, too, he would have. Flora, please believe that I never did it. I kept Archie's demands a secret because I thought I could protect all of us and still help you get what you wanted so badly. I'm sorry I failed."

She wanted to believe him. But he'd already shown he was willing to do anything to secure their safety. The end of the Mount Washington race flashed in her mind, the moment when he'd wrenched the steering wheel from her hands and destroyed any chance she had to pass those last two cars and win. He hadn't cared what she wanted then, much less trusted her to get it on her own. He did what he thought would protect her physically, no matter how much it ended up hurting her emotionally.

A moan rang out from the overturned car. They both jumped to their feet and rushed over, one on each side of the vehicle.

Flora dropped to her knees and pressed her cheek against the ground, straining to look underneath. "Mr. Franklin? We're here, but we can't move the car. Sam went for help."

On the opposite side, Jensen forced his way as far under the car as he could get, reaching out toward the trapped man. "Do you hear us, Archie? Can you move at all?"

Another moan was the only answer, no movement that Flora could detect. Dropping back onto the ground next to the car, she forced her breathing into a regular pattern instead of the gasps her lungs wanted to take. The reality of what they faced was sinking in, pushing away worries about whatever Jensen may have done.

This was all so reminiscent of what she'd imagined when she learned about Henri's accident. Had she been the cause of another lethal crash? For all her words to Jensen about healing, the pain of her part in Henri's death ripped her heart open all over again. How many lives would have to be lost because of her actions?

For what felt like an eternity, Flora and Jensen took turns trying to get as close to Mr. Franklin as possible, talking to him all the time. But there was no improvement, only an occasional moan that told them at least he hadn't died. Yet. Flora couldn't imagine the extent of injuries that could be caused by a car as heavy as the White Steamer pinning a man down for so long.

At the sound of an engine rumbling toward them, Flora raced to the top of the embankment while Jensen remained with Mr. Franklin. Her heart sank as not one but two teams approached, slowing near the group on the embankment. The first driver pulled his car to a stop on the bridge and pushed up his driving goggles to examine the scene. "Anything we can do?"

There were only four of them between the two cars, not enough to lift the Steamer until more arrived. "We have a doctor and local help coming. It might be beneficial to have your help when we move the car, but I don't know how long it will be before they return. And you'll risk losing your position in the tour."

In both cars, the men exchanged glances. The first pair whispered together for a moment. Then they apologized even while restarting their vehicles. The two teams resumed their journey, taking care to move with caution until they were well away from the creek.

Flora tried not to let getting passed distract her from the more important situation in front of them. She'd made a choice for their team, the right choice. The consequences weren't unexpected. She'd known when she decided to stay that they would lose any chance to finish in first place. But deep down, she'd hoped somehow they wouldn't lose too many positions.

As time wore on, she stopped counting how many teams passed over the bridge, some stopping to see if they could help and some simply driving by slowly, but none agreeing to wait until there were enough hands to move the car.

When another engine rumbled toward them, Flora stood on the bridge until she could see that it was, indeed, the Decauville. Fred and another man sat in front, while Beth and Sam sat in the back. "They've come back, Jensen. It looks as if they have a doctor."

Fred had hardly stopped the car when Sam jumped out of the back. "There's a wagon of men coming behind us to help, but the car is faster. It'll be a few minutes before they get here."

The doctor nodded a solemn greeting in Flora's direction as he picked his way down the hill with Fred and Sam. Along with Jensen, they all lined up along one side of the White Steamer and started lifting, trying to tip it over on its side to free Mr. Franklin.

But it wasn't enough. Sam dropped to the ground after their third failed attempt. "It's too heavy. He couldn't survive this unharmed, could he, Doc?"

The doctor assessed the situation from his spot next to Fred, his lips pressed into a tight line. "I don't know. Assumptions won't help. We need to get him out and see what his injuries are. Then we'll deal with what may be."

The wagon filled with six more local men finally clattered over the bridge, and the entire group joined together on the higher side of the car. Again, they all lifted and pushed as one, trying to tip the car over from its top to the side.

And this time, they succeeded. A cheer rang out

as the car crashed farther down into the creek. Flora got as close as possible to the spot where the car had been, peering between the shoulders of the men now surrounding the site. The doctor leaned over Mr. Franklin, blocking Flora's view while they all seemed to hold their breath, waiting for his evaluation.

When Sam pushed his way through the group and lost the contents of his stomach into the tall grass a few feet away, then collapsed on the ground, pale and shaking, Flora grimaced. It had probably been a good thing that she couldn't see the wrecked car and its injured occupant. She sat beside Sam, both of them listening for any updates.

After far too long, the doctor finally stood and addressed the group. "Thanks to all of you working together, this man will live. But he's in very bad condition. Mr. Lerner, can we use your wagon to transport him back to town? The car will be too small for him to remain stretched out."

A sob burst from Sam as the other men started working together to move Mr. Franklin into the wagon.

Flora put her arm around Sam's shaking shoulders. "It's all right. At least he'll live."

"But at what cost? What kind of life is it if his legs are crushed beyond use?"

Flora's stomach clenched at the harsh description of Mr. Franklin's condition. "Many people have lived through injuries as bad as that and had fulfilling lives."

Sam stood and pushed his way after the others. "I'm going along. Nothing I do could ever make this better, but staying with him is at least something."

A melancholy pall settled over everyone as several men helped the doctor lift Archie and maneuver him up the hill and into the back of the wagon. Sam climbed in the back and sat with him while the doctor squeezed onto the narrow seat next to the farmer who owned the wagon. With a flick of the reins, the horses headed back toward town with the men who had come to help walking behind, the procession as somber as if they were headed to a funeral.

Jensen trudged to the top of the embankment, surprised to see how little daylight remained.

Handing Jensen the jacket he'd discarded in the grass hours ago, Fred offered a weary smile. "Pittsfield isn't far. Let's get to the hotel so we can eat and rest. We all need it."

The half-hearted group returned to the Decauville. Flora started the car, and they rode the rest of the way to the last tour stop in silence. It was dark by the time they arrived.

Jensen hoped to get to Flora's side as soon as she stepped down from the car, but Fred stopped him before he could reach her. "I'm going to take Beth to get freshened up and rest for a few minutes. Do you and Flora want to visit Sam and Archie at the hospital after that?"

Turning to see Flora marching straight to the nearest official to take on the difficult task of explaining what had happened, Jensen knew what her answer would be. "Yes, I'll let her know, and we'll meet you in the lobby in an hour."

Fred slipped his arm around his wife, and the couple trudged toward the hotel. Jensen hedged closer to Flora, trying to stay nearby without getting in her way as she recounted the events of the day for the officials. Getting past the herd of cows, trying to hold off Archie, racing to the bridge. While she never laid blame on anyone, the consequences of Jensen's actions rang in every word of the story. This tragedy was his fault, just as it had been with Gregory.

Flora finished her conversation with the officials and didn't wait to watch them inspect the car. Instead, she immediately strode toward the hotel without even a backward glance at Jensen. She was angry with him. And for good reason, if she believed what Sam said and doubted Jensen's weak explanations.

But he intended to keep trying. He wasn't going to lose her without a fight.

But when was the right moment to push? Should he explain the entire story of how Archie blackmailed him? Or wait until she had time to process all that had happened that day?

In the end, he simply ran to catch up with her, following her into a hotel that was smaller and rather plainer than most they'd stayed in during the tour. Inside, a noisy party was underway in the dining room. Flora paused in the doorway, watching the other teams as they gathered to celebrate the last night of the tour. Jensen stood as close to her as he thought she'd allow, close enough that he could see tears forming in her eyes. It wasn't difficult to understand why. Tomorrow they would all pull across the finish line, where they'd started in front of the AAA headquarters, and a winner would be declared.

But after choosing to stay with Archie, the Harrison Goods team was out of the running.

The majority of the teams still hadn't lost a single point. There was no way all of them would do so before arriving in New York City the next day. That fact must have hit Flora as she spun around and trekked across the hotel lobby. But their day wasn't over . . . yet.

Before she escaped to her room, Jensen rushed to grab her arm, stopping her as gently as he could. She froze, then met his gaze. It was only a brief moment, but enough longing enlivened those chocolate depths to encourage his heart. She might be angry, but she also cared. "Fred asked if he and Beth could walk over to the hospital with us after we clean up. To visit Sam and Mr. Franklin. If you're up to it."

His awkward invitation was met with a curt nod. "I'll be down in a bit," was her only response.

Jensen let her go, praying that rest and time would open her heart to hear the truth—that he never actually did anything to hurt their chances of winning the tour.

Upstairs in his room, Jensen splashed water over his dirt-smeared face and neck, then changed out of equally dirty clothes into a pair of nicer trousers and a clean—if wrinkled—white shirt. He brushed his jacket off the best he could. At least he'd been warm enough to remove it as soon as they went down the embankment, so it had been saved from most of the mud his other clothes were covered in.

Then he immediately felt terrible for thinking about his clothing when a man was lying in the hospital with grave, possibly fatal injuries all because of Jensen thinking they could beat him in a race.

Abandoning any further efforts to freshen up, Jensen headed back downstairs, past the boisterous dinner, and outside. Fred and Beth were already waiting next to the plain clapboard building. Jensen's heart ached at the drawn expression on Beth's tired face. A woman expecting a baby didn't need this kind of strain.

But that was nothing compared to the grief

ravaging Flora's face when she joined them. She'd been crying, he could tell. And he longed to wrap his arms around her and reassure her that everything would work out.

If only he could make that be the truth for her.

The group set off on foot toward the hospital, following Fred, who had picked up the doctor there earlier and thus knew the way. He slid his arm around Beth, the couple giving each other support through their physical connection.

Jensen glanced at Flora out of the corner of his eye as she walked next to him. For the last few days, he'd thought he had a right to kiss her as he had last night. He'd imagined a future with her in it. He'd glimpsed the possibility of working through his past mistakes and regaining the life he'd dreamed of before Gregory died. But now?

A wave of sorrow almost knocked him off his feet. Would his mistakes once again tear away what was dearest in his life? Five years ago, it had been his stupid choice that cost Gregory his life and forced Jensen to reject his life's passion. Now, it was like that day all over again, except this time, he was being turned away by the one person he wanted in his life more than anything.

They reached the two-story brick hospital building, unremarkable except for the large white-and-red sign painted on the wall to identify it. Inside, they were directed by a nurse toward a room at the end of a quiet hallway. Fred stopped at the door with Beth at his side. "We'll stay out here. You two have more to say to them, and it won't help Archie rest to have a room full of visitors all at once."

Flora looked up at Jensen, uncertainty in her wide eyes. He took her hand, relieved when she let him. Then he led her through the door.

Inside, brass fixtures hanging from the high ceiling provided electric light for the room. It was silent, Archie's form lying still under a blanket on the only one of the eight beds that was occupied. There was no missing the ramifications of the accident. The length of Archie's legs under the bedding was far too short. They'd both been amputated.

Nearby, Sam was sprawled in a wooden chair with his chin almost touching his chest, heavy breathing indicating he had dozed off. Should they announce their presence or not? Jensen was ready to turn around and tiptoe out when Archie's voice croaked out his name. "Don't go. I'm awake."

At the words, Sam jerked out of his sleep, jumping up from the chair as soon as he saw them. "Oh, hello. I'll go and give you a few minutes. The doctor said he needs to rest a lot, so it can't be long."

He skirted out the door, leaving Jensen and Flora alone with Archie. They went to his side and stood in awkward silence until Archie relieved them of the pressure of figuring out what to say. "I guess I owe you my thanks. Sam told me you gave up your opportunity to win to stay with me."

Jensen shrugged. "We couldn't leave you there."

"You could have. It's what I might have done if the situation was reversed."

Flora gasped at the blunt words.

Archie barked out a harsh laugh. "You may not want to hear it, but that's the truth. I was awake enough under there that I had to think about some things, to look back at how I've been acting. And if I'm honest—which I'd like to be from here on out—I'm not sure I'd have even stopped if you were the ones upside down in that ravine." Archie fought to push himself up on the pillows.

Before he could think better of it, Jensen reached out and put an arm around the man's shoulders to help.

Archie nodded a brief thanks, then grimaced as he settled back against the headboard. "You're too polite to mention it, but no doubt you've noticed the doctor had to take my legs, both at the knees. They were too crushed to heal."

The words hung in the air between the three of them. Flora sank to the edge of the bed next to Archie. Her voice was raw when she finally spoke. "I'm so sorry. I shouldn't have pushed so hard to get to the bridge first. I hope you'll forgive me someday."

He looked up, clearly startled. "Forgive you? You didn't make me pull out there. It's not as though you drove me off the road or anything. I would have done it to you, given the chance, but no one would ever believe you caused this. I was blinded by wanting revenge and made a stupid choice. I'm just glad the one suffering the consequences is me, not Sam or any of you."

Jensen didn't know what to do with the sincere change in Archie's demeanor. "It would be better if no one had to suffer. I hate that our feud came to this. We could have cleared the air years ago if I wasn't so set on protecting myself. And here you're letting a tragedy change you for the better, something I could never manage to do."

Archie tilted his head as he thought about that. "You're right, we should have handled this a long time ago. But we didn't. Both of us are at fault for that. But we can do better moving forward."

A weight Jensen hadn't even been aware of lifted from his heart. He stuck out a hand and shook Archie's. "We can and we will."

A knock sounded at the door a second before a nurse opened it wide and gestured for Jensen and Flora to leave. "Mr. Franklin needs to rest now. You'll have to go."

They left the room with promises to visit Archie once he was recovering back in Philadelphia.

As they headed toward Fred and Beth, who had walked to the far end of the hall, Flora finally spoke to Jensen. "I want to find Sam. I need to speak with him. Alone."

Nodding, Jensen paused and watched her until she disappeared around a corner. Maybe talking with Sam would help her see the truth in what he'd tried to tell her that afternoon rather than cement the idea that he had sabotaged them. But whether it did or didn't, the conversation with Archie had brought clarity to his mind. For the last five years, Jensen had been blinded by regret for his failings. It hadn't driven him to change—instead, it had caused him to hide.

Until Flora.

Now, instead of sending him running in the wake of another mistake, her encouragement over the last week showed him there was hope that he could work through the problems his choices caused. He didn't have to remain stuck in a life that was going nowhere. And he was ready to stand and face it all if it meant he might get to have her next to him when he came through the other side.

Chapter 22

Flora found Sam sprawled in a chair in an alcove at the front of the hospital, a dim space that was empty of other visitors. The late hour and long day were starting to take a toll on Flora, and she felt as drained as Sam looked, but she needed some answers. Quite frankly, she didn't know if she could trust anything Mr. Franklin or Jensen would say to her. So she dropped onto a cushioned chair next to Sam and let her head rest in her hands.

Sam straightened in his seat and reached out to rest one hand on her shoulder. "Flora, you should go to the hotel and rest. There's nothing anyone can do here."

Looking into his grief-ravaged face, she patted his hand, trying to communicate as much comfort as possible. "No, we can't heal his body. But you both need friends around you to keep your spirits up."

"What about the tour? You can still finish."

Anguish over losing points—and their chance to win—overtook Flora for a moment. There had hardly been time during the day to think through all that the events had cost them. But Flora pushed away the feeling. She'd shed enough tears in her room earlier. There were more important issues to face now. "I don't have any right to worry about a silly car race when we almost lost two lives today."

Sam shook his head. "You have a responsibility to Mr. Harrison to finish. You should honor that. Archie and I are together here. We'll be fine until I can get him home. That will take longer than it will for the tour to finish. You have one more day, Flora. Go finish it."

Unable to sit, Flora stood and paced the small space between their pair of chairs and another set of empty ones nearby. "What's the benefit in finishing? I'll probably make another thoughtless, ambition-driven choice that will harm someone else."

Looking up in surprise, Sam's voice grew stronger with resolve. "That's completely untrue. You didn't cause this. Archie chose to try to pass at the last second. He knew we were far too close to the bridge."

No matter what Sam or Jensen said, there was surely more she could have done. But there was another pressing matter she needed to bring up before she lost the chance. "Sam, what did you mean about Jensen sabotaging our team?"

Leaning back in his chair, Sam sighed. "Every day, Archie convinced me to do more and more questionable things. First, it was cutting through properties. That didn't seem so bad. It saved us a lot of time and didn't hurt anyone. Before he started causing damage, at least. Then I learned he was paying locals to cause problems, like cleaning up the confetti markers and blocking the road with wagons. He was so determined to prove himself to Mr. Dorman and beat Jensen that he would have done anything to stay ahead."

Flora leaned forward, silently encouraging him to continue.

Sam hung his head. "I knew he had a plan to get back at Jensen for what he faced after Gregory died. I didn't know what he intended to do until I overheard Archie insisting that Jensen had to stop your team from winning. I was under the car checking the brakes, and they didn't know I heard it all. I didn't believe Jensen would go through with it, but then you had a string of bad runs and there was that day you had to stop and make repairs before the check-in. So much went wrong that I had to wonder."

Flora's head ached from trying to sort out the truth. Had Jensen contrived the situations that kept them from moving up in the tour? Had he somehow caused the loose line that made the Decauville run so badly that day? But if so, why did he repair the car before they reached the check-in?

No matter the reasons, they still lost so many spots in those first days on the tour that it could have been more than bad luck. Her concern was whether Jensen agreed to Mr. Franklin's plan in the first place. It didn't matter if he changed his mind in time.

Or did it? He'd encouraged her so much since the night she'd revealed her past at the Mount Washington Hotel. Since their first kiss. Had he been trying to assuage his guilt over causing them to fall behind? Her stomach churned with that thought. Everything he'd done and said since the midpoint of the race could have been the result of guilt. Had he felt it even when he kissed her? When he held her hand or put his arm around her?

Flora's lungs didn't seem capable of moving enough air, and her eyes swam. Sam was watching her with red eyes and slumped shoulders. "I'm sorry, Flora. I'm so sorry I let it get out of control."

Forcing aside her own pain, she grabbed Sam's hand to get his attention. "No, you have nothing to apologize for. Jensen and Mr. Franklin made these choices. You and I could have done a few things differently, but their mistakes caused this mess. Their rivalry would have ended in tragedy one way or another."

Sam's mood seemed to lighten as her words sank into his heart. She managed to put a smile on her face as she stood. "We'll see you back in Philadelphia, Sam. Take good care of Mr. Franklin for us. We'll clear the air once everyone is settled at home. But don't let your feelings lie to you about being at fault any longer."

With a final squeeze of his hand to let him know he wasn't alone in his pain, Flora bid Sam good night and went to find the others. He was right. The Harrison Goods team needed to finish the race they'd started. Whether they could win or not, Flora had to stop letting choices made by selfish men impact her life. She'd let Clement control her for too many years. Even Henri had forced his preferences on her too often. It was time to prove she could stand on her own.

Through the night, her confidence wavered. But when morning light dawned on the last day of the tour, Flora was ready. She would run the best leg she could and finish with pride. She was in the Decauville before any of her companions emerged from their rooms. The extra time alone was well spent in prayer, sending up supplications for Mr. Franklin and Sam as well as for the other teams to remain safe. And she may have thrown in a request or two for herself, for her bruised heart to heal from whatever Jensen had done when she finally sorted out the truth.

Flora leaned forward and rested her head on the steering wheel, letting the sounds of the city stirring for the day accompany her pain. Sam's words had torn a hole in her heart yesterday, but the moment she realized all Jensen's affection and support might have been out of guilt was enough to bring her to her knees.

And now she faced an entire day by his side.

She would need all the fortification she could get, and God was the only one she had left to lean on. In a moment when everyone else was failing her, His faithfulness stood out in stark contrast. So she continued in prayer, repeating the same desperate pleas for strength until the others joined her and engines started roaring to life.

As they started the final day of the tour, there was a calmness about Flora that was impossible to miss. A good thing, for after visiting Archie at the hospital, Jensen had come away feeling the complete opposite. But if someone had to suffer, let it be him, not Flora, who had already been through so much.

He regretted that he hadn't taken the chance last night—while they'd both been there with Archie—to clear the air on Sam's claim that Jensen sabotaged the team. Flora didn't seem inclined to believe him, so maybe Archie could have told her the truth in a way that would have convinced her Jensen didn't go through with anything.

But Jensen hadn't felt right about bringing it up when Archie was suffering such a great loss. Jensen kept remembering the other man's anguished face when he had to explain that his legs were gone. He would like to think he'd handle a tragedy of such magnitude with enough strength and confidence that he would emerge a better man. But it was much more likely he would have been devastated, broken, and unable to adjust to a new life. And that realization hurt as much as anything he'd experienced so far.

Jensen had always considered himself capable in his own right, strong enough to handle whatever was thrown at him. He'd lost his parents at a young age, lost his best friend in an accident of his own making, and lost all direction in his life. But still, he'd managed to get by. Maybe he hadn't led the most successful life, but he'd survived it all.

For the last few days, since he rediscovered his faith at Bretton Woods, he'd thought he was relying on God. He was making a point to live by the standards he'd been taught in church as a child. But it had become very clear as he stood by Archie's side that if he was the one in that bed, he would be trying to rely on his own strength to recover. Everything he'd done in his life had revolved around self-preservation. He'd doubted that he could trust God with his life. And where had that gotten him?

He'd been living with no purpose, no hope that the future would be better than his past, no comfort of knowing he wasn't alone. And that wasn't a joyful, fulfilling existence for anyone. The parallels between his life and Archie's were too great to ignore. He knew without a doubt that if he hadn't had Mr. Harrison and Gregory in his life, he would have ended up the same bitter, angry, vengeful man that Archie had been. He very well might have ended up in a hospital bed like Archie too. But he'd never stopped to recognize God's hand in his life, the blessing that the Harrison family was. He'd only assumed they would toss him aside at the first hint that he wasn't perfect, that he made mistakes.

He'd planned on explaining his past actions to the Harrisons upon their return to Philadelphia, but only out of fear that Archie would do it first. Now, he *wanted* to tell them. He wanted the air cleared and the past open to talk about and learn from. He was ready to move forward, not remain stuck in his mistakes.

But there was one thing he wasn't so confident he knew what to do about.

As he climbed into the car next to Flora, his heart sank when she refused to even glance his way. She greeted Fred and Beth, asking how Beth was feeling, but then she kept her eyes trained on the many cars in front of them.

Still, Jensen had to try. "Flora, can we talk before we leave?"

Without looking over, she shook her head. "I'd like to focus on the drive, please. Of course, there's no reason to push ourselves today, but I'd like to get us back to New York without any more tragedies occurring."

Pushing her probably wouldn't help the situation, so he leaned back against the plush seat and pulled out the now-worn route map. If they couldn't make things right before the finish line, at least they could have a good run for the final leg. It might be the last time Jensen ever got to sit in a car with Flora.

And that bleak thought refused to leave him in peace.

As the Decauville heaved into motion at the end of the line of cars, the truth of that reality hit him hard in the gut. He'd been assuming that if he could say the right things to Flora, she'd see that he hadn't done what Sam claimed. But there was no proof to back him up. If she chose to believe Sam, and Sam chose to believe Archie, what could Jensen say that would change either of their minds?

Had he lost Flora before he even had a chance to make her part of his life?

The bouncing of the car over rough, rutted roads was almost unnoticeable compared to the rending in his heart. For so long, he'd refused to entertain the idea of a woman in his life, of opening himself up to falling in love and having a family. He hadn't felt worthy of such a blessing. Somewhere along this journey, Flora had covertly convinced him otherwise. He'd started hoping there could be a future for them together. He hadn't even realized how much he wanted it until that dream was about to be snatched away from him.

He managed to give Flora the directions she needed to keep them on track, but he was hardly aware of doing so. Every time he looked at her, his heart ripped open a little more. If she wouldn't believe him and she chose to stay in Philadelphia with her brother but Jensen couldn't be part of her life, he would have to leave. Remaining so near her while knowing he couldn't love her the way he wanted was a torture he couldn't withstand. He would either have to convince her of the truth or leave everything and everyone else he loved in order to stay away from her.

With no reason to hurry, Flora stopped the car for a picnic lunch next to a picturesque creek outside a small town in Connecticut, where they watched birds flitting through the trees that lined the road as they ate. It was far more peaceful than any part of Jensen's heart that day. He had to take his chance before Flora was lost to him forever.

As if they knew he needed time with Flora, Fred and Beth claimed they wanted to stretch their legs and took their sandwiches for a slow walk down the creek bank. Sitting next to Flora on a blanket by the trickling water, Jensen got to the point before she could find a way to escape him. "Please hear me out. That's all I ask."

She hesitated for long enough that his heart

dropped, certain she would deny him. But finally, she responded with a curt nod.

His lungs finally took a full breath again. "Archie did try to force me to sabotage our team. He threatened to send word to Mr. Harrison that I was responsible for Gregory's death. All I wanted was the chance to explain myself, instead of an impersonal letter breaking his heart all over again. So I stalled, told Archie I'd think about it."

Her jaw tightened at that admission. Jensen nearly lost his nerve to continue. What was the point if she'd already made up her mind? But he had to tell her the entire truth, whether she believed him or not. It was time for the secrets to end.

"I managed to get through the first part of the tour without promising him anything, but then we had that rainy day with the ferry crossing and the repairs we had to make on the side of the road. I suppose he thought I went through with it and those things were my fault. He backed off and left me alone until he saw how well we were doing after the midpoint. He must have felt the need to put more pressure on me so we wouldn't beat him. He started threatening the safety of our team. And then he told Fred."

Fear of how she would respond made it impossible for Jensen to sit still. He jumped up and paced the length of the blanket Flora still sat on. "You may not believe me, knowing everything I kept from you and from those I love most for all this time. But I need to do all I can to repair the rift between us. I'm tired of secrets and worrying that people will be angry with me. I'm ready to take responsibility for all I've done, starting with the fact that I hurt you."

He looked at her then, his throat tightening at the hard expression on her face. Jensen dropped to his knees next to her and took her hand in his. She didn't stop him, but she also didn't soften. "Flora, you mean so much to me. I pray that you can forgive me and that you'll come to see my intention was never to hurt you or our team. I only did what I thought I could to protect us all. I'm sorry it went so wrong."

He searched her lovely, precious features, still seeing nothing to indicate she believed his words. He could do no more, so he dropped her hand and retreated to the car, letting his roiling emotions pour in a silent prayer that echoed through his entire being. *Lord, I did what I could. I'm going to trust You with my love for Flora. Please bring her back to me somehow.*

Chapter 23

Flora felt terrible. She hated the mournful look on Jensen's face every time she snuck a peek at him out of the corner of her eye. She wanted more than anything to fling her arms around his neck and tell him it didn't matter if he'd tried to ruin her chances to win. If only they could ignore the entire thing and chase a happy ending together.

But she couldn't do that. It did matter if he did what Sam claimed. Because she couldn't commit her life to a man who would do something so underhanded to control her and protect himself. Clement had always done whatever was necessary to protect himself at the expense of Flora and Owen, the people who should have meant the most to him. She refused to let a person like that be part of her life again.

Which would be so much easier if she didn't already love Jensen.

There was no getting around it. She did love him. When he'd taken her hand by the creek and apologized, her heart had wanted to burst into a thousand pieces. She saw a future without him stretching out before her, and it made her want to lock herself away and cry for the rest of her days.

As much as she'd thought she loved Henri,

she'd never felt such a deep need to tell him her every thought.

Such a profound feeling of loss when he wasn't by her side.

Such an ache when she imagined seeing him at family events and having no claim to his heart.

Perhaps it was for the best that they weren't in the running to win the tour anymore. Flora couldn't concentrate on the road. She followed Jensen's instructions to get them back to the finish line at the AAA building, but she was hardly aware of any of the drive. The only thing she could focus on was his miserable face when she couldn't say she believed him.

But why would Sam lie? Unless, as Jensen had guessed at the scene of the accident, Sam didn't know the truth either. Maybe Sam thought he was telling her the truth when Mr. Franklin was the one who had lied. How could she know for sure? Was Jensen the selfish scoundrel Sam made him out to be, or the kind, caring man she thought she knew?

It was too much to sort out while trying to finish what should have been a triumphant experience in her life. Flora had driven well during the tour. She'd almost gotten them clear up through the field into a winning position before the accident. She should be proud of herself and her team for persevering and making it through despite all the obstacles they'd had to work around.

Instead, she was miserable.

Because she only wanted to experience such a moment if she could enjoy it with Jensen, and that was no longer possible.

They drove over the finish line to the sound of shouts and cheers from a crowd of onlookers, but Flora couldn't help feeling they didn't deserve much praise for a twentieth-place finish. Not after having a real chance to win and losing it because of a feud. Not after the relationship she'd come to rely on had been fractured.

The team climbed from the car and joined the other competitors who had all gathered in the AAA reception hall. It was time to find out the winner of the tour, but the Harrison Goods team mustered little excitement for the celebration.

Once the last few teams arrived, one of the head officials moved to the podium, and the entire room fell silent. "Well done, ladies and gentlemen!"

Cheers and applause filled the room, and the official waited with a grin until it quieted down enough to continue. "The Glidden Reliability Tour was quite a success. We set out to introduce the idea of automobiles as part of daily life to the country, and we achieved that goal. Newspapers around the world have followed your progress over the last ten days, and the public has been captivated by the stories you created." He paused for effect, and there was more applause, less raucous than the first round but still too cheerful for Flora's mood. "I know you're all aware that there is still one item left before we can conclude the first running of the Glidden Reliability Tour—and that is to determine the winner."

The crowd cheered again, but the official went on, raising his voice over the widespread speculation that began flying around the room. "Since the tour was run on a points system and you are all such skilled drivers, the majority of the finishing teams had perfect scores. As we explained in the beginning, each person who drove or rode in the tour gets a vote for the team that was the most skilled and sportsmanlike, the one who will best represent the good names of Mr. Glidden and the American Automobile Association."

As the man left the podium, other officials started handing out ballots and directing people to a locked voting box at the front of the room. Unable to bear the frivolity any longer, Flora slipped out amongst the disarray of team members and passengers debating who they were voting for. She found a quiet spot at the farthest end of a long hall and sank back against the wall to gather her thoughts.

Before she'd had enough time, Beth joined her, looking flushed after spending time in the hot, crowded reception room. Flora offered her the closest thing to a smile she could manage, but

Beth wasn't fooled. Nor was she about to beat around the bush. "What's going on between you and Jensen? Before yesterday, I was certain there was romance in the air. I saw him take your hand on several occasions. He looked at you like a man falling in love. What happened?"

Flora sighed. She'd been naïve to think she could escape Beth and Fred noticing anything going on, with them all being in such tight quarters for so long. "You're right, I thought we were falling in love too. But then Sam said Jensen sabotaged us, that he jeopardized our chances of winning to protect himself. Jensen says Mr. Franklin tried to force him to do it, threatening to hurt the Harrisons with his secret about Gregory, but that he still didn't go through with it. I don't know who to believe."

Beth chewed at her lower lip. "I have to believe Jensen. He's been so concerned about keeping us all safe this entire time. He wouldn't do anything that could harm us."

"But quitting the tour—or being unable to finish because of damage to the car—would have meant we'd go back to our safe lives without continuing to risk anything."

Tipping her head to one side, Beth thought that over. "I can see the logic in that. But I still don't think Jensen would do it. He's too good a man to go along with something so underhanded. Are you certain that's what happened?"

Flora started pacing the narrow hall, her steps matching the rapid rhythm of questions that hadn't stopped running through her mind since the day before. "I'm not certain of anything right now, Beth. Sam is a good man too. I don't believe he's lying. And Jensen admitted to keeping things from others, thinking he could protect himself and them. Look at how long he lived with the truth of his part in Gregory's death, not telling a soul. He's very capable of hiding things when he thinks it's in someone's best interest."

Beth considered that. But then she straightened and gave Flora a soft smile. "Sometimes you have to trust the person you love. There are moments when it looks hopeless, when we feel so hurt by the behavior of someone we thought cared about us. It's happened to me and Fred too. We're all human with the flaws and sins that accompany that state. You'll hurt him, too, break his trust, even. You may have already. The difference in a relationship that lasts is that each person is humble enough to realize that they're just as broken and capable of causing hurt as the other. Neither person holds any regretted, confessed actions against the other. Part of commitment is choosing to offer forgiveness as God offers it to us."

Beth went to Flora, and they wrapped their arms around each other. After a long embrace, she leaned back to look at Flora. "Don't miss the chance to experience love with Jensen because you're afraid of the hurt. Work through this with him instead of striving against him. It will be worth the effort."

With one last encouraging smile, Beth left Flora alone in the hall and returned to the party. Flora still wasn't in the mood to celebrate much of anything, but a tendril of hope wound its way through her heart. Could a decision to trust Jensen repair the damage from all the bad choices that had been made? It might be too simple to solve all of their problems, but perhaps it was the only way to start.

Jensen had noticed when the ladies slipped from the room, but he was confident following them wasn't his best course of action, no matter how much he wanted to plead his case to Flora again.

He knew he'd made the right choice when Beth returned and headed straight toward him. Standing with her hands on her hips, she was clearly on a mission. "Jensen, did you sabotage the car?"

"No. Archie was trying to force me to, and the timing of our issues on the road made him and Sam believe I did. But I didn't do it, I promise you."

Beth relaxed, resting one hand on her stomach while the other pointed at the door. "Then you better figure out a way to prove your trustworthiness to Flora before it's too late."

"Too late?" Fred looked back and forth between them, blinking with a frown.

Beth gave her husband an indulgent pat on the arm. "They're falling in love, Fred. And you know I couldn't stand to see a good love story ruined by one stupid mistake and all this confusion."

Jensen's heartbeat started a racing staccato. "Falling in love?"

"Now, it isn't my place to say things you two need to say to each other. Just find a way to prove it to her, Jensen. A gesture that means she can trust you with her heart, one she can't deny. Now, Fred, I see cream puffs over there and must have one. Or a few. Let's go."

Stunned, Jensen watched the couple weave their way through the reveling teams with their arms entwined. In the background, he heard the announcement of the winner, Percy Pierce, who received more than twice the votes of any other driver. Mr. Pierce made his way to collect his trophy as Jensen sank into a nearby chair. Could Flora feel the same way he did? He was desperate to believe she might love him but hadn't let himself even dream it with all that was standing between them.

If she did, Beth was right. He needed to prove himself to her. But how? How did a man make up for so many mistakes?

It was a question that plagued him the entire way back to Philadelphia the next day. The drive flew by without a hitch. Fred and Beth were cheerful, exclaiming over how glad they were to finish their visit with the Harrisons before returning home to prepare for the baby. Flora was quiet but not as cold to Jensen as she had been since talking to Sam at the hospital in Pittsfield. He even thought he caught her looking his way more than once.

But that could be wishful thinking.

As Flora drove them through Philadelphia toward Harrison Goods, Jensen's mouth got drier and swallowing became all but impossible. By the time she parked the car at the edge of the street in front of the store, Jensen had never been both so relieved and so reluctant to step foot inside.

Fred and Beth went into the store as soon as Flora turned off the engine. But Jensen hesitated outside the door, visions of what might happen when he spoke to Mr. Harrison growing more dramatic in his mind by the minute.

A gentle hand on his arm reminded Jensen that Flora was still standing with him, bolstering his resolve. Her voice was soft when she spoke. "What's wrong, Jensen?"

He examined her face, and there wasn't anger in her eyes anymore. Had she decided he was telling the truth? Hope swelled in his chest, but there was still work to do. Beth was right. He had to make a gesture that would prove to Flora he was worthy of her love. He just hadn't figured out what that was yet.

But he was awfully glad to have her by his side for what was ahead. "I'm wondering if there's anything left for me in there. I'm sure Owen has stepped into Mr. Harrison's place while I was gone. He's much more capable of it than I ever was. And now I'm not even sure if there's a relationship with Mr. Harrison for me to return to, once I tell him everything about Gregory. What if he blames me? Gets angry and makes me leave?"

Flora's fingers rubbed his arm, sending a thrill through Jensen. He put his hand on top of hers as she spoke. "You won't know until you try. Mr. Harrison is a reasonable man, and he loves you like his own children. I can't see him holding your actions against you. He'll forgive you as Fred did once you laid out the entire truth."

He noticed she didn't include herself in forgiving him, but that was a matter for later. Drawing and releasing a deep breath, Jensen led the way into the store and through the merchandise displays, which were noticeably neater and more interesting than he remembered. The new leadership at Harrison Goods was already an improvement. As they crossed the showroom, Owen nodded to acknowledge their return while helping a customer.

Jensen held the door that led to the offices open

for Flora, appreciating the confident smile she sent his way as she passed him. They reached Mr. Harrison's door as Fred and Beth emerged.

Fred patted Jensen's shoulder, nodding in support. "You can do this, Jensen. We'll all be better off with things out in the open. I'm going to take Beth to the house to get some rest and tell Mother the good news."

Flora said goodbye with hugs for both of them while Jensen found all the words he wanted to say stuck in his throat. Then it was time to enter the office where he'd spent so many hours trying to learn the Harrison family business with little success.

Mr. Harrison greeted them from behind his nearly empty desk with a wide grin. "Welcome back! Fred told me how the tour ended, but I can't even be disappointed with the results after hearing the wonderful news that I'm going to be a grandfather. Sit, please. Tell me all about the trip."

For several minutes, Flora entertained him with tales from their journey. But eventually, she got around to Archie's actions. "Fred told you about the accident that ruined our chance to win, but he may not have told you everything. Mr. Dorman's driver, Archie Franklin, felt he needed to cheat his way through the race. He even tried to get Jensen to sabotage our car and eliminate us from the tour."

She looked at Jensen, encouragement in her eyes. His heart thumped when it sank in that she said Archie *tried* but didn't succeed.

Mr. Harrison, however, stared at him with a furrowed brow, his fingers pressed together under his chin, bringing Jensen's attention back to the matter at hand. "And why would he believe you'd ever go along with that, Jensen?"

Not sure he could meet the man's pointed gaze, Jensen focused on the only decorative piece that remained on Mr. Harrison's desk, an ornate wooden globe Mrs. Harrison had given him for their wedding anniversary one year. "Sir, he had some information that he knew I didn't want to become public knowledge, and he threatened to use it to hurt those I care about."

"And what is that information?"

Jensen swallowed hard. Between the chairs they sat in, Flora reached out to squeeze his hand. Her support spurred him on. "That I had a part in Gregory's death, which I've been keeping from you all these years. It was my urging that made him agree to the race. He was hesitant at first and wouldn't have agreed to it if I hadn't let Archie get to me and insisted Gregory could beat him. Then I changed my mind at the last minute and left him to race on his own without a lookout. His death is my fault."

The silence in the room pressed down on Jensen's shoulders. He still couldn't look up, terrified to see judgment in his mentor's eyes. Until Mr. Harrison's chair squeaked as he rose and moved to kneel by Jensen. When he finally glanced at Mr. Harrison, the tension drained from Jensen's body, for only concern and love mixed with the tears filling the older man's eyes.

"Now listen," Mr. Harrison said, "Archie and Gregory made their own decision. No matter what your involvement in the situation was, it doesn't mean you're to blame. The entire thing could have been avoided if Archie hadn't goaded you both. I saw how he teased you two for years, and I've felt that if I'd put a stop to that rivalry when it started, it wouldn't have come to such a tragic end. We all try to blame ourselves for these things. But that doesn't mean our feelings of guilt have any basis in reality."

Lurching forward, Jensen threw his arms around the man he'd viewed as a father for most of his life. Relief weakened his knees when the embrace was heartily returned. All the shame he'd felt for the last five years disintegrated, leaving him wondering why he'd waited so long to talk about it.

Mr. Harrison ended the hug and wiped at the tears that had gathered in his eyes. He turned to Flora, his tone returning to its usual business-like efficiency. "Flora, I'm most impressed with what I've heard of your driving on the tour. I hope you're not planning to leave Philadelphia any time soon. I'd like the opportunity to talk with you about our plans for the racing team."

Flora straightened and smoothed a loose hair back from her forehead as she answered. "I'm not sure my future is here, Mr. Harrison. I'll have to consider that before I can commit to anything. But I appreciate your faith in allowing me to represent your racing team."

Ending the conversation with a promise to go see Mrs. Harrison right away, Jensen watched Flora return to the showroom. She made a beeline toward Owen while Jensen turned to go to his office, giving her time to reunite with her brother. His heart felt lighter than it had in years, knowing Mr. Harrison didn't despise him for his mistakes. Forgiveness had a beautiful way of healing long-painful hurts.

Now the one issue that remained hanging over his head was how to convince Flora of his love for her before she left Philadelphia for good.

Chapter 24

A week later, Flora fanned herself as she walked the busy sidewalk in the blazing afternoon sun. After spending most of the week exploring Philadelphia with Aggie, she was getting better at finding where she needed to go.

Just in time to leave for whatever her next adventure might be.

It was starting to feel like time for her to move on. The first day or two, it had been wonderful to relax and enjoy spending time with Owen, Aggie, and Isabelle. After so many days on the road, sitting in their still, quiet home felt like heaven.

The only thing missing was Jensen, who had been conspicuously absent the entire week.

To pass the time, Flora and Aggie—with Isabelle sometimes tagging along—had visited all the museums, historic churches, and lovely shaded parks Philadelphia had to offer. That had filled the rest of the week pleasantly enough. But it was becoming clear to Flora that the newlyweds yearned to adjust to life together without long-term guests in their home. And Isabelle kept talking about finding a place of their own and starting the life they'd come to Philadelphia for.

As much as that sounded nice, Flora couldn't bring herself to solidify any plans. She knew what she was waiting on, but was there any hope it would happen?

Since some time apart would do them all good, Flora had relieved Aggie of hostess duties by declaring a desire to amuse herself for the day. She'd thought a solitary walk would help clear her mind to focus on what she would do next, how she and Isabelle were going to survive when their small inheritance ran out.

If only it was that easy to bring her wayward heart back into reality.

Mr. Harrison hadn't contacted her about driving for his team again, but she knew he was waiting for her to broach the subject when she was ready. The problem was, every time she even looked at the Decauville now, she saw Jensen in the passenger seat, memories of the dashing smile that too rarely graced his face making her heart ache. She longed to see him there again, ready to help her drive to victory.

The idea of running a race without him felt empty and pointless. But what else could she do? What was her purpose if not racing?

Crossing a busy street, Flora scurried to avoid a quick-moving milk wagon, then she paused to admire a beautiful display in a jeweler's window while she caught her breath. At least for today, a distraction had arisen to keep her busy. Mr. Franklin had been discharged from the hospital in Pittsfield, and he and Sam were back in

Philadelphia. They'd sent a note asking her to visit them.

Whatever the reason Mr. Franklin had sought her out, the opportunity to learn the truth of what happened during the tour was too important to pass up. She was sure now that Jensen was telling her the truth—and had been telling the truth the entire time. But hearing the details from Mr. Franklin would put to rest any lingering doubt that might haunt her in the future.

Arriving at her destination, Flora examined the rather dull-looking boarding house, a disappointing view after the charming neighborhoods she was used to traveling through in Philadelphia. She rang the bell and was escorted to the parlor by the cheerful proprietress. There she found Mr. Franklin in a wooden chair that was mounted on large wheels with a blanket thrown over his lap. It was far too warm a day to need the wrap, with no hint of a breeze stirring the curtains at the open windows, so Flora assumed it was meant to cover the result of his injuries. Sam rose from an upholstered chair next to Mr. Franklin and greeted her with a smile, seeming much more at peace than the last time they'd spoken.

As she took a seat on a worn but comfortable damask sofa facing the men, Flora focused on Mr. Franklin. "It's so good to see that you made it home. How are you feeling?"

Mr. Franklin shrugged, and although there were

shadows of pain in his eyes, his voice reflected the same peace Sam seemed to have found. "As well as you could expect. It's not easy getting used to my legs being gone and needing to wheel this chair around all the time. But Sam's been kind enough to help me as I learn."

Sam smiled. "It's the least I can do. He's still my teammate."

Flora let herself relax back against the plush divan. She'd been so unsure of what to expect when she received the invitation to visit them. There had been so much bitterness and regret in Mr. Franklin's words the last time she'd seen him. "You both look as though you've made some peace with what happened."

Nodding, Sam answered first. "I spent time with a pastor who visited patients at the hospital after you all left. He said some of the same things you said, Flora. That the blame didn't rest on any one of us. We all made choices that led to what happened. But that God always uses our mistakes to bring about some kind of good."

Mr. Franklin leaned forward, drawing her attention back to him. "That's why I had Sam invite you today. I want to take responsibility for my part instead of blaming others as I've always done. I know you believe Jensen sabotaged your team, and I have to set everyone straight. He didn't do it. I thought he had, at first, and I told Sam so. But when I confronted Jensen about it at Bretton Woods, he said he didn't. I was still trying to blackmail him then, so there was only risk involved for him to deny it. That's how I know he wasn't responsible for anything that happened to your team."

The tension that had gripped her since the accident released, letting Flora draw a deep, cleansing breath.

Rubbing one hand over his jaw, Mr. Franklin grimaced. "I regret all the trouble I caused. I see now what a waste these last few years have been. I spent so much time wrapped up in thoughts of revenge and hatred when I could have been building a good, respectable life. And it culminated in harming so many of you along with me. I hope you can forgive me someday."

Flora reached out and patted his hand where it rested on the arm of his wheeled chair. "You're forgiven now, Mr. Franklin. As Sam said, we all made mistakes on the tour. Yes, some with farther-reaching effects than others, but God sees fit to forgive them all, so I will too."

A grateful smile spread across his face. "Thank you. Now, I hope you'll go tell Jensen he's forgiven as well. You can't hold something against him that he didn't do."

A flush worked its way up Flora's neck. "I was so quick to assume that he did it. He tried to tell me, and I refused to believe him. What if *he* doesn't want to forgive *me*?"

Sam and Mr. Franklin both burst into laughter, startling Flora. Sam recovered first. "Oh, he'll forgive you."

Mr. Franklin grinned even wider now, happier than Flora had ever seen him. "He's a man in love. He'll forget your doubts in a second if you admit you love him too."

Flora's back tensed, and she found herself responding more harshly than she intended. "Why do you believe you know so much about my feelings? What makes you think I'm in love with him?"

"Did you think no one saw you two kissing and holding hands?" Sam laughed again, and Flora looked away, crossing her arms as the heat seared farther up her cheeks.

But she couldn't deny they might have a point. If he did love her—as everyone seemed to think—and she went to him ready to apologize for her doubts, would he offer forgiveness?

And what would it mean for her future if he did?

Shaking her head, Flora let the irritation over their assumptions go. "You're right, I suppose. But don't let it go to your heads."

With smiles all around, they chatted for several more minutes. Then Flora stood to leave with a promise to visit again before she left town. *If* she left town. Sam smirked when she added that.

She returned to Aggie and Owen's house to find

it empty, save for Isabelle, who the cook told her was napping. Flora retreated to her room to get ready for dinner at the Harrisons' home, which Mr. Harrison had called a celebration in the invitation he sent. What they were celebrating, she wasn't sure. But, despite his absence the rest of the week, she couldn't imagine the entire family would gather without Jensen there.

So she donned her favorite dinner gown, one made of *point d'esprit* and Chantilly lace in black and cream. It might be several years old, but it was still quite acceptable, and she felt her most confident in it. Sitting down at the vanity, she pulled and twisted and stuck pins in her hair until it resembled something her maid in France might have arranged. Close enough, anyway.

But the closer it came to the dinner hour, the more she found herself critiquing her look. And wondering if Jensen would like it. Perhaps she would look better in pink?

Owen found her pacing by the front door when he descended the stairs to wait on the others. "You look beautiful, Flora."

She tugged at her skirt. "Do I? I'm not sure this is the most appropriate gown."

Tilting his head, he examined not her gown, but her face. "Flora Montfort, are you worried about what Jensen will think?"

Throwing up her hands, Flora dropped down to sit on the stairs, not caring if it was unladylike to do so. "You're not the first one today to assume I'm concerned with Jensen's opinions."

Owen's eyebrows rose, and a half grin started on his face.

Flora had the urge to wipe it off by pulling his ear as she'd done when he'd teased her as children. "Fine. I am. Owen, I believed some terrible things about him that I now know to be untrue. He's aware I didn't believe him when he told me the truth. How can I make that right?"

Her brother, the only champion she'd had for so many years, knelt in front of her. "Flora, you were married. Didn't you and Henri ever argue?"

She thought back to their fiery fights, of which there were many. "Of course. But we never took the time to work through it. I've told you before, our marriage was not healthy."

A wide grin brightened his face, and he stood when Aggie appeared at the top of the stairs, elegant in dark-green velvet. He spoke with warm candor. "Well, I've only been married a few weeks, but I know a sincere apology can go a long way. Start there and back it up with action when you get the chance." Then he stepped up to meet his wife.

Everyone seemed so confident that Jensen would forgive her without hesitation, but Flora wasn't so sure. It would take more than simple words to show him how sorry she was and how much she longed to continue building the relationship they'd started on the tour.

As Isabelle joined them and they prepared to go to the Harrisons' home, Flora considered ways to put action with her words. And she could only think of one thing that would prove Jensen was more important to her than anything else.

After years of fighting for it, Flora was ready to give up racing.

In the Harrisons' parlor, Jensen couldn't help remembering another dinner party in the same room, the one where he'd first met Flora. On this night, it was only Mrs. Harrison, Fred, and Beth who chatted across the room while he sat with Mr. Harrison. Before the others arrived, Jensen had requested a moment of Mr. Harrison's time.

And that was the biggest difference between the earlier party and this one. Now, rather than fighting his passion for mechanics, Jensen was prepared to find a place doing what he loved.

Mr. Harrison sat facing him on a matching pair of sofas arranged at one end of the room, waiting expectantly. "Well, Jensen, what did you want to speak to me about?"

Letting a deep breath calm his nerves and the memory of Flora's beautiful, smiling face strengthen his resolve, Jensen laid out his plan to win her trust. "I know Flora hasn't answered you about driving for your racing team yet, but I hope I have a way to encourage her to accept. I'd like to join the crew as a mechanic. I know you've already filled most of the positions, so don't feel it has to be anything other than a shop mechanic. But I want to be there for Flora. And I want racing to be part of my life again because it's part of hers."

Eyebrows raising, Mr. Harrison mirrored the surprise Jensen had felt when he realized showing Flora he wanted to be part of her racing career was not only a way to prove his love but something he wanted for himself too. The older man rubbed his chin. "A shop mechanic? I'm not able to do that, I'm afraid. Those positions are all filled, as you mentioned."

Jensen nodded, but his stomach clenched. Now how would he convince Flora his goal in life was to give her everything she dreamed of?

But when he glanced up at Mr. Harrison again, he saw a teasing glint in the man's eyes. The older man chuckled. "I'm not refusing you a job, Jensen. I've been holding the lead mechanic position, hoping you would come to this decision. You're made to work on cars. There's no one else I would trust with my team's equipment. The job is yours."

A warm energy coursed through Jensen, and he couldn't help jumping up to shake Mr. Harrison's hand. "Thank you, sir. I'm so relieved you still want me on your team after everything that's happened."

Voices at the door brought their attention to the others arriving. Jensen stood with Mr. Harrison, nervous energy causing his fingers to twitch. What would Flora say when he told her his plan for their future? Would she see his earnest love for her? Was she ready to trust him?

When she finally walked through the door after Owen and Aggie, the air disappeared from Jensen's lungs. The lace gown she wore highlighted her graceful figure and made it impossible to take his eyes off her. His palms grew damp, and he had to clear his throat several times before he could swallow.

Not seeing her the entire week had been torture, and now that she was in front of him, Jensen's heart swelled. He loved her so much.

If he could only make her see it without ruining things again.

Jensen followed the others to the dining room, barely able to look at Flora for fear his nervousness would be written all over his face. He'd spent the entire week thinking up and rejecting plan after plan. He'd known what he needed to do—what God had intended for him from the beginning—but he'd fought it for so long. Now it was time to see if it would be enough to win Flora back.

Everyone took their assigned places at the

long table in the Harrisons' dining room, and the servants began setting plates in front of each guest. Jensen found himself at the far end of the table from Flora, who was seated next to Mr. Harrison. It was frustrating to be in the same room with her but still so far away. He reminded himself there would be plenty of time to talk with her. The rest of their lives, if things went as he hoped. What he needed to say was much too personal for this setting, anyway.

Fred and Beth were busy filling the older Mrs. Montfort in about how Beth was feeling and her plans for their nursery once they returned home. At the head of the table, Mr. Harrison and Flora were deep in conversation, one that looked serious. Were they discussing Flora driving for the team again? If Mr. Harrison revealed Jensen's decision to work with them, would Flora give agreement as well? Or would she refuse because of it?

The dinner courses dragged on, and Jensen grew more anxious with each one. He longed to take Flora's hand in his, to pull her close and show her his feelings in the most undeniable way. The sentiment "absence makes the heart grow fonder" was all too true. He'd missed her. He'd thought of her every waking moment and dreamed of her at night. It had been madness.

He had also spent much time in prayer, a new habit that would lend stability to their relationship as they started fresh. If she would believe him this time. He'd prayed quite a bit that she would. And that prayer was the only thing giving him the strength to remain seated and wait until the right time to present Flora with his plan.

Finally, dessert was brought out. Once most of them had finished the final course, Mr. Harrison stood to get the attention of the group. "Most of you were a bit confused that I called this dinner a celebration, but I have several good reasons to do so. First, even if our team didn't win the Glidden Tour, we made a strong showing for our first event. I can't be too disappointed when the Harrison Goods team is being touted as a fine example of good sportsmanship and compassion for their fellow racers after stopping to help a team in need."

Mr. Harrison paused to let the congratulations pass before he continued. "I know we've all heard the most exciting news to come out of that trip, but I'll say it again with pride. Fred and Beth, we're so pleased about your coming addition to the family. We pray for good health and blessings as you bring this new life into the world."

Another round of best wishes went up, this one even more joyful. "And my final reason for celebration isn't news to any of you, either, but it's still something I'd like to commemorate. We're having the first meeting of the new Harrison Goods racing team at the shop tomorrow. Flora and Jensen, I'd particularly like both of you to attend, since you were our first driver and mechanic."

Mr. Harrison looked around the table, his eyes growing misty. "I'm so thankful to God for bringing the four of you back to us. I can already see you've all grown in significant ways, and I hope that will lead you forward into a joyous and fulfilling future."

Questions swirled in Jensen's mind as the others all returned to their conversations while rising from the table to adjourn to the parlor. Mr. Harrison said he and Flora *were* the team's first driver and mechanic. Had she turned down the driving position? Was she unwilling to work with him, maybe even still unable to trust him? With no way to sort it all out, he could only look toward Flora, longing to see answers in her eyes.

Instead, he found them shining with unshed tears.

Not caring what any of the others might think, he moved to the chair next to her and took both her hands in his. The room emptied, leaving them to the moment he'd been praying over all week. "Flora, did you decline Mr. Harrison's offer to be our driver?"

As if she couldn't bear to speak the words, her mouth opened and then closed again. Finally, she just nodded. The pain of losing her already began to sting his heart, and he rushed to get out the statements he'd rehearsed all week. "I know you lost faith in me. But I didn't damage the car during the tour, and I'll work as long as it takes to prove it to you. You're an amazing woman and the best driver I've ever met. I can't apologize enough for my part in everything that happened on the tour, for keeping things from you and causing so much pain. Can you give me the chance to earn your trust again?"

She shook her head and his heart dropped. She was going to refuse to accept his apology.

Then she lunged forward and threw her arms around his neck. Jensen held her, unable to keep his hands from caressing her back as she sniffled against his shoulder. His heart was beating so hard she must be able to feel it. What did this mean?

Finally, she leaned back and spoke. "Jensen, I need to tell you I spoke to Mr. Franklin today."

Blinking in confusion at the change of subject, Jensen's mind raced to determine what his former rival might have said that made her refuse to drive for Mr. Harrison. "I didn't know he was back in town."

Nodding, she bit her lower lip. "I'm the one who needs to apologize. He confirmed that you've been telling the truth. Sam only thought you'd gone through with it because Mr. Franklin believed you had and told him so. But Mr. Franklin confirmed that you refused to give in to his manipulation no matter what he tried and that you were honest and trustworthy at every turn. I'm sorry for assuming the worst about you."

Jensen's heart lightened, despite his fear over where the conversation was headed. "Apology accepted, without hesitation. Archie has changed, hasn't he?"

She smiled, but sadness tinged its edges. "I think we all have."

Silence fell between them as Flora picked at an invisible spot on her skirt. If Mr. Harrison had offered her the job again at dinner, had he also told her about Jensen's participation? Should Jensen tell her that he'd taken a step of faith for her and joined the team? Or did she need time to trust him again, even though she knew the truth now?

Before he could decide what to do, she rose from her seat. "I suppose we should join the others, then."

Crestfallen, he tried to read the emotions crossing her face without success. "If you'd like. Will you be at the shop tomorrow as Mr. Harrison requested?"

She offered only a short nod before heading toward the door, leaving Jensen more unsure of his position in her heart than he'd been before dinner. Replaying the conversation in his mind, he tried to see where it had gone wrong but came up empty-handed.

The only thought that carried him through the rest of the evening with Flora sitting across the room from him was that he had one more chance to show her how much he loved her. Tomorrow at the shop, he would have to convince her to stay.

Chapter 25

Flora straightened the jacket of her plaid suit and drew one last deep breath while standing in front of the door to the racing shop. It was exactly three minutes before the meeting started, and she would rather be anywhere else at that moment. But she *was* there because she couldn't disappoint Mr. Harrison after the kindness he'd shown over her abysmal failure in the tour.

It had nothing to do with Jensen.

She certainly wasn't standing in front of that familiar door because of the longing she imagined in his eyes the night before as he watched her across the Harrisons' parlor.

Nor because of the way he'd held her when they were alone at the table, his touch sending shivers up and down her spine.

Her respect for Mr. Harrison drove her to finally step inside the shop, which was still shiny and clean despite the work they'd done on the Decauville before the tour and the disassembled Packard that now sat at the first workstation. The men who were already gathered all turned to watch her trek across the smooth floor to join them. She smiled at the crew members she recognized. But she couldn't bring herself to look at Jensen.

Not that she doubted him any longer. After speaking to Mr. Franklin, Sam, and Owen, she'd been able to see all the ways Jensen had proven himself time and again. His apology the night before had been a balm to her soul. Yes, he made mistakes and occasionally took over in his efforts to protect her. But his heart was as different from Clement's or Henri's as it could be. His actions always stemmed from concern for those he loved.

The problem was that he hadn't yet said that she was a person he loved.

As the men talked amongst themselves, she snuck a glance at Jensen, finding his gaze already on her, warm and inviting. A thread of worry weaved its way through her heart. He'd said so many things she wanted to hear the night before, all spoken in genuine remorse. But he hadn't made any mention of feelings that matched hers, of caring that went beyond friendship.

She'd turned Mr. Harrison's job offer down during dinner because she believed Jensen would see it as a sign of her willingness to build a life they were both comfortable with. But he'd seemed so upset with her decision. Then, faced with doubts about his affections, she'd fled from her plan to explain her choice when they had a moment alone. Questions and regrets had plagued her ever since.

The door opened again, and Mr. Harrison entered the shop. Flora managed what she hoped was a pleasant smile as he greeted her on his way to stand in front of the group and start the meeting. "Thank you all for coming. Some of you have been working with us already, preparing the Packard for our next event, a track race in Buffalo. But you'll notice several newcomers joining us today."

Mr. Harrison gestured toward Jensen and grinned, a gleam brightening his eyes. "I'm thrilled to present our new lead mechanic, Jensen Gable. Most of you know him already. He'll bring a wealth of knowledge and experience to our crew."

Flora's trembling hand rose to adjust the narrow bowtie at the base of her throat. Jensen was working with the team? Why hadn't he told her?

She didn't have much time to dwell on the question, though, because Mr. Harrison continued. "I'm hopeful we'll have the question of our driver settled soon enough. For now, I'm going to let you all get acquainted a bit with each other and the shop, for those who are new. Feel free to look around."

Pulling Flora aside while the men began milling around, Mr. Harrison got right to the point. "I'm still holding out hope that you'll change your mind and agree to drive for us. Jensen seemed sure you would want to once you learned he's joined the crew."

Letting her eyes stray to where Jensen stood with a few of the others, Flora's conflicting emotions clouded her mind. "As I said last night, it may be best for me to leave Philadelphia. Isabelle and I might settle somewhere warmer. Or spend some time in New York where we'll be close to a few of her distant relatives."

Narrowing his eyes, Mr. Harrison watched her for a moment. "Jensen didn't declare himself last night, did he? I'd hoped the boy would follow his grand gesture with the proposal we all know is coming."

His words made her want to fling something across the room. "Everyone keeps telling me that he has some kind of deep, meaningful feelings for me, but I'm starting to believe you're all wrong. He didn't declare any feelings. He didn't even mention he'd changed his mind about working in racing again. He must see me as a friend, a former teammate. Nothing more. And I'll thank you all to stay out of our business from here on out."

Realizing her voice had grown louder than she'd intended, Flora saw with horror that most of the men were looking her way.

Including Jensen.

If only he'd said he loved her, this choice would be easy.

But he hadn't. He'd said sweet, encouraging things. Mr. Harrison seemed to believe he'd faced his fears for her. But now that she was being presented with the very thing she'd wanted for so long—and the independence to finally choose for herself—she found racing wasn't what would make her happy, after all.

She wanted Jensen's love.

She'd been willing to give up the dream-fulfilling offer that was within her grasp if it meant he would offer what she wanted more than anything.

It was time to face the reality that he wasn't going to do so.

Flora pressed one hand to her aching chest. "I'm sorry, but I can't accept the position. I'm grateful for the offer, Mr. Harrison, I truly am. Please excuse me."

Then she spun and fled the shop. She tried to amble along the sidewalk at a proper pace but soon found her footsteps increasing in speed until she was dashing toward a nearby park. Spotting the corner of a bench that was barely visible behind the huge trunk of an oak tree, she headed straight toward the private sanctuary.

Sinking onto the stone seat, she tried to focus on the yellow blooms of some summer flowers planted in neat clumps nearby. But all she could see was the green-gold depths of Jensen's eyes. Resting her elbows on her knees, she buried her face in her hands. Everything she'd been longing for had been right in front of her, and she couldn't bring herself to reach out and claim it. All because she'd let her heart get involved. As Clement had always said, emotions were trouble.

A cold wave stilled her thoughts in their tracks. Now she was agreeing with Clement. What had falling in love with Jensen done to her? Would this pain lead her to become bitter and controlling like her brother?

If Flora had learned anything through this mess with Jensen, it was that focusing on the truth was freeing. So she sat for a few minutes reminding herself of all the ways she was different from Clement. She thought of the ways the Lord had led her through the years of abuse from Clement and then the contentious relationship with Henri. Without a doubt, He would continue to guide her steps.

Even if the journey He took her on didn't include Jensen, God's will was still good.

Footsteps on the brick path caught her attention. She froze, trying with all her might to blend into the tree at her back. While she was feeling calmer, she didn't want to talk to anyone at the moment. Unless it was Jensen coming to declare his love for her.

As if summoned by her thoughts, he appeared around the tree a moment later. Sunlight caught on his features, highlighting the line of his nose, the curve of his lips. A memory of kissing him on the porch of the Mount Washington Hotel flashed through her mind. Would she ever experience that again? Was it worth being at his side every day in hopes she might?

Jensen joined her on the bench without a word. Her heart raced so fast she worried it might overtax itself and stop altogether. What would he say to her running out of the shop?

As it turned out, he didn't say anything. Jensen took her shoulders in his hands. Slowly, giving her time to refuse, he pulled her toward him. A small part of Flora thought she ought to resist him until he made his feelings clear. But her heart didn't care. It only wanted to feel his nearness again.

So she let him fit his lips over hers. Heat speared through her, and her eyes drifted shut. If she was about to find he didn't share her feelings and this was their last kiss, she might as well enjoy it.

Reaching up, she let both hands tangle in his short hair, enjoying the surprising softness of it. Their bodies pressed as close together as possible with the strange angle of sitting side by side.

After several moments that weren't nearly enough, Jensen pulled back, leaving both of them gasping for air. Flora tried not to meet his gaze, terrified of what she would—or wouldn't—see in his eyes. But his fingers slid down her arms to grasp her hands, and he said her name with such raw emotion that she immediately looked up.

And she saw everything she'd been praying to find.

Desperate to keep her from running away again, Jensen prayed Flora would see his heart in his face, that she would hear it in his words. When she'd left the shop in such a rush, he'd been too stunned to stop her. But Mr. Harrison had pointed out the problem before the door even closed behind her. "Jensen, that young woman is in love with you. Didn't you reveal your feelings last night? We all left you two alone in the dining room to give you the chance."

Jensen was ashamed to admit that he'd delayed doing so out of fear. "How can you be sure? She refused the job, most likely because she can't stand the thought of working with me."

Mr. Harrison had laughed then, actually laughed right at Jensen. "Preposterous. She refused out of concern for you, an attempt to prove that your worries about racing matter to her. Her feelings are obvious to all of us. She's waiting for you to declare yourself. You better find her and do it before she leaves for good."

So he'd run out of the shop, hoping he was going the right way when he headed toward the park. It had taken longer than he wanted, but he finally spotted a corner of familiar plaid fabric peeking out from behind a large tree. And when he rounded the trunk, there she was, sitting on a bench with her face in her hands. Jensen's heart had wrenched. He'd done that. He'd upset her by giving in to his fear and not speaking the words she needed to hear.

Now, sitting next to her and drinking in her beauty, there was one burning question he needed an answer to right away. "Did you refuse the driving job because you don't want to work with me?"

Her lips parted in surprise. "Of course not. I had no idea you'd agreed to join the team. I refused *for* you."

Relief spread through his chest. He searched for the words to convince her of his heart. "Mr. Harrison reminded me that I should have said something more to you last night, something that I hope will change your reaction to his job offer. You've helped me rediscover the blessing of the family God gave me, along with a purpose I never thought I'd be able to face again."

She blinked and stared at him, waiting.

Now was the time to practice what he'd learned during the tour. Avoiding risk might protect him in the short term, but it would only lead to long-term loneliness and emptiness. It was time to lay out everything he'd been feeling. Jensen took a deep breath. "You're the reason I agreed to take the job as the lead mechanic. You helped me find a passion for working on cars again. You showed me how to face my fear and find healing. I'm not sure how to make it flowery and romantic as you might expect, so I'll just say it. I love you. And if you love me, too, I can do anything with you at my side."

Finally, she threw her arms around him, and Jensen reveled in the feeling of holding her once again. She mumbled something against his neck, but he couldn't hear her. Putting as little space as possible between them, he pushed back to examine her face, praying he would find the glow of love.

Instead, he found eyes glowing with mirth. It started with a giggle and soon turned into a full-fledged laugh.

He wasn't sure he understood the humor in almost losing her, though. "What's so funny?"

"Jensen, I only turned down the job because I thought leaving racing behind was the best way to prove you're more important to me than anything in this world. We've both been trying to sacrifice for each other, and we didn't even recognize it."

Realizing she was right, merriment welled up in his chest too. "So does that mean you'll drive for our team? And maybe even consider spending time with a grumpy old mechanic?"

She rested her head on his shoulder as she responded. "You don't know how happy driving and working alongside you will make me."

Hesitating, he reached for the answer he was

desperate to hear. "And do you think you can come to return my feelings?"

She turned her face up to reveal a brilliant smile. "I already do. Jensen, I've loved you since the moment you kissed me on the porch in Bretton Woods. You've proven to me that being in love doesn't mean giving up control of my life. God is the only one who can control anything, anyway. There's nothing but freedom in loving a good man like you."

He crushed her to him, sharing an endless number of kisses until her lips were swollen and her cheeks pink. He grinned. "You look thoroughly well-kissed. Want to go announce the good news to the team now?"

Her cheeks flushed an even deeper pink as she tried unsuccessfully to straighten her hair and make herself look as though they hadn't been doing what they had. "Yes, I'm ready. You know, Beth will never let us forget that she was right this entire time."

Grinning, he pulled her up and steered them back toward the shop. "It took a number of our family members to convince me you might return my feelings, so I think they'll all feel as though they played a part."

She offered a shy smile, a look he wasn't used to from Flora. "The same with me. Why did it take so much trouble for us to believe in each other?"

He tucked her hand through his arm as they approached the shop door. "We both had a few things to overcome. But now, thanks to God's perfect plan, we don't have to wade through our problems alone anymore."

She rested her head on his shoulder again. Could a heart explode from the amount of love filling it? "No, we're not alone."

All the members of the Harrison Goods racing team turned to watch them enter the shop.

Jensen couldn't help grinning as he gently pushed her to stand in front of him. "Gentlemen, I have good news. Allow me to announce the driver for our team, Mrs. Flora Montfort. She's the most qualified race car driver I've ever seen, and I can't wait to start tallying up victories with her."

The men cheered, and many stepped forward to welcome Flora with excitement. Jensen stood back and watched her in her element, talking cars and racing set-ups with a crew that respected her. For the first time since Gregory died, the future felt hopeful and bright.

A hand on his shoulder turned Jensen's attention away from Flora to find Sam standing next to him. "Sam, what brings you here?"

The younger man looked sheepish, and Jensen realized they had some things to work through, the same as he and Flora had. Sam pulled Jensen away from the others a bit. "Mr. Harrison asked me to come. He's offered me a job running operations here at the shop. But I needed to make sure you and me are on good terms before I accept. Jensen, I'm sorry I doubted your loyalty to your team. I can't believe I ever believed you would sabotage them."

There was nothing but warmth in Jensen's heart as he listened to Sam's genuine apology. He was ready to forgive the past and move forward. He pulled Sam into a hug. "Apology accepted. Now I don't want to hear another word about it. We all made mistakes on the tour. And we all have another chance to do it right next time. I'm thrilled to have you on our team, Sam."

When they separated, Sam was beaming. "I'm going to go talk with the others. Are you coming?"

Jensen nodded, but he paused a moment, looking over the scene before him. There stood the woman he loved—who loved him back—in the middle of the racing shop where he was going to begin work. The difference between this moment and two months ago was night and day. Before Flora, he'd been lost in self-pity and unable to accept God's love or anyone else's. Now he could recognize the gift he'd been given in the Harrison family. They might not have been his by blood, but they were still as loyal and loving as any family could be.

Not only that, but he had a future, faith to

sustain him, and a career where he could thrive on the horizon. The twists and turns of his road in life had been difficult to navigate, but God had led him through to a better place than he ever could have imagined.

Reaching Flora's side, Jensen took her hand in his and let hopes for their shared future swell in his heart. For the first time in years, he could look forward with confidence and put their dreams into motion. And all of it was possible with Flora by his side.

Chapter 26

The jail in Syracuse, New York, smelled like the darkest, dampest alley in Paris.

Flora sat on a rough wooden bench that was scarred with the carvings of what looked like hundreds of prisoners before her. Across the ten-foot jail cell, Sam sat on an identical bench, using a sliver of wood to add his name to those already chiseled into the seat. He looked as if he didn't have a care in the world. As though he could sit there as long as it took for help to arrive.

Waiting for Jensen to eventually get them out of this mess wasn't appealing to Flora, though. He was busy managing the three teams Harrison Goods was fielding in this street race. It could be hours before he learned where she and Sam were and came to save them.

She jumped up and returned to the corner of the cell closest to the door leading to the front of the jail. Ignoring their cellmates, two men who smelled strongly of some kind of drink she never wanted to experience, she banged on the bars until the door opened. As soon as a uniform started to appear, she launched into the argument she'd tried on every officer involved in this debacle.

"Excuse me, but you have no reason to hold me or my partner. We were only driving that fast because we were in a car race. It's sponsored by the American Automobile Association, and your department should have been informed it was happening today. You have no grounds to hold us."

The young officer who had come this time looked bored. "Ma'am, I'm sorry, but we received no such notice, and your driving was quite reckless. Our senior officers are discussing what to do with the two of you right now, so you'll have to wait until they've decided and take it up with them then."

The young man didn't listen to her continued pleading, instead walking away without another glance and closing the door firmly behind him.

Flora flopped down on the bench next to Sam with a sigh. "It's been five hours. Where on earth is Jensen?"

Sam smirked, never looking up from his carving. "He's probably taking his time to teach you a lesson."

Flora threw up her hands. "I didn't do anything except try to get around that Napier on a tight turn. And they call that reckless. I was in complete control. I've done far crazier things than that this year, haven't I?"

"That's one way of putting it." Sam continued smiling as he began work on a particularly intricate part of the design he'd started etching next to his name.

Flora let her head fall back to rest between the thick metal bars behind them. Driving for Harrison Goods racing had been a dream for the last year. She adored working side by side with Jensen every day. They'd developed the ability to support and adapt to each other without hesitation.

And yet, Jensen still hadn't spoken of marriage.

Snoring from one of the drunks lying on his back under a tiny, high window distracted Flora for a moment. It irked her that racing was still considered so illicit that she'd ended up in jail for running in an organized event, and not for the first time. She smiled thinking about the last instance when Jensen had to rescue her from an over-eager officer. Jensen had been downright frantic, rushing to the jail as soon as he'd heard, demanding that she must be released immediately.

This time, it seemed he was in no hurry.

She occupied herself with thinking about next week's race until keys jangled in the heavy door again. To her relief, this time, the young officer appeared with Jensen behind him. Jensen wasn't sporting a look of agitated worry as she'd expected, but one of amused tolerance. Meeting his eyes the moment he stepped through the door, all she could do was shrug, bringing a grin to his face.

How she loved that grin and the newfound happiness it represented.

The officer unlocked the cell while Jensen came to stand in front of Flora with the bars between them. She speared him with her best look of disapproval. "It took you long enough to come and get us. What caused the delay?"

He shot her a smile that held more humor, but also a hint of something intriguing she couldn't put her finger on. "I had a stop to make on the way."

Sam and the officer went through the door to the front of the jail while Flora hesitated just outside the closed cell, standing so close to Jensen that it would have only taken a breath for her to touch him. "What stop could be more important than rescuing us from unjustified incarceration?"

Jensen fixed his gaze on her, so much love there that it stopped her breath altogether for a long moment. His voice was husky when he responded. "It was a matter of our future. A rather important one that required a visit to a jeweler's shop."

A thrill hit Flora with all the force of the Packard race car waiting for them outside. Was he finally going to ask her to marry him? An especially loud snore from the cell behind them brought Flora's awareness back to where they stood. She put both hands on her hips. "Jensen

Gable, you had better not propose to me in a smelly jail."

Jensen laughed as he slid his arm around her waist and led her toward the door. "I wouldn't dream of it, my love. But it's coming. We've gotten to know each other as well as two people ever could, and I've saved enough to buy a comfortable home for us with plenty of space for Isabelle too. So I'd say it's about time, wouldn't you?"

Leaving the jail with Jensen, Flora reflected on how different her life was now from when she'd first set eyes on the man at her side. There had been plenty of turns in the road, but God had used them to bring her and Jensen together, happier and healthier than either of them could have imagined. And she agreed with her whole heart. "There was never a better time."

Author's Note

I'm fascinated by stories about women doing things society didn't expect them to. While Flora was a character that had been in my head for some time, it wasn't until I was reading about women in turn-of-the-century sports that I discovered her passion for auto racing.

This was inspired by a real woman, Joan Newton Cuneo, who was active in racing in the early 1900s and drove in the 1905 Glidden Tour. She had to fight to enter and only managed to do so because the American Automobile Association (AAA) had failed to explicitly state in the rules that women couldn't drive. And this was only left out because they assumed driving was for men and no woman would dream of it, anyway.

Mrs. Cuneo was a vocal advocate for female drivers in the early days of automobiles. She raced until women were officially barred from AAA events and then continued to set speed records and promote safe driving practices and infrastructure while racing in any events she was allowed to enter.

I followed the schedule and recorded incidents of the 1905 Glidden Tour with one large exception. The accident at the end of this book actually took place on the first day of the tour and involved Joan Cuneo. On a bridge, she was forced to swerve to avoid a car that had stopped suddenly and ended up rolling her car into a creek. Thankfully, she was unharmed and her car, though damaged, could still be driven. The repairs gave out on the last day, and she wasn't able to finish the tour, but it's incredible that the vehicle held on for nearly 870 miles after that tumble!

One of my favorite scenes is the Climb to the Clouds race, which started in 1904 and continues to this day. The first-place driver in the 1904 Climb to the Clouds finished in 24 minutes, 37.6 seconds. In 1905, the winner took only 20 minutes, 58 seconds to reach the top. These days, because of all the hairpin turns, it takes the average driver a half hour to reach the top of the 7.6-mile road, and the record for fastest race time stands at 5 minutes, 44 seconds!

While I included Flora in the hill climb, unfortunately, Joan Cuneo wasn't allowed to drive it in 1905. There's some belief that she eventually did find a way to do it because she tried in 1905, and it's the sort of challenge she would have fought to conquer. But I couldn't resist the opportunity to include Flora in such an interesting event.

Thank you so much for reading Flora and Jensen's love story! These characters are so dear to my heart, with all their hurts and the big hurdles they have to overcome. I adore stories of two broken people helping to lift each other up and point each other toward the Lord. If you would, take a moment to leave a review online. Reviews are vital for authors to get their books out there and help readers find stories they will enjoy.

I hope you'll connect with me to learn about upcoming releases. You can find me on:
Facebook (AbbeyDowneyAuthor),
Instagram (abbeydowney),
Pinterest (abbeydowneyauthor),
or my website (abbeydowney.com).

About the Author

Abbey Downey started writing inspirational romance stories during naptime when her kids were babies and found she couldn't stop. She previously published two books with Love Inspired Historical under the pen name Mollie Campbell. She also works with Spark Flash Fiction producing a quarterly digital magazine that contains love stories under 1000 words.

A life-long Midwestern girl, Abbey lives in central Indiana with her husband, two kids, and one rather enthusiastic beagle. She loves watching her kids play sports and fixing up a 1900 farmhouse with her husband. Connect with Abbey at www.abbeydowney.com.

Center Point Large Print
600 Brooks Road / PO Box 1
Thorndike, ME 04986-0001 USA

(207) 568-3717

US & Canada:
1 800 929-9108
www.centerpointlargeprint.com